LISA WORRALL

LAUREL
HEIGHTS

Laurel Heights

2nd Edition - Copyright © 2014 by Lisa Worrall

1st Edition - Silver Publishing - Copyright © 2012 by Lisa Worrall

All Rights Reserved.

Editor: Jae Ashley

Cover Designer: Meredith Russell

TRADEMARKS ACKNOWLEDGEMENT

The author acknowledges the trademarked status and trademark owners of the following wordmarks mentioned in this work of fiction:

Martha Stewart: Martha Stewart Living Omnimedia, Inc.
Super Bowl: National Football League
GQ Magazine: Advance Magazine Publisher, Inc.
Tylenol: The Tylenol Company
Q-tips: Chesebrough-Pond's, Inc.
Days of Our Lives: Columbia Pictures Industries, Inc.
Boy Scouts: Boy Scouts of America Corporation
Prius: Toyota
Hershey bar: Hershey Chocolate
and Confectionary Corporation
Clorox: The Clorox Company
Superman: DC Comics
Bubble Wrap: Sealed Air Corporation (US)
Bubblicious: Cadbury Adams USA LLC
Corona: Cerveceria Modelo
Dirty Harry: Warner Bros/Malpaso Productions
WoW: Blizzard Entertainment
Greyhound: Greyhound Lines, Inc.
Guitar Hero: Activision Publishing, Inc.
Led Zeppelin: Joan Hudson/Plant, Robert A/Page, James/
Baldwin, John AKA John Paul Jones
Harlequin Romance: Harlequin Enterprises Ltd
Sleeping with the Enemy: 20th Century Fox
Knots Landing: Warner Bros. Television
Camaro: General Motors Corporation
Pogo's Adventures: Nick C. Scime
Romance Writers of America: Romance Writers
of America, Inc.

A Note From The Author:

Thank you for your purchase of this title. I sincerely hope you enjoy this read but would ask that you please remember that the only money authors like myself make from writing is from the sales of my books. If you like my stories, please feel free to spread the word and tell others, but please refrain from sharing this book in any form, as I depend on sales to support my family. If you see this book or any other written by me offered on pirate sites, please report the offending entry to lisaworrall69@gmail.com

DEDICATION:

I would like to dedicate this book to my sister, Teresa, without whom this story wouldn't have come to fruition. I thank her for having a dream, giving it to me for the bones of this story and for letting me go nuts with it. I also thank her for her support, her love and her innate ability to be the only person I know who *really* tells it like it is. So if she says it's good… it must be.

Without her shoulder to lean on, her ear to bend and her hand to slap me when I'm being stupid, the last eighteen months would have been so much harder, and there are no words to express how much she means to me.

CONTENTS

PROLOGUE

The gated housing development of Laurel Heights was quiet in the early hours. The houses were dark and their occupants asleep. Nobody heard the muffled shot that rang out into the still of the night. A shot, quickly followed by another. Shots that left two members of their exclusive community dead.

****

"Where are you going? It's two in the morning."

Will pulled his T-shirt back on and raked his fingers through his blond hair. "Early start tomorrow," he said picking up his wallet and his cell. Checking he'd not received any messages while he was otherwise engaged he shoved them both into his pocket, and sat on the edge of the bed to slip his feet into his boots. Will closed his eyes at the feel of soft lips feathering across the nape of his neck, warm breath lifting the strands of his short hair where it sat against his skin, and sighed. He hated this part, the leaving. Especially when the sex had been good, which it had. Ignoring the insistent pulling of impatient fingers at his shirt, he laced his boots and stood up.

"Do you want my number?"

"Sure," Will replied, taking out his cell. He moved his fingers over the pad and pretended to put the number recited to him into his contacts. He wasn't sure why they were going through this charade. The man staring up at him wasn't fooled by Will's actions, yet he continued to reel off the numbers. Pushing his cell back into his pocket, Will leaned down, ran a quick hand through curly blond hair, and kissed the offered lips. He pulled back before it could become anything more and crossed the room. Pausing in the doorway he raised a hand, scrabbling desperately for the guy's name and failing, so throwing a lame goodbye over his shoulder instead. At least he had the decency to blush slightly when the cold reply followed him out into the hall.

"It's Jack, asshole."

****

Scott threw his head back, lost on a sea of sensation as he pounded relentlessly into the willing body beneath him. "Fuck, *yes,*" he cried out when the heat around him tightened and he lost it. His orgasm pulsed through him and he thrust mindlessly, chasing the last of his pleasure. When his breathing had calmed enough to move, he grabbed the end of the condom and pulled out then turned to flush it down the toilet beside them. Club bathrooms were never exactly the easiest places to have sex in, but eyes across a crowded room and all that. Tucking himself back into his pants, Scott gasped as hands grabbed his face and turned him around into a searing kiss.

"My place?" The gray eyes gazing into his were hopeful.

Scott shook his head, his lips curving into a regretful smile. "I'm sorry, I have an early meeting," he replied, softening the dismissal with a kiss. "But I had fun; maybe we can do it again some time."

"Ah, so you're one of those guys who gets his rocks off and then isn't interested, huh?" The other man's tone was angry, as he glared up at Scott.

Scott's eyes hardened and he pulled himself up to his full height of almost six feet before unlocking the door of the stall. "I'm never interested in some twink who'll let me fuck him before I've even asked his name." Ignoring the stunned look on the other man's face, Scott walked out into the crowded bathroom, and kicked the stall door closed behind him. After quickly washing his hands, he ran his fingers through his short, black, sweat-dampened hair, and then made his way back out into the club.

Surrounded by a sea of writhing bodies, Scott looked at the illuminated hands of his watch and yawned when he saw that it was two in the morning. Lowering his head to avoid anyone mistaking a glance for a come on, he began to push his way through the throng toward the exit. Even though the guy in the bathroom had thought he was being blown off, he really did have an early start tomorrow. Outside in the cold New York air, he hailed the first cab he saw and clambered into the back.

I

Staring down at him, Grace wondered what time Scott got home from the club last night. Although she knew he was aware they had to be in early this morning, she also knew him well enough to know that that was where he'd undoubtedly spent his evening. It also annoyed her that he could still look good after a night of drink and debauchery, when she would have looked like warmed over shit. She smiled at Scott's groan as she pulled the bedclothes off his body, and chuckled as he made a desperate grab for them at the last minute to cover his modesty.

"What the fuck are you doing?" he growled, opening his eyes and glaring at her.

"Getting your lazy ass up," she said in a matter of fact tone. "What time did you leave the club last night?"

"Who said I went to the club?" he muttered, pulling the duvet back over his head.

"I did," she replied, yanking at the covers again. "Come on, it's nine-thirty, and we've got a shitload of paperwork to get through." She walked across the room and paused in the doorway, turning to grin wickedly at him. "Never give a woman the key to your house, Scott. Not if you don't want her to use it."

"You're not a woman," he grumbled. "You're a Rottweiler, now get out." Grace Cassidy laughed as she made her way into the kitchen to put the coffee on, her long blond hair flowing behind her like a curtain. She had been Scott's partner for just over a year and she was the only one in the department who knew he was gay. He'd shared this piece of information with her after working with her for only a couple of months, a fact that she was both humbled and touched by. That he would feel comfortable enough with her to tell her what he considered to be his deep, dark secret practically right off the bat had touched her, and she was fiercely protective of him. She'd told him that she had no problem with his sexual preferences, if anything it was a relief because it meant that she could actually work the job instead of worrying about him looking up her skirt.

She'd understood the reasons why he didn't want it made public knowledge, although she was of the opinion that it was probably better to come right out with it. That if he was upfront and weathered the storm, the fallout from his honesty would be quieter and fizzle out sooner than if someone found out by other means. But Scott wouldn't be swayed. So Grace had simply taken the secret he had entrusted her with and guarded it closely.

Searching the cupboards for two cups, she placed them on the counter and then reached up for the open sugar packet. She hastily dropped it when she opened it and came face to face with a very large and desiccated spider. "Jesus fucking Christ, Scott," she hissed, throwing the entire bag in the trash. "For a gay guy you're such a slob."

"Jeez, stereotype much?" Scott chuckled, wandering into the kitchen, rubbing a towel over his hair. There were damp spots on his dress shirt and his tie was lop-sided, obviously having been tied in a hurry after he'd re-defined the term quick shower. "I'm hardly here. You know the hours I work, hell, you work 'em with me."

"Yes I do, moron," Grace retorted. "But even I manage to put food in the cupboards once a week and check that I haven't got dead bugs everywhere. But then I suppose you are a man, after all."

Scott laughed as he poured the coffee Grace had made into the two mugs and slid one across the counter to her. "Exactly; just because I like to suck dick doesn't mean I'm Martha Stewart in the kitchen."

Grace's gaze traveled the length of Scott's body as she drank her coffee. She took in the muscular six foot frame, made up of broad shoulders, slim waist and lean hips. Scott was beautiful, plain and simple, and she often told him that he was doing a disservice to women everywhere by not even attempting to go down the straight and narrow. His short black hair was always gelled to give him that "I just got out of bed" look, even though she knew that if she attempted that look it would take her half an hour to get it to look like she didn't have a cat on her head. She smiled at the thought and openly studied his handsome face.

Rimmed with long, dark lashes that Grace herself would personally kill for, his eyes were of a brown so dark they were like limpid pools of chocolate. Scott's aquiline nose had a slight bump in the middle, but the slight imperfection only served to make his face more beguiling. Below that, he sported an expertly groomed five o'clock shadow which gave the impression he hadn't shaved that morning, when in fact it looked like that on purpose. It didn't hurt that he had full, voluptuous lips just made for kissing, that drew your eye whenever he spoke. She'd seen many a female suspect confess without even realizing she was doing it, while concentrating on those lips. Grace sighed at the lyrical tangent she had wandered off on and put the now empty coffee cup in the sink. Picking up her badge, she fitted it to the waistband of her trousers, and then holstered the gun she had put down on the counter.

"You're staring again," Scott muttered a complaint. He put his cup in the sink next to hers and picked up his jacket from the back of the chair, rolling his eyes when he caught Grace's gaze and pushed his arms into the sleeves.

Grace grinned and gave him the once over again. "Are you *sure* you're gay?" she asked hopefully.

"Shut *up*," Scott replied, his cheeks flushing as he pushed her toward the door.

Laughing loudly, Grace waited for him to lock the door behind them and then trotted down the drive beside him. God, he was fun. She would have thought he was well used to her quick witted responses and open teasing by now; but his face flushed quicker than a toilet every time. Consequently, for her, it never got old.

Grace depressed the button to unlock her cherry red sedan and slid behind the wheel, unable to contain her snigger when Scott all but threw himself into shotgun, his expression petulant. Starting the engine, she headed the car toward the White Plains City Police Department. Regardless of their easy banter, they *did* have a shitload of paperwork to get through. Hopefully, being Sunday, a supposed day of rest, no one would decide to kill anyone so they could get on with it.

****

"Would you please stop gloating," Julie Bates, Will's partner, complained, keeping her attention on the computer screen in front of her. "What are you? Twelve?"

Will snorted and carried on transferring details from the arrest sheet he was reading on to his PC. "I'm not gloating. Hey, if Turner can't drag himself away from last night's floozy, far be it from me to complain because we got here first."

Admittedly—although he hadn't exactly spent last night alone—for him it had been the first time in two months; he was sure Scott '*next please*' Turner could make no such claim. He'd been just as surprised to find himself in someone's bed last night as Julie obviously was from the look on her face when he filled her in en route this morning.

When he'd decided to go to the bar for a quiet drink last night, he'd actually intended to have a quiet drink. But once he'd locked eyes with the gorgeous guy in the corner booth, he'd thrown caution to the wind and accepted the beer that had been sent over. Of course, the evening could have ended a little better, you know, he could have remembered the guy's name—but hey, nobody's perfect.

Looking up at his partner of eight months, Will grinned. He ignored her eye roll and combed his fingers through the gelled spikes of his honey-blond hair, returning his concentration to the paperwork beside him. Glancing up, his gaze followed Turner and Cassidy as they came out of the elevator and walked to their desks. Turner sported the hesitant gait of someone who had over indulged the night before, not that that was a huge surprise. "*Afternoon*, guys," he couldn't resist teasing as they sat down.

"Wow, were you here with the dawn chorus, Harrison? Did you bring the Cap a nice shiny apple?" Scott drawled, taking out his gun and putting it in the top drawer of his desk. "Waiting for the arrival of your plaque as chief suck up?"

Will's eyes narrowed as he looked at the other man. "Aw, poor baby, wouldn't Cassidy put out last night?" His tone was filled with mock sympathy, and sarcasm dripped from every syllable. "Or did you only make your way through four girls instead of the usual six?" A satisfied smile spread across his lips as he watched Scott rise from his chair, and Cassidy put her hand out to restrain him. "Ooh, did I hit a nerve? Didn't Scottie get his fill last night? You should keep him on a leash, Gracie."

"Shut up, Will," Grace tapped a warning on Scott's forearm and waited until he returned to his seat before picking up the first file on the mountain of files on her desk. "Jules and I are getting pretty fed up with the two of you. So grow up, grow a pair, grow what the fuck ever, but stop bickering like Paris Hilton and Nicole Richie for five minutes, and get the fuck along."

She stood and walked around the back of Will's chair, and he froze as she slowly ran her hand down his chest. Will gasped when her glossed lips brushed his ear and the tip of her tongue licked around the sensitive shell as she intoned huskily, "And by the way—I *always* put out."

Will scowled at her as she walked behind Julie's chair on her way back to her own desk, and held out her hand for the high five that Julie slapped onto it, before sliding into her seat. The two of them took great pleasure in making him feel like a gawky schoolboy, which afforded her and Julie seemingly endless amusement. The fact that Scott enjoyed his discomfort, too, didn't help. However, he felt slightly vilified when she turned to glare at Scott, the look stilling the man's laughter as though she'd pressed a mute button and growled at him.

"I don't know what *you're* laughing at, Sparky. You're just as bad. Now shut up, we've got work to do."

Will grumbled under his breath as he started up his PC and picked up a file while he waited for it to whir into life. Three days ago they'd finally managed to close a long running case that the four of them had worked their asses off on. For six months, they'd been trying to close in on Dean Kinkade, a wealthy industrialist who had faked a burglary in order to murder his wife and collect on her life insurance.

Six months of subpoenas, interviews, knocking door to door, and going through paperwork; anything just to get a break, and then they found it. He hadn't quite covered up the paper trail for the knife he'd used, and they'd got him. Instead of sunning himself on a beach in Cancun, Kinkade now found himself in the

Westchester County Jail, awaiting arraignment, where Will was pretty sure they didn't have a pool or bikini clad hotties.

Although they were still on a high from their success, there was now the obligatory mountain of paperwork to transfer onto computer; hence their early arrival at the office on a Sunday, their collective day off. Will sighed heavily as he pushed his reading glasses onto the bridge of his nose and then logged into his PC. This was going to take forever.

****

Two hours later, their Captain barked a command from the open doorway of his office. "Cassidy, Bates, bring your girlfriends in here!" Slamming the door behind him, he returned to his desk and handed a box of tissues to one of the other two men in the room. "Are you sure you don't want something to drink?" Glenn Hall asked for the third time since they'd arrived. He sighed as his cousin shook his head, for the third time. "You look like shit, Damon," he said quietly.

Glenn had been the Captain of the White Plains Homicide Team for six years and not once, in all those years had he had a member of his own family involved, albeit very loosely, in a murder. His gray eyes narrowed as he watched Damon blow his nose again, and dab at the tears rolling down his cheeks. Glenn had appointed himself Damon's surrogate brother while they were growing up and they were very close. He ran a hand through his salt and pepper hair and looked up at the knock on the door. "*Come!*" he yelled and watched his four best file into the room. "Sit," he instructed, waiting until the two women had taken seats and the two men were standing behind their respective partners.

"Damon, Cal, this is Turner, Harrison, Cassidy, and Bates. People, this is my cousin, Damon Hall and his partner, Cal Perry," he began by way of introduction and waved his hand at the two men.

"You remember the murder/suicide over at Laurel Heights a month ago?" Glenn leaned back in his chair and folded his hands across his stomach as he stared at his detectives. "Damon and Cal live in Laurel Heights, and they were friends of Jon and Cory, the accused and the victim. I know it looked pretty much open and shut, but Damon and Cal aren't so sure and, now, neither am I." Turning to his cousin, he smiled softly, uncaring if his affection for the other man was clear to anyone else in the room. "Damon, you wanna take it from here?"

****

Scott leaned against the bookcase he was standing next to and watched Damon from beneath lowered lashes, as the other man stood up and walked over to the window. It was obvious that the man was upset and by the shake of his shoulders, Scott surmised that Damon wanted to regain his composure before speaking. While they waited, he took the time to study the couple.

Hall bore a slight resemblance to his cousin, but only in the twice-removed kind of way. Whereas Hall's hair was a shortly cropped, rusty brown, liberally sprinkled with gray; Damon's was black, and fell in a widow's peak across his forehead. His eyes were blue, as opposed to smoky gray, and he was clean-shaven with full, pouty lips, whereas the Captain liked to sport a neat beard and mustache. His gaze fell to Cal Perry, who still sat in the chair, watching Damon anxiously. Cal was a very striking man, with skin the color of ebony, limpid brown eyes, a thin mustache and neatly trimmed, barely there goatee. Scott felt the man's genuine concern for his boyfriend, rolling off Cal in waves, and he watched the way he twisted his hands nervously in his lap while he waited for Damon to speak.

No one needed any explanation regarding Laurel Heights itself. The purpose-built, five-house cul de sac was famous in White Plains *before* the incident last month; now it was the 'in' topic on everyone's lips. Laurel Heights was an exclusive gated community in the leafy suburb of North White Plains, seventeen miles outside of White Plains, and in a very sought after area to live, by the wealthier population of the city. There was, however, one stipulation to owning a property in Laurel Heights. You had to be a couple and you had to be gay.

The murder/suicide had happened just over a month ago when Cory Philips had, apparently in a fit of rage, shot his partner, Jon Webber in the head at close range. In his grief, it would appear that Philips had turned the gun on himself. The other residents of Laurel Heights had been interviewed and had testified as to the volatile nature of Jon and Cory's relationship, and the fact that they had been fighting on and off the day of the incident. As the Captain had said, pretty open and shut. Scott watched Damon slowly turn from the window and waited patiently for the man to collect himself before he began.

Damon wiped futilely at the tears still coursing down his cheeks. "I'm sorry," he said, his voice thick and raw as he took the clean tissue that Cal held out to him. "It's been very hard." He took a deep steadying breath and began again.

"I know the other residents of Laurel Heights said that Cory and Jon had a volatile relationship, but it's simply not true. They were young, in love and deliriously happy." He wiped at his nose and sank into the seat beside Cal before continuing. "They were the sweetest couple I've ever seen and I just don't believe a word of it. There is no way that Cory would have done that to Jon. No way on this earth. He would rather have cut off his own hand than hurt that boy. He *loved* him."

"Mr Hall, why would the other residents lie about the nature of Mr Philips' and Mr Webber's relationship? What reason would they have?" Will's deep voice echoed around the room.

Cal reached out for Damon's hand as the man dissolved into more tears, and picked up the story. "Detectives, I know that Laurel Heights is, shall we say, an unusual community, but there is more that goes on behind those closed doors than you or anyone else realizes." He glanced at Hall for affirmation and took a deep breath when his boyfriend indicated his acquiescence. "Look, we're not ashamed of it, although it is not to everyone's taste. There are certain practices once a month at Laurel Heights. We don't always indulge, but we have done and we know that Cory and Jon did too. We think whatever happened that night had to do with the part of Laurel Heights that only the residents see. That there was a reason they had to be silenced."

"When you say "events", Mr Perry, what exactly do you mean?" Julie asked politely, a reassuring smile on her lips.

"Orgies, partner-swapping, that sort of thing," Cal replied, his gaze unwavering as he looked at Julie, obviously waiting for the slight woman to judge him in some manner. His gaze softened when he realized that he was looking for contempt where there was none.

"And you say that Cory and Jon indulged in these monthly gatherings?" Grace asked, leaning forward in her chair to face Cal. "Were you and Mr Hall at any of these "events" at the same time as Cory and Jon?"

"We did indulge in some partner-swapping with Cory and Jon," Damon replied with a nod of his head, his fingers still entwined with Cal's. "That's how we know they could never hurt each other. Jon was with me and Cory was with Cal and neither of them could do anything. They were happy to participate in the orgies or the soft bondage when it was the two of them being together, but not if it involved another person. They were so in love with each other, that although they were happy to have sex next to you, they wouldn't have sex with you."

"Basically," Hall piped up, leaning forward to place his elbows on his desk and look at the four detectives in front of him. "We need to have a root around in Laurel Heights, and find out exactly what's going on behind those closed doors. Apparently there is a rigorous interview process that the Resident's Committee puts you through to get a house in Laurel Heights. Damon and Cal have got you a foot in the door and the Committee is looking to rent the empty property." He apologized quickly for his thoughtlessness as Damon burst into fresh tears, and handed him more tissues.

"So, Harrison, Turner, you have an appointment at three tomorrow afternoon. That should be enough time to get your stories straight. You know the usual; how you met, how long you've been together, what the other likes to eat for breakfast, all that sort of shit." He jabbed a finger at Grace and Julie. "You two are gonna work together here, liaise with the boys while they're in situ and get them any information they need."

Will cleared his throat and a confused frown creased his brow. "I'm sorry, sir. I'm not following."

"Jeez, thought you were supposed to be top of your class…" Scott trailed off when he was hit with a glare from Hall.

"You two listen to me, and you listen real good. Every other male detective in this department is either married or too old for this community. You two are the only ones who fit the bill." Hall pointed his finger agitatedly at the two men. "I'm sick of hearing you two bitch about each other and I'm here to tell you right now, I don't care. You hear me? I don't care if Harrison stole your marbles or Turner took your lunch. I have no interest in your pathetic squabbles or playground scuffles. You *will* suck it up and you *will* pull this off. I wanna know if someone pulled the trigger for those boys. Do you understand me? My *family* is in there and I want them protected. You're going undercover boys and you *will* act like you think the sun shines out of each other's asses, do I make myself clear?"

Will and Scott did the only thing they could do when Hall had that tone in his voice—they nodded.

II

Will cupped his hands under the running water and splashed his face. Lifting his head he gazed at his reflection. He reached out for a paper towel and dabbed the moisture from his skin. *This was not happening to him. This couldn't happen to him.* He'd worked so hard to build this persona. For God's sake, as far as everyone in the department was concerned, he'd been in a committed relationship with Amanda for three years and they were living the perfect apple pie life. No one knew the girl in the photograph he kept on his desk was the model who came in the photo-frame.

He'd been fourteen when he'd realized he was more interested in the way the T-shirt stretched across his best friend's chest, than with the way the buttons almost popped off on some of the tight blouses his older sister's friends wore. Sixteen when Matt Hayes popped his cherry in the back of Matt's pick-up truck on Lookout Point; eighteen when he came out to his family.

After the initial shock had worn off and his mother had taken a couple of moments to mourn the loss of the grandchildren he would never give her, she'd gone back to her needlepoint and his father had turned the sound back up on the Super Bowl; thus further cementing his belief that he had the coolest parents in the world. It had been later that night that his father had sat on the end of Will's bed and talked about what being openly gay in the police force might mean for him.

"Not that I would ever suggest you deny who you are, son," Frank Harrison had said softly. "As far as your mother and I are concerned, it doesn't matter whether you fall in love with Betty or Bob. I'm just saying that there're folks out there who would go out of their way to make things difficult for you, just because you prefer Bob, if you get my meaning."

Frank had been right. Will had realized that the moment one of his roommates, Billy Roberts, had admitted to being gay. Some of the other cadets in their class had set up a campaign of ridicule and torment that had the man packing his bags after three weeks. Will had walked into their room when Billy had been packing his suitcase. He'd moved around the room in silence, handing Billy clothes from the drawers and helping the other man gather his belongings, knowing he wouldn't talk Billy out of his decision to leave. "I'm sor—" Billy had stopped Will's apology with their first and only kiss. He would never forget the look on his friend's face when he closed the lid of his suitcase and took one last look around the room. Billy had pulled Will into his arms for a brief hug and murmured into Will's hair, "Don't tell them, Will. Don't let them take away your dream, too."

Billy's words hit home, and from that moment on, Will had become Mr All-American. He had a picture of his 'girl back home' on his dresser and laughed along with the ribald stories of the other cadets. Not that he would have been able to find a girl's g-spot with a road map and a flashlight. He'd sailed through the academy with flying colors and graduated in the top ten of his class, and no one had any idea he was planning on spending graduation night in a hotel room with his boyfriend, rather than at the big party with the rest of the guys.

Will had begun his career in the Greenwich Police Department, working his way up to Detective. Eight months ago he had been promoted to Homicide and transferred to White Plains, where he'd been introduced to his new partner, Julie Bates. It had been the first time he'd really be relying on a partner and, after six months of working together, and deciding that if they were to be holding each other's lives in their hands they should know everything about each other, he told her he was gay.

Of course, he'd stressed to her that he wanted it kept a secret, that everyone else thought he was straight and he wanted to keep it that way. His private life was his own and he didn't want some homophobic colleague trying to force him out of a job he'd worked damn hard for and was damn good at.

Julie had been extremely laid back about the whole thing, informing him with a twinkle in her eye that he wasn't telling her anything she hadn't already figured out for herself. At his incredulous expression, she had reassured him that he played his part very well and no one else in the department had any suspicions. Her brother, who was a paramedic in the Fire Department, was gay and she understood only too well the prejudice that was still rife in both the police force and the fire department. She'd watched her brother go through a really tough time after he first came out to his colleagues, and she totally got the reasons why he wanted to keep it a secret. She'd thanked Will for taking her into his confidence and he'd known that no one would ever find out from her.

Now, now everything was going to hit the fan. How the fuck was he supposed to pretend to be gay? More importantly, how the fuck was he supposed to pretend to be the yin to Scott *'asshole'* Turner's yang? Will gazed into his own eyes and saw panic, bordering on unabridged terror reflected back at him. Running a hand over his face, he pinched the bridge of his nose between his thumb and forefinger. He wasn't going to be able to do it. He'd never pull it off. They'd see through him like a pane of glass. How the hell was he supposed to convince a room full of strangers he was in love with Scott *'I'm so far up my own ass I can see what I had for breakfast'* Turner?

He remembered the first time he'd seen the other man. Hall had taken him around the department and introduced him to everyone. Turner and O'Malley, another detective, had been in the middle of a ribald conversation about Turner's conquest the night before.

Will had remembered how uncomplimentary Turner had been about the poor girl, who had probably thought she'd found her knight in shining armor, and his stomach had turned, forcing him to swallow against the acid that burned in the back of his throat. Unable to help it, all he'd managed was a curt nod when Hall had made the introductions, and had quickly moved on to the next desk. Turner was everything he despised in a man. Cock-sure, brazen, thought he'd done it all and knew it all, ruffling his feathers and strutting around like Cock of the Walk. The man was just an ass who got by on his dark, devilish looks and his charm, and nothing the man had said or done in the last eight months, had made Will change his mind.

Will shuddered inwardly and rubbed at the throbbing in his temples. He couldn't imagine what Turner would do with the information that he was gay. The asshole would have a goddamn field day. Leaning his forehead against the mirror, Will's shoulders slumped in defeat.

This was never going to work.

****

Scott stared at the coffee machine as if he were trying to commit the menu to memory. *What the fuck was he going to do?* The captain had just thrown him into a nightmare situation. Part of him wondered if the vindictive son of a bitch knew the truth about his homosexuality. And that for the last eight months he'd craved Will *'I'm fucking beautiful and don't I know it'* Harrison as if he were Scott's own particular brand of crack.

He remembered the first time the man had walked into the department. Scott had nearly swallowed his tongue as one hundred and eighty pounds of tight abs and lean hips had sauntered across the floor with the captain. He'd been talking with O'Malley, doing his best to convince the man that he'd been with some nympho-maniacal redhead the night before, when he'd glanced at the approaching men and his words had stilled in his throat.

Scott didn't think he'd ever seen anything like Will Harrison. The guy was about the same height as him, but Will's broad shoulders, made it seem like he towered over Scott. His instant reaction had been to wonder what it would be like if Will put all that muscle to good use and he'd been dreaming about it ever since. At first glance, he'd thought maybe he would be able to find out; that he'd seen something flicker across those incredible dark brown eyes, as he'd been unable to prevent his gaze from raking over the man in undisguised admiration. Then he'd heard Will talking with Gracie about a girlfriend and Scott had felt disappointment unfurl in his gut. He'd cursed his stupidity for getting the hots for the straight guy. He should have known someone that hot would be out of his reach. Burying how he really felt behind a veil of sarcasm and snappy rejoinders, he had become so good at it he had everyone, including Will, convinced that Scott couldn't stand him.

He'd seen Will's look of disgust when the admin girls had fawned over him at the Christmas party, and anger had burned through him. Who the hell was Harrison to look at him that way? To judge him? The look on Will's face had Scott giving the girls even more of a show than he'd intended. Hell he was a man after all and attention was attention. Especially when you wanted to hide the fact that you'd much prefer six foot of Will Harrison rubbing up against you instead of Tina from the typing pool. Scott had become extremely adept at maintaining the facade he had created for himself. God knows he'd had enough practice. Until Grace, he'd only made the mistake of coming out once before.

****

"Goddamn queers."

Scott didn't take his gaze off the eight ball. If he made this shot, he would actually beat the great Paul Turner for the first time in his seventeen years. "Sssh," he hissed through his teeth, his tongue sneaking out of the corner of his mouth in concentration. "If you're trying to distract me, Pop, it's not gonna work. I'm taking you down."

"Who do they think they are? Coming in here and flaunting their perversions."

Scott sighed and lifted his gaze from the ball to the object of his father's consternation. His stomach lurched when he saw the two men at the end of the bar. Everyone who knew Paul Turner was aware of the man's bigotry—especially his son. Not that Paul wasn't an equal opportunities bigot, he was. He had something to say about all minorities, but if he had to pick the one he reviled the most, it would be homosexuals. Or fudge-packing, shirt-lifting, ass-loving abominations of God, as he liked to call them.

Which was probably why Scott felt it best not to let his father know that last Friday night his mouth had been around Jake's, the taller man of the two, cock while his face had been fucked with lust filled abandon. *Yeah, that would go down real well.* Or the fact that, after he came, Jake then pounded Scott's ass so hard he felt him for the best part of a week.

His gaze locked with Jake's and his stomach lurched again when the other man raised surprised eyebrows in recognition. Scott gave him an almost imperceptible shake of his head, letting go of the breath he'd been holding when Jake's eyes flitted from him to Paul and back again. Message received and understood—thank God.

"You know they even let 'em into the factory now?"

"What?" Scott looked up at his father again, a frown creasing his brow. "Are you gonna let me take this shot or not?"

"The queers. We've got one of 'em working at the factory," Paul repeated, downing the rest of his beer, his fifth Scott noted, but then he was counting. "Fucking fairy."

"Pop, come on." Scott's stomach was now filling with a thousand anxious butterflies. He knew that look on his father's face and, fueled by alcohol, there was no telling what kind of scene Paul would create. "Let's just play the game, okay?"

Paul turned cold blue eyes on Scott and his lips curled into a sneer. "You telling me what to do, boy? When did you get so big for your breeches that you thought you could tell *me* what to do?"

"Pop—"

"No, come on, hotshot. Fill me in." Paul waved his beer bottle perilously close to Scott's face. "I wanna know when you decided you could tell me what to do!"

Scott flinched as the beer bottle in his father's hand was slammed onto the pool table. His gaze scanned the room and his cheeks flushed with embarrassment to find they were the center of attention—as they usually were when Paul had too much to drink. "I just meant—"

"Been listening to your mother again, boy? Do you think I'll listen to you any more than I listen to her?" Paul's face grew red in anger as he snarled at Scott. "What is it? Huh? Sticking up for the queers? Hoping to get a little kiss are you?"

"Dad, please," Scott tried to reason, keeping his tone calm. His gaze widened when he saw Jake push himself away from the bar and walk toward them.

Fuck! No! He could see the concern on Jake's face and while a part of him was grateful for it, the greater part wanted him to stop his approach and just turn away, pretend he hadn't heard a single word. He shook his head quickly at Jake and his heart sank like a stone to the bottom of the lake behind their house. Paul Turner had seen the gesture.

"Do you know him?" His gaze flitted between Jake and his son. "Do you know this faggot?"

Scott felt the blood drain from his face as quickly as realization flooded his father's. He didn't need to utter a word. Paul knew. He stood, frozen to the spot as his father approached him—afraid, but unwavering, even when Paul Turner spat in his face and stormed from the bar.

Paul Turner had barely spoken to Scott again in the remaining year he spent at home before entering the police academy. His face held no pride when his son shook the dust of their town from his feet and left for the city, only contempt and disappointment. Paul had died three years later, having never repaired the damage his bigotry had caused to their relationship.

Grace was his second partner since Scott had come to work in homicide, and he'd waited six months before he'd told her he was gay. His previous partner, John Norton, had been a dyed in the wool redneck, with three daughters and two sons, who came from a background where gays in the department would not be tolerated. Scott had decided his working life would not have been worth living if John had known where his preference really lay. But Grace, Grace had been different. From the start he felt as though they'd known each other their whole lives. The longer they spent together, the fewer reasons he could find *not* to tell her. He trusted her with his life and knew that she understood his reasoning and would hold onto his secret until the day she died.

Scott was brought back to the here and now by the plastic cup dropping into the tray as the machine whirred into life and filled the cup with coffee. He stared at the steady stream of black liquid and blinked, not realizing he had even pressed the buttons. Picking up the coffee, he hissed when some of the hot liquid spilled on his fingers.

But now—now the shit was going to hit the fan. Now he was supposed to pretend to be in love with Will *'I'm built like a Greek God'* Harrison? How did he convince complete strangers he wanted the man mountain? He sighed heavily and headed back to his desk. Convincing them wouldn't be the difficult part. The difficult part would be not being *too* convincing.

This was never going to work.

****

Two hours later, Scott looked up from his computer screen to find Grace and Julie standing beside his desk. Grace was holding a pizza box and Julie was holding a large A4 notepad. "What?" he asked, blinking owlishly at them.

"The four of us are going into the boardroom where it's nice and quiet, so we can hash out your story," Julie smiled, her eyes twinkling with glee, which was not a good sign as far as Scott concerned.

"My what?" Scott said, rubbing at the bridge of his nose. He'd been staring at the screen for so long, a decided ache had settled behind his eyes. By the look on the women's faces, it was only going to get worse.

Grace grabbed his hand and pulled him to his feet. "Come on, Turner. We need to put our heads together and get your cover story straight. You too,

Harrison. We're gonna sort out the Will and Scott big gay love story."

Scott glanced over at Will as he re-entered the department with a cup of coffee in his hand. "Gracie, come on," he complained, "we've still got eight depositions to get on the database."

"The cap has given them to Brown and Logan, no excuses."

Scott's gaze was pleading and her hand tightened momentarily on his and he was grateful for the reassurance before she followed Julie out of the department. He heaved a sigh, knowing he sounded like a disgruntled five-year-old and rubbed his eye with a closed fist for good measure. Stomping across the room and down the hall after the two women, his shoulders slumped in defeat. He knew they were gonna have way too much fun with this. Out of the corner of his eye he saw Will fall into step beside him, the man's stance mirroring his own—shoulders slumped, feet falling heavily on the tiled floor. *At least he looks as happy about it as I do.*

"Okay," Julie drew the word out for effect. "You two will have absolutely *no* problem convincing people that you're the love of each other's life. *No* problem whatsoever." Her tone oozed sarcasm as she looked from one to the other.

Will's expression showed his discontent and Scott could only imagine that his was a mirror image. He lifted his feet and stretched his legs out, resting them on the table, wishing she would stop gloating and get on with it already.

"Just get on with it."

Scott's gaze flitted to Will across the table and he swallowed down the chuckle bubbling in his throat. They were definitely on the same wavelength with this thing. Which certainly made a change. He tried to ignore the way the short spikes of Will's hair slipped through the man's fingers as he ran a hand through them and cleared his throat, turning his attention to Julie. "Um… we need to keep it short and plausible. What sort of questions are we going to be asked?"

Grace took a slice of pizza from the box and pushed it toward the center of the table. Scott waited, he'd like to say patiently, but he'd be lying, while she scanned the sheet of paper in front of her and chewed thoughtfully on her pizza. Finally she mumbled around her food, "A ton of boring stuff. How you first met, how long you've been together, what you do for a living, when did you know he was 'the one'?" She swallowed the bite of pizza she'd been masticating and frowned. "What the fuck do they wanna know that for? You wanna move into a house, not join the Romance Writers of America." She gaze carried on down the rest of the list and Scott frowned when her pink glossed mouth dropped open in surprise.

"What?" Julie beat him to the question as she leaned forward in her chair and picked up another slice of pie to accompany the one he'd just watched her inhale.

"They want to know who the top is and who's the bottom?" Gracie's tone was incredulous and she gazed at Scott in stunned amazement. "How the hell do they get normal, sane people to answer these questions in an interview to rent a house?"

"I'm guessing they can ask whatever the hell they want," Scott replied, rubbing at the bridge of his nose again as his headache intensified. "Every gay couple with enough money in New York is trying to get into the five houses in Laurel Heights, plus they want to make sure they have the right kind of person living behind those security gates. Someone who is open, liberal, and not gonna pass out if one of the neighbors turns up on the doorstep wearing a cock ring and a smile."

"Nice," Julie said, screwing up her nose, bringing a smile to Scott's lips as she tossed her half eaten pizza slice back into the box and grumbled. "Now I have a vision in my head of old Mr Lannerman who lives next door coming to borrow a cup of sugar, and it won't go away."

Scott chuckled at the look on her face and reached for a slice of pizza. He didn't exactly have much of an appetite, but his stomach had other ideas as it rumbled beneath his ribs. Rolling his eyes as Will knocked on the surface of the table, he slid the box across to the other man. "Can we hurry this along? I had a late night and I wanna get home."

"Who was the lucky ho last night?" Will said sarcastically around a mouthful of melted cheese. "Or were there so many you can't keep track?"

"Aww, missing the little woman? At least I was with *someone*, Captain Masturbation," Scott shot back, annoyed by the tone in Will's voice. "If Amanda doesn't get back from her course soon, you'll have to see the doc about the calluses on your palms."

"Boys, boys, boys," Grace admonished. "Don't make me turn your chairs to face the wall. Suck it up. Two men are dead. Can't you two put aside your bitching for five minutes?"

Scott ducked his head and mumbled a sorry for their insensitivity and he heard Will do the same. The girls were right. This was serious and they were prepping for an assignment, no matter how bizarre it might be. He was a cop for God's sake. Trained to go deep undercover. He could put his own feelings aside and get with the program. Hell, wasn't that what he'd been doing for years?

"Good," Julie said, turning over the cover of her notepad. "Okay, I'm gonna write the story down and then I'm gonna give you both a copy so you can study it before your appointment tomorrow. Jeez, this is going

27

to be so much fun—not. Right, are we sitting comfortably? Then I'll begin. How did you first meet? Gracie, what do you think?"

"Well—"

Scott's gaze narrowed when whatever Grace had been going to suggest was cut off as Will piped up, "I was working out in the gym when Scott followed me into the showers and asked me if I wanted to drop the soap." He held his hands up to his chest and clasped them together. "I just knew he was the one for me."

"I think you'll find, *sweetums*," Scott said, his eyes darkening in irritation. "I was minding my own business as I walked through the park when you called out from behind a bush, 'Hey big boy you wanna suck of my lollipop?' As soon as I saw you in that trench coat, I was a goner." He fluttered his eyelashes at Will and grabbed another slice of pizza. Two could play at that game and he'd been playing longer than Harrison.

"Aww, *hunnybun*, yet again you've got it wrong," Will replied, his voice dripping with barely disguised anger. "I believe we first met when you were pole-dancing at that strip joint and when you stuck your g-string in my face, you made my heart skip a beat."

"*Pumpkin*," Scott countered quickly with a sneer. "Didn't we meet at the library? I asked you if you had any books on *suckling* pigs and you asked me if I wanted to *suck* your pork."

"All right asshole, that's it!" Will ground out through gritted teeth and jumped out of his chair, much to Scott's amusement as he took in the fists clenched at Will's sides as Will glared down at him. "I'm not fucking working with this amateur."

Scott started when Julie's voice cut across their verbal war, "Shut the fuck up! Both of you!" Julie's angry yell echoed around the room as she stood and banged the notepad down onto the table. "Did you not hear what Gracie said? Two boys are dead! You will sit down and you will shut up, while we concoct some reason why you two would be together!" Scott had to bite the inside of his cheek when she held her hand up as Will opened his mouth. "Sit!" It was even more amusing when Will immediately sank back into his seat, his arms crossed and a petulant pout on his face. Scott studied Julie from beneath lowered lashes, trying to look suitably chastised as she returned to her chair and said, "You both seem to have a hell of an imagination, so Will can be a writer. Scott, you can be—"

"Annoying, childish, drunk?"

"Shut up, Will," Julie spat and turned her attention to Grace. "What do you think?"

"IT Consultant," Grace said with a smile. "He knows enough about computers to bluff his way through anything anyone asks him. He can say he works freelance, from home and writes software or something. Perfect."

"Okay," Julie scribbled frantically on her notepad. "What kind of books does Will write?"

"Don't we get a say?" Scott griped, watching the girls throw ideas back and forth to each other like a tennis double team.

"No!" They replied in unison and he leaned back into his chair, crossing his arms and sure that his face held the same petulant pout as Will's.

"I've got it! Children's books," Grace said, nodding at Scott. "Scott's got a niece. That's how they met. Scott took his niece to one of Will's signings. Their gazes met across the table and it was love at first sight and all that shit. How *romantic*." She pitched the tone of her voice a little higher on the last word.

"Are you two for real?" Scott spluttered.

"Did I *say* we were finished?" Julie ground out, scribbling ferociously on her pad. "I'm thinking they've been together for two years. That's long enough to know most things, but not so long that they would be expected to know every tiny detail."

Grace nodded in agreement as Julie continued writing. "Okay, I'm thinking you should bottom, Scott."

"Me?" Scott choked on a piece of pizza and had to wash it down with some water before continuing. Gracie was having way too much fun with this. Her blue eyes positively gleamed. "Why me?"

"Have you seen the size of Will's feet?"

Scott stood and pushed back his chair, ignoring Will and rolling his eyes at the two women who were laughing hysterically. He'd had just about enough and needed to get out before visions of being the bottom to Will's top stiffened his dick any further. "Just write the fucking notes. I'm going home."

"See you later, *sweet cheeks*," Will drawled, lifting his hand and blowing Scott a kiss.

Scott dealt with the gesture in a mature fashion befitting his age—he flipped him the finger and slammed the door, stomping off down the hall to the elevator. Shaking his head and muttering "Asshole," he stabbed the button for the elevator.

****

Scott's head was pounding when he rode up in the elevator to the department the following day. His sunglasses weren't quite keeping out the glare of the lights and his stomach rolled as the elevator lurched to a stop. "*Fuck*," he whimpered when the doors opened, every whir and scrape of metal grating on his over sensitive ears. He made his way to his desk, via the coffee machine, and slid into his chair, resting his head in his hands. Last night had seemed like such a good idea—at the time.

When he'd left the boardroom yesterday, his anger at the situation he found himself in had reached fever pitch and he needed to work it out of his system. Needed to get drunk and hopefully laid, preferably in that order. In the club, he'd enjoyably participated in both when, after five beers, he had found himself in a locked bathroom stall, his hands curled in soft dark hair while the man tried to literally suck Scott's brains out through his cock. Then there had been dancing, a lot more alcohol and Scott bending the muscled young thing over the hood of a car in the alley behind the club. He desperately tried to ignore the fact that if the guy had been a few inches taller and his hair a couple of shades lighter, he could have been Will's double.

Laying his head on his desk, he sighed at how good the cool surface felt against his hot skin. He shouldn't have had those last four shots, and the slice of toast he had forced down his throat for breakfast had not managed to settle his lurching stomach, but only increase his nausea.

"Are you fucking kidding me?" Will's voice said from behind him.

"Stop yelling," Scott moaned, not bothering to lift his head, not that he thought he'd be able to if he tried.

"You went out and got drunk the night before we're supposed to go undercover?" Will spat. "You're already *four* hours late and we've only got two hours to get our story straight. We've got to be at Laurel Heights at three. Are you even conscious?"

"Fuck off. Just get me another coffee. I'll be fine in a minute," Scott said quietly, wincing as Will's voice reverberated through his skull like a thousand shards of glass. He could feel the weight of Will's disapproving gaze on the back of his head and he really didn't give a shit. Why was the asshole still here? Why wasn't he getting coffee like he asked? How hard could it be?

You put the money in, pressed the button, and picked up the cup… surely even Harrison could manage that. Yes, he was aware that going out to drink last night was probably not his most mind-blowingly fabulous idea. He was also aware that being hung-over for the interview at Laurel Heights was low on the good idea list, too. But he'd needed something to stop him from thinking about living with the annoying ass glaring at him now. The great big, beautiful, sex on a stick, annoying ass. "Are you still here?" He mumbled into the table and breathed a sigh of relief at the huff Harrison gave and smiled feebly as the sound of Harrison's footsteps carried him away.

****

When Will returned from the store twenty minutes later, Scott was in exactly the same position he had left him in. Well, almost. Someone had decided it was a good idea to stick "Got Any Spare Change" to the back of his shirt. Will snorted at the small hill of coins that had accumulated beside Scott's head and curled his fingers around Scott's bicep, hauling him to his feet. "Come on, princess," Will said, and he led Scott from the room.

"Christ, Harrison," Scott hissed, his free hand going to his head. "Warn a guy would you? Get the fuck off me."

"Sit down and shut up," Will snarled, pushing Scott into a chair in the boardroom and dropping the brown paper bag in his hand onto the table. Walking over to the small cupboard in the corner, Will pulled out two glasses and put them in front of Scott. Opening the bag, Will withdrew a box of eggs and cracked two of them into one glass. He smirked when, out of the corner of his eye, he saw Scott give a dry heave. Returning his hand to the bag, Will pulled out a carton of Passion Fruit juice and filled the empty glass to the brim with the orangey liquid. "Here, numbnuts." He held the raw eggs out to Scott. "First this and then the Passion Fruit."

Scott gazed up at him over the top of his sunglasses and shook his head slowly. "Are you certifiable? I'm not drinking that. I'd rather feel like shit."

"Think of someone other than yourself for once, Turner. We can't just coast through this interview. We *have* to get in." Will shoved the glass into Scott's hands. "Either you do it yourself or I pour it down your throat. The choice is yours."

"I am glaring at you right now. I just want you to know that. I'd do it for real, but my eyes would probably dribble down my chin." Scott took the glass and looked at the two yolks bobbing in a sea of clear viscous fluid. "Are you shitting me or does this really work?"

"It really works," Will insisted with a nod of his head. "I read it somewhere once. Down the eggs, swallow them whole, and then knock back the juice. The eggs are protein and the juice is full of fructose which will burn the alcohol out of your system quicker." He glanced at the clock, frowning at the amount of time they *didn't* have. "Come on, hot shot. We need to get you sober or we're gonna be fucked."

Will watched, thoroughly enjoying Scott's discomfort as the man closed his eyes, held his nose and put the glass to his lips. He couldn't help but grimace as Scott swallowed the eggs then slammed the glass down on the table and grabbed frantically for the juice, knocking it back in three gulps and motioning to Will to pour him more. After his third glass, he burped inelegantly, dry heaved, and laid his head down on the desk. His voice was muffled as he said, "I just want you to know, for the record, I hate you."

Snorting, Will sat down in one of the empty chairs and pulled his notes out of his pocket. "Hah, you hate me now—wait 'til you live with me."

III

An hour and another carton of Passion Fruit juice later, Scott was quite surprised that he actually felt halfway human again. He'd also visited the bathroom six times, but considered that a small price to pay. Scott could feel Will's eyes on him as they sat at the table in the boardroom, but he didn't lift his head as he studied the notes in front of him.

"So, are you ready to do this? All the lights on? Raring to go?" Will's voice was heavy with sarcasm.

"What do you want to do, practice making goo-goo eyes at each other?" Scott retorted, not even looking up. He ignored the muttering that came from the other man and picked up the sheet of paper in front of him. "Okay, so according to Jules' chicken scratch, we met at a book signing. What if they ask you what books you write?"

Will stabbed at the paper in Scott's hand with his forefinger. "It says there, dumbass, children's books."

"I know that, cheese dip," Scott bit back. "Don't they have a name? What if they wanna know the title?"

Will frowned and Scott watched a slow smile eventually lift his lips. "I'll tell them I write Pogo's Adventures under a pseudonym. I know enough about that series to cope with any questions," he said, quoting the title of a series of children's books. At Scott's raised eyebrow, he flushed slightly. "You're not the only one who's an uncle. I've got a nephew."

"Huh," Scott replied. "Okay. So we met at a book signing. I brought Ella to meet you and it was, *love at first sight*?" he finished incredulously. "Are they trying to kill us? I can't believe we put our lives in these women's hands on a daily basis." He groaned.

"So Ella is your niece?" Will wrote the name on his notes. "How old is she?"

"Four," Scott replied, looking up. "What's your nephew's name? In case they ask."

"Why would they ask that?" Will met Scott's gaze in surprise.

Rolling his eyes Scott yawned. "What if they ask me what inspired you to write Pogo's Adventures? What am I gonna say? 'Gee, I don't know, but he likes it doggy style?'" Ignoring the narrowing of Will's gaze he continued, "Look, I can tell them that you just made up a story to tell your nephew at bedtime and he loved it so much you were encouraged to write it down." He glanced up at the clock to see how they were doing for time. "Come on, Stretch, we've gotta go in thirty. Keep up will ya?"

"His name is Scottie and he's six," Will replied grudgingly. "And don't call me Stretch. When did you know he was the one? Gimme a break. We are never gonna pull this off."

"Why? It's just one big game of pretend," Scott drawled, leaning back in his seat, feeling better now that his stomach had stopped threatening to empty its contents at any moment. "You pretend to like me. I pretend to like you. How hard can it be?" He stood, about to make his seventh trip to the bathroom before they left. As he passed Will's chair, he couldn't resist the temptation and a small, wicked smile curved his lips. Reaching out his hand, he gently brushed his fingers through Will's short, blond hair, biting back a laugh as Will's head turned so quickly the man was in danger of whiplash. "See—I know how to pretend," he murmured huskily, leaving Will staring after him with his mouth open as he closed the door behind him.

****

They wasted ten minutes in the parking lot arguing over which car to take. Will's almost brand new SUV, or Scott's 1982 Camaro. Finally, after words like, nouveau riche, bucket of rust, and ass-wiping shithead, were thrown around, they settled it like men. They flipped a coin. Which is why they were driving out of the parking lot with a smiling Scott behind the wheel of the bucket of rust and a very sullen looking ass-wiping shithead beside him.

They were five minutes into their thirty minute journey when Will couldn't contain himself anymore. He knew that Scott was only trying to get a rise out of him in the boardroom, but if the moron thought that this was going to be a chance to make Will as uncomfortable as possible, he could think again. "What the fuck was that in the boardroom?" he asked, turning in his seat to glare at Scott.

"What?" Scott said, not taking his eyes off the road as he eased into the traffic on the freeway.

"Why did you touch my hair? What were you trying to prove?" Will huffed.

"I wasn't trying to *prove* anything, Captain Paranoia," Scott replied, opening his window and resting his arm on the door. "Did it not occur to you that we may have to touch each other? Haven't you ever heard of PDA?" Scott glanced at Will. "For God's sake, even an uptight prude like you must hold pretty little Amanda's hand when you're out together. How are we gonna convince them we've been in love and living together for the past two years if there's a ten foot gap between us?"

"*Shit!*" Will hissed. PDA hadn't even crossed his mind. He was too busy trying to fathom how the hell he was going to manage spending time in the same house as Scott, now he had to touch him as well? *Will someone please just wake me up?* "No it hadn't occurred to me—" The words stilled in his throat and he swallowed hard before continuing. "Exactly how much PDA are we talking about?"

"How the fuck am I supposed to know?" Scott scrubbed a hand over his face, making his opinion of this conversation clear. "Let's just play it by ear. Now please shut the fuck up. I don't want to walk in there with bruised knuckles where I've punched you in your stupid face."

"Eat me," Will retorted and turned away to look out the window. Why did Turner insist on antagonizing him? It was hard for the both of them. Why did he have to make things worse. It was bad enough that he had to work with the moron, live with the moron, now he had the specter of public displays of affection hanging over his head. *This is fucking torture.*

After another ten minutes of total silence, Will heard Scott's sigh and glanced over at the stony faced 'love of his life', who growled, "So, tell me more, who are we meeting at this interview?"

Leafing through the file he pulled out of the briefcase at his feet, Will scanned the paper in front of him, grateful for the distraction from the heavy silence hanging like a fog in the car. "We're going to be interviewed by one half of each of the four remaining couples in Laurel Heights. They're the self-appointed Residents' Committee. Jay Randall, David Taylor, Marcus White, and Cal Perry, whom we've obviously already met.

"The interview is being held at number one, which is the Randall and Walker house. Jay Randall and Erik Walker are actually the architect and designer that built Laurel Heights. So this little "community" is their baby."

"Tell me more about Cory and Jon."

"Cory Philips, twenty-four, the son of prominent businessman Arthur Philips. He never worked a day in his life. Never needed to, had a trust fund bigger than your ego. Jon Webber, twenty-two, similar story. Wanna-be artist living off Mommy and Daddy," Will stated, not missing Scott's eye roll at the slur upon his character, or the raised eyebrow of condescension.

"That's a shitload of silver spoons. How long were they together?"

"Um, three years," Will replied. "They met at some retreat or other, which I think is just rich speak for 'I sit around on my ass all day'. Apparently they were inseparable from that moment on. They'd been living in Laurel Heights for just over six months before the shootings." Will closed the file and put it back in his briefcase, shutting it with a snap. Half-turning in his seat he gazed at Scott, a frown marring his forehead. "I talked briefly with Jon's father yesterday. They're all shell shocked, Scott. It seems Damon and Cal aren't the only ones who thought they were the perfect couple. In fact, both families are so convinced that Cory didn't shoot Jon and then himself, they're thinking about filing a Civil Action suit against the community."

Will recalled his conversation with the victim's father. The older man had been distraught, not that you would have been able to tell from his stance. Jon Webber Sr was an astute businessman and he remained stoic throughout the interview, apart from the almost imperceptible shaking of his hands.

"Shit, what did you say to that? That sort of crap could make it difficult for us to find out anything." Scott took the next exit and Will listened to the monotone of the voice on the sat nav as it told them there were four more minutes to their destination.

"What do you think I did? I put them onto Hall. He managed to convince them to wait and see whether we come up with anything before they file papers with the court." He leaned against the headrest and shrugged. "But I'm inclined to believe them, you know? Something just doesn't sit right. Those boys had everything to live for, money, good families who accepted them and their relationship. Jon's dad even told me Cory had asked him for Jon's hand in marriage two days before the incident. I just can't see him pulling the trigger."

"Well, let's hope we find out. We're here," Scott said, pulling up to wrought iron security gates. Will craned his neck and noted that behind the gates were five large, opulent houses situated in a semi-circle. "Jesus Christ," Scott mumbled, the expletive drawing Will's gaze from the houses and back to his partner. "It's like Knots Landing. How the hell are we gonna pull this off?"

The gates opened with a rumble and a moan— their arrival had obviously been noted. Trying to cover his own nervousness, Will snorted in reply, "Getting cold feet, Turner? I thought you could pretend. Well, you're not the only one." Will reached out, and a ridiculously childish urge to pay Scott back for the hair thing had him caressing Scott's thigh. With satisfaction, he felt the muscle jump beneath his fingers and intoned in a voice as sweet as molasses, "Come on, *honey*, we don't wanna be late." He removed his fingers and dropped them into his lap, staring at his hand as though he had never seen it before. Why were his fingers tingling? Why had a spark of something he had no intention of thinking about, shivered up his spine? This was Scott '*would you like to be a notch on my bedpost'* Turner. He couldn't stand him… right?

"Dick," Scott muttered and steered the car toward the first house in the semi-circle.

Will mentally berated himself as Scott straightened his tie and climbed out of the car. By the time Scott had walked around to the passenger door and opened it, he was quietly reminding himself of all the things he disliked about the man waiting for him to get out.

"What are you waiting for?" Scott hissed through his teeth.

Will glanced up at the easy smile on Scott's face and swallowed hard. He pasted a smile that he hoped matched Scott's and clambered out of the car, nudging the door closed with his hip. Will's eyes widened as Scott's hand came up to fiddle with the knot on his tie, long fingers brushing against his throat. Desperately trying not to slap Scott's hand away, he clenched his jaw and grinned. "What're you doing?"

"We have an audience," Scott countered, directing Will's gaze to the big bay window beside the heavy oak front door. "It's show time."

Will wasn't expecting Scott to kiss him so soon, and he thought the fact that he hadn't punched his lights out, showed marvelous control on his part. But he was expecting even less to feel Scott's lips against his after it was over. If you could even call it a kiss. It was barely there, a mere brushing of skin against skin, but Will's thighs had trembled at the contact. He just hoped Scott hadn't noticed.

****

They didn't have a chance to ring the bell before the door opened to reveal a tall, handsome man with piercing blue eyes and hair so black it had a blue sheen in the sunlight as it fell across his forehead. "You must be Will and Scott. I'm Jay Randall," he said, a welcoming smile on his face as he held out his hand, his gaze traveling appreciatively over Will, much to Scott's annoyance. "Wow, Damon said you had muscles. He wasn't exaggerating."

"I need the muscle to make sure this one doesn't get out of hand," Will chuckled lifting his arm and laying it across Scott's shoulders. "Nice to meet you,

Jay. I'm Will Harrison." Scott almost rolled his eyes at the open adoration on Jay's face when Will flashed him one of his one hundred watt smiles. Luckily, he managed to stop himself.

"And you must be Scott Turner. IT Consultant extraordinaire." Jay grinned, clasping Scott's hand in both of his. "Damon was right about you, too."

Shaking Jay's hand, Scott slid his other arm around Will's waist and huffed out a laugh. "Really? What did he say, only good things I hope?"

Jay beckoned them into the foyer of the house. "It depends on whether or not you consider the fact that he thinks you have the most beautiful eyes he has ever seen and cock sucking lips to die for good things."

If Jay was testing the water to see whether or not he was going to shock them, he was in for a surprise. As was Scott when Will lifted his hand and swiped the flat of his thumb across Scott's lower lip. Scott's gaze widened momentarily before he regained control as Will said softly, "Trust me, Jay, they really are."

Jay guffawed as Scott playfully nipped at the pad of Will's thumb. "I like you two already. Come on in, guys, and meet the others." Walking ahead of them down the hallway, Jay did not bear witness to Will elbowing Scott in the side for the nasty nipple twist he'd received in retaliation for the lip remark. When they reached the door at the end of the hall, he turned and Scott quickly pulled Will into his side, noting the way Jay's gaze took in the way their hips brushed as they walked. "We're in here. It's all pretty informal." Jay opened the door and they followed him into a large living room with deep burgundy carpets and cream walls.

"Wow," Will murmured, gazing around the room. "You have a beautiful place here, Jay." He scanned the room, taking in the huge ornate fireplace surrounded by a marble mantle. The room housed four plush, cream couches and on two of them were the other members of the Residents' Committee.

"Let me make the introductions," Jay said and led the two men to the occupied couches. "Okay, here we go. David Taylor lives with Brent Miller at number two. Marcus White lives with Todd Campbell at number three and last but not least, Cal Perry who, as you know, lives with Damon Hall at number five. Guys, this is Scott Turner and Will Harrison, who are hoping to join our little group."

Scott and Will walked the length of the sofa and shook the hands of each man, both of them accepting a hug from Cal as if they were long lost friends.

"I'm glad you could make it, guys," Cal grinned, waving a hand toward the cream sofa opposite the one the Residents' Committee was seated on. "Sit, sit, and make yourself comfortable. Damon sends his love and his apologies. He wanted to be here, but the studio is booked solid today and he just couldn't get away." Cal leaned back against the cushions beside Marcus. "By the way, he told me to tell you that the photographs he took of you last week will be ready tomorrow."

Scott smiled at the other man, reassuring him with a glance that his message had been received and understood. Damon Hall was one of the most sought after photographers in White Plains and Cal had obviously told the Laurel Heights' residents that they were old friends. "Great," he enthused, lifting a hand and putting it on Will's thigh. "We've been anxious to see how they turned out. Haven't we, honey?"

Will placed his fingers on top of Scott's, squeezing them a little tighter than was necessary. "Absolutely, babe." Turning, he addressed the rest of the room. "Damon took some standard shots for us as Christmas presents for our families. Along with some more," he chuckled softly, "personal shots, just for us."

"I wouldn't mind seeing those," David drawled, his gaze traveling the length and breadth of Will's body, leaving Scott wishing he hadn't noticed the way the man's gaze, lingered on the taut muscles of his abdomen and the impressive bulge in his pants.

Scott kept his face as impassive as he could when Will stiffened beside him under the weight of David's gaze. Torn between wanting to punch David for leering and trying to remain nonchalant, he was surprised to find his hand turning beneath Will's, palm to palm, locking their fingers together. *Staking your claim, Turner? It's just pretend—remember?*

Jay sat down next to Marcus and picked up a small clipboard, attached to which were several sheets of paper. "I live here at number one with my better half, Erik Walker. We're responsible for Laurel Heights. I'm the architect and Erik is the designer. We've been partners for ten years and we've experienced all kinds of prejudice toward our life choices, as I'm sure all of us have. Anyway, after one particular incident, we decided to set up our own development and rent them exclusively to couples on the same life path as us. We wanted an environment where we were free to be ourselves and not have to conform to what," he air-quoted, "normal people wanted us to be."

"God forbid, we should ever conform," Marcus interrupted with a chuckle. His ice blue eyes studied Will and Scott, and he smiled softly. "What Jay is saying is there are no closets in Laurel Heights. What you see is what you get. We tend to be in and out of each other's houses and we all manage to get along real well. So far, anyway."

"We're not exactly what you would call conformists," Scott said, rubbing the back of his hand on Will's thigh. "Are we, babe?"

"Nope, we're always open to new ideas." Will extricated his fingers from Scott's, lifted his arm and draped it around Scott's shoulders.

"That's nice to hear," Marcus said, settling back against the cushions. "We have a set of standard questions for you to answer then we'll have a break and discussion between ourselves. If we all think you'll both fit in well with our set-up, we can discuss the extra activities that Laurel Heights has to offer and see where we go from there." He gave the two men a reassuring smile. "We fully understand that Laurel Heights may not be to everyone's tastes—so if, at any time during the interview, you feel that this is not the place for you, just say. Please don't think that you have to answer everything, especially if there are some questions that make you uncomfortable. You won't hurt our feelings."

Scott smiled, his gaze roaming over Marcus. He was a broad shouldered, handsome man with a gentle smile and laughing blue eyes. Scott was usually a good judge of character and he liked this guy's easy manner and air of calm.

Cal leaned forward in his seat and put his hand on Will's knee. "I already filled Scott and Will in on some of the finer points of Laurel Heights life." He dropped a wink at Marcus. "I don't think we'll shock them too much."

"Yes," Will agreed, glancing down at the man beside him. "Scott's pretty much un-shockable, aren't you, sweetie?"

Scott pasted a smile on his face and lifted his hand to give Will's cheek a pat that felt a lot heavier than it looked. "I've seen you first thing in the morning, peaches. Nothing shocks me anymore." His comment and Will's mock-affronted expression drew a laugh from the group of men. Although he was grateful that no one could see the hand that curled around his side, or the hefty pinch of the meat of his ass that was Will's retaliation.

"Well, let's get this show on the road shall we?" Jay said, his gaze falling on the clipboard resting on his knees.

They made it through the standard questions easily enough. Where had they met, how long they had been together, etc. With Will rolling his eyes when he had to prompt Scott on the date they met. Scott couldn't help but smile along with the other men at some of Will's descriptions of the stories he was supposed to have written and how his nephew had reacted to them. This was a side of Will he had never seen. The man beside him was charming, engaging, and Scott found himself laughing out loud on more than one occasion.

Then they got to one of the "play it by ear" questions.

"Okay, when did you know he was "the one"?" Jay asked, leaning back against the cushions of the couch and rubbing his shoulder against Marcus's beside him.

"Why don't you take this, Scott? I can't answer it because I knew you were the one from the first moment I saw you." Will leaned in and nudged his head against Scott's in an apparently affectionate gesture.

"Sure, peaches. When did I know he was the one? Well," Scott appeared to be absentmindedly picking at a thread on Will's pants, but what he was actually doing was searching his head desperately for an interesting story. He wasn't having much luck with fabrication, so decided to stick as close to the truth as he could.

"Before I decided to go into business for myself, I worked as the in-house IT for an insurance company and I think we'd been dating for, what was it Will, about four months before Christmas?" He glanced at Will as if for verification although, of course, Will had no idea what Scott was going to say. In fact he looked almost as enthralled as the other men as he nodded.

"Yeah," Scott continued, "it was about four months and we were allowed to bring partners to the Christmas party."

He took a deep breath as he let his mind wander back to when he had looked up at the sound of Will's rich laugh across the room. "I took Will with me, and he was mingling with some of my colleagues, charming the socks of them, of course, as I knew he would. I remember I'd been kidnapped by one of the secretaries for a dance and I heard him laugh. It was weird, you know? I mean, I'd heard him laugh a million times before—but when I looked at him, it hit me, out of the blue, and I just knew." Scott looked up into Will's eyes, for the first time ever, able to let his real feelings shine through, even though Will would think it was all part of the act, he didn't have to hold back. "I wanted to hear him laugh for the rest of my life." He cleared his throat, embarrassed he'd let his control slip and smiled at the others, his cheeks flushing. "That was when I knew."

"Wow," David said, softly, an almost dreamy smile curving his lips.

"Yeah, wow," Will murmured and Scott's gaze widened as the other man bent his head to capture Scott's lips in a gentle kiss. It didn't last for very long and he pulled back with a soft snick, holding Scott's lower lip between his own for a few tantalizing moments before he released it and smiled at their audience. "Sorry, I love that story."

What the fuck is he doing? Scott's lips tingled where they'd touched Will's. By the look in Will's eyes, he was thinking the same thing.

"Okay, guys. That's most of our questions answered on the standard bit," Jay said, standing up. "We'll just go and make some refreshments and have a little chat and we'll back in about ten minutes or so." Jay walked from the room, followed by the others, and Cal closed the door as he was the last one to leave.

"What the fuck?" Scott hissed as soon as the door clicked shut. He wiped at his mouth with his fingers and glared at Will. "You freak out at the thought of PDA and then you kiss me in front of everyone?" He was stunned by Will's actions. "What is wrong with you?"

Will shrugged, lowering his voice, his cheeks aflame. "It was a good story, I got—" He stumbled over his words. "I just got caught up in the moment." He ran a shaking hand through his hair and punched Scott in the bicep. "Stop looking at me like that, asshole. You kissed me outside! You said to make it look real."

"I meant holding hands, and the odd peck on the cheek," Scott hissed back, using anger to cover his own confusion. Not to mention the urge to throw Will down on the sofa and kiss him senseless. "Not that you should stick your tongue down my throat in a room full of people. Does Amanda know how into the part you're getting?"

"Oh, fuck off," Will's mouth dropped open in amazement. "I did *not* stick my tongue down your throat. Stop griping, they're coming back."

David opened the door for Cal, who carried a tray laden with cups filled with steaming liquid. He gave them a beaming smile as he put the tray down on the table and handed them each a cup of coffee. "It's looking good," he muttered and he held out the sugar bowl. Scott noted his astonishment as Will spooned three heaped teaspoons into his cup.

"He's got the palate of a five year old," Scott shrugged, declining sugar for his own coffee. "You'll have to forgive him. It's a miracle he has a single tooth left in his head."

"What?" Will said, his gaze flitting between the two men. "What did I do?" He frowned when Cal and Scott merely grinned at each other, and sank back against the cushions to concentrate on his coffee.

Marcus helped himself to a cookie from the plate next to the sugar bowl and sat down, waiting for the others to join him. "Okay guys, if you're ready, we'd like to go on with the other set of questions. Are you happy with everything so far?" He grinned as both men nodded. "Great, here goes. Once a month, the ten of us get together and indulge in some activities that might not be in every one's comfort zone."

"What kind of activities?" Scott asked politely, sipping at his coffee.

Scott watched as Jay lifted a hand and followed the curve of Marcus's jaw with a fingertip, smiling softly when the man leaned into his touch. "Partner-swapping, S&M, Dom/sub, that sort of thing." He ran a hand through his thick, black hair. "We mostly keep it between the residents of Laurel Heights, but sometimes we do include outside parties, to add a little spice to the mix. Is that something you would feel comfortable sharing with us?"

David put his coffee cup down on the table and smoothed a hand down Cal's thigh. Scott didn't like the way his dark brown gaze never left Will's face as he stroked the man beside him, his fingers inching closer and closer toward the growing bulge in Cal's pants. "It's nothing too far out there," he said softly. "Certainly nothing we discuss outside these gates." He glanced at Will's arm, still around Scott. "I mean, the two of you are obviously a very close couple, and this might not be for you. I don't know how open your relationship is. No one is out to wreck anyone's relationship here, guys. It's just a little fun between friends. We're not saying that you have to indulge in *everything* that goes on at our 'gatherings', but you would be expected to attend and participate in whatever you're comfortable with."

"Obviously," Marcus said conversationally, unashamedly tilting his head so that Jay could lick at his ear. "You could end up with either one of us, or all of us together, depends on your mood. But we're looking for a couple who will fit in with both personas of the community, the public *and* the private. How about it guys? Do you think you could live here?"

Scott gazed at Will, taking in the flush on his high cheekbones at the four men's open display. Raising his eyebrows at him as if he was asking for Will's decision, he turned back to the waiting men when Will nodded. "I think we could," he smiled, dropping a kiss onto Will's hair. "It sounds perfect."

****

The journey back to the office was spent in silence, both men lost in their own thoughts. When they finally pulled into Scott's parking space, Will sighed in frustration. "What did you think?" He half-turned in his seat and frowned. "They all seemed really nice guys. Hardly the type to kill two all-American boys."

Scott turned put the car in park and turned off the engine, taking out the key. "I agree. But then apparently Ted Bundy was a nice guy, too. For now, everyone is a suspect."

Will clambered out and waited for Scott to do the same and then lock the car. They walked to the elevator in silence and when the ancient doors opened with a grinding of metal against metal, they stepped inside. Pressing the button for the fifth floor, Will leaned back against the faux carpeted walls of the small metal box and his lips lifted at Scott's groan when Barry Manilow's voice began to bounce off the walls.

"I swear," Scott grumbled mutinously. "If maintenance doesn't change the music in this thing, I'm gonna bust some heads."

Will glanced over at the other man leaning nonchalantly against the handrail, glad that Scott's eyes were closed. It gave him an opportunity to study him from beneath lowered lashes and wonder what Scott was thinking about. He wished he could say he hadn't been taken aback when the four men began their casual display. Obviously he wasn't a blushing virgin, but his experience was made up of the grand total of two one night stands and three relationships. He knew he was probably old-fashioned in his thinking, but sex for the sake of sex had never interested him. Scott's features had remained carefully schooled throughout and Will wondered if anything fazed the man.

Scott's eyes fluttered open and Will pretended to study a scratch on the elevator wall with great interest. Scott didn't say any more after the music remark, but Will felt his gaze on him. *What the fuck is going on?* His head swam, a thousand desperate thoughts bouncing off his skull like a crazed pinball. Thoughts he never imagined would have even entered his head.

Scott *'my middle name is dickhead'* Turner was the most irritating man he had ever met and nothing in the eight months since Will had been working with him, had changed his mind about that. He'd always thought that if ever there was a reason for selective breeding, it was Turner. Now everything had changed. Why did his lips tingle every time he thought of them pressed against the other man's? Why did it feel as though Scott's hand was imprinted on his thigh? Why did the thought of living in the same house as Scott Turner now fill him with an altogether different kind of dread? *Don't think about it William,* his inner voice whispered comfortingly, *don't think about it and it will all go away.* Taking a deep breath as the elevator ground to a stop, Will only hoped that his inner voice was right.

Grace and Julie were obviously waiting anxiously for their return, because Will noticed how they jumped to their feet before they'd barely stepped foot into the department. "How did it go?" they said in unison.

"I think it went okay," Scott said, sitting down in his chair and dropping his cell and keys onto his desk. "They seemed real nice and we answered all their questions. When they started making out in front of us, Will nearly passed out," he teased, "but apart from that it went well."

"Will?" Julie asked. "What do *you* think?"

"What?" he said quietly. Julie raised her eyebrow and he nodded, her words finally filtering through the sludge that used to be his brain. "Yeah, it was good. I think we pulled it off." He looked back down at his pile of phone messages and pretended to concentrate.

When a rolled up ball of paper hit him on the head about half an hour later, he looked up at Scott, his irritation clear in his voice, "What?"

"Are you even listening to me?" Scott said, screwing up another piece of paper. "That was Cal on the phone. For fuck's sake, Harrison." Will watched in confusion as Scott picked up the pen holder on his desk and held it up in the air. "And the Oscar goes to."

"What the hell are you talking about?" Will repeated.

"We can move in at the end of the week."

IV

"Are you going to tell him?"

"Tell who, what?" Scott replied, glancing at Grace where she was sitting cross-legged on the end of his bed. He was trying to pack his case. The house at Laurel Heights was fully furnished, so he only needed his laptop, clothing and toiletry essentials. Grabbing some more underwear from his top drawer, he threw it on top of the pile he'd already accumulated.

"Will."

Scott padded into the en suite and grabbed his toiletry bag from under the sink. He opened the medicine cabinet and began to fill the bag with everything he would need on a daily basis. "I can tell you're in one of your cryptic moods," he called from the bathroom. "I'm gonna need a little more, babe."

"Are you going to tell Will that you want in his pants?" It wasn't a question, it was a statement.

Scott's hand froze on its way to the toiletry bag and his gaze flew up to his reflection in the mirror. Swallowing hard, he dropped the shower gel into the bag and forced what he hoped was a confused frown on his forehead. "Are you high, Cassidy?" He walked back into the bedroom and tossed the bag into his case.

Grace tilted her head and raised her eyebrows at him, not speaking, just waiting. Waiting until Scott's shoulders slumped and he sank to the bed beside her.

"How long have you known?" Scott asked quietly, avoiding her gaze.

"A while," Grace replied, putting a hand on his forearm. "Don't panic, honey," she said. Scott knew the horror he'd felt at her remark was clear on his face, because she added reassuringly, "No one else knows."

"Then how?"

Grace shrugged, her smile sympathetic. "Because I know *you*."

Scott sighed and stood, closing his case and zipping it up. "It's not a big deal," he said, his tone casual. "So I've got a crush on the cute straight guy. It's not the first time it's happened and I'm sure it won't be the last."

"That's a very healthy attitude, Scott." Grace leaned back on her elbows and stretched out her legs, crossing her ankles. "Shame you're lying through your teeth." Scott glared at her. "It's hard enough for you to disguise how you feel when you only had to work in the same room as him. How the fuck are you going to cope with living in the same house?"

"Gracie, you're making a bigger deal out of this than it is. I've got a job to do, trust me, Will Harrison is the last of my worries. I can handle it," he said, hauling his case off the bed. Picking up his laptop bag, he hooked it over his shoulder. "You gonna wave me off or what?"

"Sure." Sighing heavily, she stood and followed him out of the house. "Make sure you keep me and Julie updated, so we can follow up on anything you find. Oh, and Scott," she said, as he slid behind the wheel and started the engine. "Be nice."

Scott slipped his sunglasses onto the bridge of his nose and smiled, dazzling her with a row of sparkling white teeth. "I'm always nice," he replied, putting the car into drive and gunning the engine. At the end of the drive, he turned left and headed toward Laurel Heights.

****

"Jesus Christ, Stretch," Scott huffed, picking up a box from the back of Will's SUV and carrying it toward number four. "What the fuck have you got in here?"

"My weights," Will replied, looking at Scott as if he had just dribbled on himself. "You know, they're big round things. You get them at the gym."

Scott rolled his eyes. "I know what they are, moron. I'm just wondering why you felt the need to bring them with you." He turned, hefting the box higher into his arms and heading into the house.

Following him with the bars that the weights attached to, Will motioned for him to put them down in the kitchen. "Because I like to stay in shape," he drawled sarcastically. "Unlike *some;* I'm not clubbing it every night. I don't want to get flabby." Before Scott had a chance to reply, Will had left to get the next box.

Scott laid his hands on his lean belly and shrugged, huffing out a breath. "I am not fucking flabby," he muttered. Opening cupboard doors he located a glass behind the third door he opened and took one out. He turned on the faucet and held the glass under the stream of cold water, gazing out onto the back yard while the glass filled. The lawn was green and lush and stopped at a wooden fence sixty feet from the house. Beautiful flower beds adorned either side of the winding path through the middle of the lawn down to the summer house. The view was a far cry from the patch of earth that was his own back yard. Turning off the faucet, Scott lifted the glass to his lips and moaned softly when the cold water slid down his dry throat. He was mid-swallow when a deep voice said from behind him.

"Welcome to the neighborhood."

Unsure how he managed to swallow the water he had in his mouth without choking, Scott turned on his heel and came face to face with a man he had never seen before. His cop's eye immediately gave the stranger the once over. He judged him to be in the region of five feet eleven, and his slender, but obviously muscled body was hidden behind an expensive and well cut, navy suit. The pale blue of his shirt served to make the man's deep blue gaze appear darker in his handsome, angular face.

Scott wasn't quite sure why the other man made the fine hair on his arms stand up, but he did. Maybe it was because the guy was looking at him as if he wanted him served up on toast. Scott was used to his looks attracting attention but, when someone looked at him the way the man seated at the kitchen table was looking at him right now, Scott's dick usually ended up in their mouth.

The man's deep blue gaze traveled over Scott from head to toe, the expression on his face predatory and insolent. Scott tried to show no reaction when the man lingered on his torso beneath the black tee he wore, then stared at the obvious bulge of Scott's cock and the muscled thighs under the blue jeans. His heavy-lidded gaze studied Scott and his thin lips parted on a smile when he finally reached Scott's face. "I'm Brent Miller, David's partner. I thought I'd drop in and introduce myself. I hope you don't mind."

Scott forced a smile to his lips and shook the hand that was offered to him. "Not at all. I'm Scott Turner. I take it you met Will outside?"

"I did, indeed," Brent drawled crossing his legs and leaning his elbow on the glass topped kitchen table. "I understand from David that you're an IT Consultant."

Scott nodded and leaned against the counter, crossing his ankles. "That's right. I started up my own business about a year ago. It means I can work from home and I don't have to spend as much time away from Will. What do you do?" Scott folded his arms across his chest, suddenly all too aware from the glint in Brent's eyes that the T-shirt he was wearing was a size too small and clung to him like a second skin.

"I own a club in the city, you may have heard of it. The Rose. It's over on Second Avenue," Brent replied, smiling as Scott nodded at the mention of the well known gay club in New York. "David is my silent partner, but only in the business. Everywhere else he's *very* vocal." Brent laughed softly at his own wit.

Scott chuckled politely, a grateful smile curving his lips when Will entered the kitchen carrying another cardboard box with 'study' written on the side. "Hey," he said softly. "Is that the last of them?" He reached out and picked an imaginary piece of fluff from Will's sweatshirt. "Brent was just telling me that he owns The Rose, on Second Avenue."

"Wow," Will smiled as he leaned against the counter beside Scott. "The Rose is a great club. We've been there a few times ourselves. It's got a nice vibe."

****

Will listened quietly as Brent chatted to Scott, noting that the guy could barely take his eyes off his partner, despite the fact that Will was stood next to him. Not that that bothered Will, he didn't particularly want Brent leering at him, but he wasn't overly impressed with the way the man was leering at Scott either. A couple of times Will caught Scott glancing at him out of the corner of his eye and the other man's stance stiffen beneath the weight of Brent's intense gaze.

Inwardly rolling his eyes and cursing Scott '*all of a sudden I'm shy?*' Turner, Will reached out a hand and slid a couple of fingers through one of the belt loops on Scott's jeans. He pulled him away from the counter and he noted the way Scott's eyes widened almost imperceptibly, but the other man went with it and allowed Will to guide him so that his back was against Will's chest. Lifting his arms, Will slid them around Scott's waist, taking his weight.

Scott stiffened slightly, but after a pause, placed his hands on top of Will's and relaxed against him, as if it were an everyday occurrence, while he continued to chat with Brent. Will tried to ignore the spicy scent of Scott's cologne, or the gentle stroking the other man had set up on Will's hand. But most of all, he tried to relax enough to make having his arms around Scott Turner look as natural as possible. "I'm sorry," he said, when Brent finished making his point, although he wasn't quite sure what the point was, he was too busy trying not to be distracted by the heat of Scott's body through the fabric of his shirt. "I've forgotten my manners. Would you like a coffee or tea, or something?" He gave a slightly sly smile. "Scott makes a mean cappuccino, don't you, honey?" Will felt Scott's fingers pause in their soft circular motion and bit the inside of his cheek to stop himself from laughing. Everyone in the department knew Scott could barely boil water.

Brent stood and stretched, shaking his head. "No, thank you. I'm fine. I just came to welcome you both to our little community and to let you know that we're going to make it an official welcome next Saturday night." His blue gaze glinted with wicked anticipation as he looked at Scott's muscled forearms where they rested atop of Will's and it was all Will could do not to choke the man with his own tie. "Coincidentally, one of our "gatherings" is taking place next Saturday, so we thought we'd turn it into a double celebration. To welcome you into your new home and, of course, to welcome you into our circle."

"Wow. So soon?" Will tried to sound enthusiastic, although his feet were a little squashed inside his sneakers, because his stomach had just joined them. "That's great." He squeezed Scott a little tighter in what he hoped would have easily been mistaken for affection—rather than the sheer panic it actually was.

"We've been looking forward to settling in, haven't we, babe?"

"I'm sure the others will be around to say hi over the next few days, so I'll leave you to your unpacking. It's good to have you with us, gentlemen." Brent's gaze raked over Scott once more. "It's going to be *real* good."

"Holy shit." Will let out the breath he had been holding after Brent had left, leaving the front door ajar. "Next Saturday? How the fuck are we going to get out of that?"

"Um...Will," Scott said, tapping Will's hands lightly. "He's gone, you can let go now."

Will dropped his arms from around the man's waist as if Scott were suddenly on fire. "Oh, sorry, man. You looked a little nervous," he said, running a hand through his hair and trying to appear casual as Scott stepped away. "I think he liked you." Will couldn't resist the tease.

Sitting down in the chair, Scott flipped him off and sighed. "Now I know what meat on a slab feels like," he joked. "I thought he was going to take a bite." He smiled genuinely at Will. "Thanks for that. He was starting to make me feel really uncomfortable."

"Well that's a first. I wouldn't have thought anything made you uncomfortable." Will pushed himself away from the counter and picked up the suitcase he had left by the kitchen table earlier, ignoring Scott's glare. "Okay, which bedroom are you having?"

"The same one as you," said a voice from the doorway.

Turning to see Damon and Cal smiling at them, Will frowned in confusion. "Excuse me?"

"Look guys, you are now living in a community of gay men," Damon drawled as he and Cal padded into the kitchen and sat down at the table next to Scott.

Damon indicated the empty chair and Will sank onto it, frowning in confusion at Damon while he waited for the man to continue. "We're nosy and we're voracious gossips. Every member of this community is going to be traipsing through your house and they will use your bathroom, look in your cupboards, and check out your bedroom. You can't give them any indication that you're sleeping apart."

"I am not sleeping in the same bed as him," Scott said heatedly, crossing his arms like a petulant child.

"Damon's right, guys," Cal chuckled. "If anyone discovers that you don't sleep together, your cover will be blown on day one. I already know Brent has been here and the others will come by, if not tonight, certainly tomorrow, and trust me, they will be all over you like white on rice."

"For once I agree with Turner," Will said firmly, with a shake of his head. The thought of having to lie in the same bed as Scott made his palms decidedly clammy. He was confused enough. He didn't need the point compounded. "We are *not* sleeping together. We're *not* gay, Damon."

"Glenn said you'd be like this," Damon sighed, throwing his hands in the air. "He told me to tell you I will be reporting back to him, and if you are not doing *everything* you can to fit in here at Laurel Heights, he will bounce you back to traffic cops quicker than you can say—" He turned to Cal for assistance. "What was the expression he used, honey?"

"Quicker than you can say license and registration," Cal replied, accepting the soft kiss his boyfriend gave him, with a smile.

"*Fuck!*" Will and Scott muttered the expletive in unison, and glared at each other.

"You'd better not snore," Scott hissed.

"I do *not* snore," Will replied huffily. "Just remember to keep your cologne to a minimum. I don't want to choke in my sleep."

"Fuck you," Scott harrumphed, standing up. "I'm going to get the rest of the stuff." He stomped from the kitchen, and Will heard the slam of the front door.

"Princess," Will mumbled. "Now he's gonna expect me to get up and open the fucking door for him, asshole."

****

Scott lifted the last of Will's boxes from the back of the SUV and put it down on the ground. Scratching his fingers through the beard growth on his chin, he sighed. He could still feel Will's chin resting on his shoulder, as if he had branded him—left his mark. How the fuck was he supposed to sleep inches away from Will in the same bed? How was he supposed to keep his hands to himself? *He's straight, Turner,* his inner voice whispered. *Don't you think I fucking know that?* he hissed back.

When he'd been enfolded in Will's arms in the kitchen, all he'd been able to concentrate on was how easily their hips fit together and the way Will's scent pervaded his nostrils—the musky, spicy smell of the man's cologne and, beneath that, the unmistakable tang of sweat. He'd always been so careful. Not to get too close. Not to let anything give him away. Hiding behind the wall he had surrounded himself with. Now it was all going to come crumbling down and he didn't know how to stop it. Stupid Will *'I'm so straight I can't even bend down to tie my shoes'* Harrison. It would be so much easier if the moron were gay. He could just fuck him and get it out of his system.

"Hey, Scott!"

Scott was startled from his inner monologue by Marcus White calling his name as he walked across the cul de sac toward him. He was holding the hand of a man Scott didn't recognize. "Hey," he greeted, raising his hand in acknowledgement. Scott had been of the same opinion as Will in so far as Marcus White was concerned. He'd felt relaxed with Marcus from the get go. There had only been warmth and reassurance in Marcus's gaze during their interview and he'd gone out of his way to make them feel comfortable.

"This is my boyfriend, Todd Campbell," Marcus grinned, introducing the man beside him. "We thought we'd stop by, say hello, and see if you need any help moving in."

"Hi, Todd. Good to meet you." Scott shook hands with the slender, blond haired man, noting the way he almost clung to Marcus's side. "It's just the box on the floor and then there's one more in the back of the truck. If you grab the one on the ground, Marcus, that would be great." He threw a grateful smile at Todd. "If you wouldn't mind closing up the truck, it would be appreciated." Reaching inside the truck, Scott pulled out the last box and heaved it into his arms and waited until Todd had closed the back of the SUV with a slam. "Thanks, guys. Please, come in for a drink. Damon and Cal are in the kitchen with Will."

"I've been looking forward to meeting you both." Todd followed the two men to the front door, and Scott couldn't help but notice the way his fingers curled into the back of Marcus's T-shirt. "Marcus tells me you're in computers, Scott. I don't want you to think I'm taking advantage of you already, but I've been having a lot of trouble with my laptop. Would you take a look at it for me?"

"Not a problem." Scott replied with an easy smile, shifting the box in his arms. "Just bring it on over and I'll see what I can do." He hoped to God there wasn't anything intricate wrong with the thing, because he'd be flying by the seat of his pants. Grace's faith in his computer knowledge may have been slightly misplaced.

The door was answered by Cal, and Scott headed into the living room, where he put the box he was carrying onto the coffee table. "Thanks," he grinned up at Marcus when the other man did the same, and gestured toward the kitchen. "Let's go get that coffee, shall we?"

"Todd! Baby, how are you?" Damon cooed when the three men entered the kitchen. He stood and enfolded the other man in his arms, pressing a soft kiss to his hair. Scott's cop's eye made a mental note of the obviously genuine affection between the two men as Damon steered Todd to a chair. "Todd's been a little under the weather since Jon and Cory, well, you know."

"I'm sorry for your loss," Scott said, reaching out and patting Todd on the shoulder. "We both are." He raised an eyebrow at Will, who got to his feet and slipped an arm around Scott's waist.

"Yes," Will said. "We realize how hard this must be for you all, seeing someone new in this house." He held out a hand to Todd and gave the other man a reassuring smile. "I'm Will. It's nice to meet you, Todd."

While the others sat around the table, Scott set about pouring the coffee that Will had already made. After making sure everyone had a drink, he eased himself up onto the kitchen island, as all the seats were occupied and sipped slowly at his own coffee. Joining in the conversation where needed, Scott sat back and watched Will work the room. He'd seen him at the station interviewing suspects and dealing with victims, and he knew how persuasive and charismatic Will could be. Scott had watched him stare down a hardened criminal and then softly elicit a statement from a frightened witness—but he'd never seen the real Will.

But then he guessed Will could say the same about him. The happy go lucky persona in front of him was new and one he had only glimpsed in their interview. He liked it.

He also watched Marcus and Todd interact with each other and those around them. Marcus appeared to be a very mild mannered, outgoing sort of guy. Easily over six feet and broad across the shoulders, his dark hair was closely cropped and his blue eyes were kind. They learned that Marcus was a record producer, who owned his own company and had several well known names signed to his label—including Todd.

Scott's gaze fell on Todd, noting how very quiet and introverted the young man seemed. Todd's fine, blond hair fell in a curtain around his face, his green gaze darting continually to the door. Scott wouldn't have thought, from his body language alone, that Todd would be the liberal, open minded type. Not for a community as "free-loving" as Laurel Heights. Watching the way Todd clung to Marcus's hand, even while they drank their coffee, Scott worried at his lower lip with his teeth. The guy seemed to be on the verge of flight the whole time, one leg constantly moving up and down as if he was ready to leap at any time. He made a mental note to get Grace and Julie to run a check on Todd. Something wasn't quite right.

"Well," Damon said, about an hour later, when no one showed any signs of moving. "I think we should let these boys get settled in. I'm sure they'll want to start christening the rooms."

"Will would probably want to catalog his toiletries first," Scott said, his tone teasing. "He's a bit anal that way. It's like being in *Sleeping with the Enemy*."

The other men laughed as Will poked his tongue out and padded to the kitchen island where Scott was perched. "I guess that makes you the pretty woman then," Will drawled, dropping a kiss on Scott's forehead. "Besides, we've only got the bathroom and the bedroom left. We got here early, didn't we, hot stuff?"

Scott forced what he hoped was a natural sounding chuckle up his throat, as Will's fingers dug into his shoulder. "Well, let's just say the years of yoga are finally paying off," he responded, sliding off the counter and following the other men to the door with Will behind him.

"You guys are great," Marcus laughed as he shook Scott and Will's hands again at the front door. "You're gonna fit in well here." He turned to Todd, who was still clinging to his hand. "You ready, babe?" At Todd's nod, Marcus followed Damon and Cal down the path, leaving Will and Scott to close the door behind them.

"Alone at last," Will drawled sarcastically as Scott slid the safety chain across the door.

"Pretty woman?"

"Unbunch your panties, Turner," Will retorted, turning toward the living room. "You know you're the pretty one." Scott's gut tightened at the flush in Will's cheeks when the words had tumbled from his mouth. The man looked like he wanted to grab the words and stuff them back in, but it was too late, they were out there, hanging between them like a fog. They stared at each other for a long pregnant moment and then Will picked up his suitcase. "I'm going to unpack. You wanna order takeout?"

Scott nodded, not saying a word as his eyes followed Will up the stairs. He knew he hadn't been hearing things. Will had called him pretty. *Don't go getting all Harlequin Romance over an offhand remark, Turner!* He moved into the living room and busied himself with setting up the laptop on the coffee table. After clearing a space on the table top, Scott plugged the power lead into the closest outlet and then into the back of the computer, leaving it to charge. He gazed around him and took a moment to really look at the décor for the first time. The fireplace wall was painted in a deep burgundy, creating a warm atmosphere as soon as you walked in. The plush carpeting was the same color as the focal wall and it was inlaid into a six inch strip of polished oak flooring all the way around the room. The three remaining walls were painted a neutral cream and the huge bay window was hung with wooden slatted blinds. The sumptuous house was nothing like his humble one bedroom home, lovingly restored by him on his free weekends.

Picking up his cell, Scott sank down onto one of the three cream sofas that provided the seating in the living room. Pressing speed dial for Gracie, he waited for her to pick up. "Hey," he said, two rings later, toeing off his sneakers and resting his socked feet on the coffee table.

"Scott!" she said, her musical lilt trilling down the line. "We were beginning to think the two of you were already at one of those 'gatherings'."

"Very funny," Scott retorted, glancing up at the ceiling when he heard a crash from upstairs. "Unpacking takes time you know and we've had some of the neighbors nosing around already. Although I'm sure they'd call it being neighborly."

"Okay, I've gone into the boardroom. I'm alone," Grace said in a hushed tone.

"If you're alone, why are you whispering?" Scott drawled sarcastically.

"Shut up," Grace replied at a normal level. "Spill. How's it *really* going?"

"It's going fine. I told you. We've been playing the perfect couple for the neighbors," Scott said dismissively. "I need you to check out the residents we've already met. Have you got a pen? Okay, we've got, Brent Miller. He owns The Rose nightclub in the city, over on Second Avenue. Next we have Marcus White. He's a music producer who owns Smooth record label. He's got a studio in the city."

"Got it. Anyone else?"

"Yeah." Scott scratched behind his ear. "Marcus's partner is a guy called Todd Campbell. He's a country singer and he's signed to Marcus's label but there's something not quite right there."

"How do you mean?"

"Well, he just doesn't seem the Laurel Heights type. You know what I mean? He's really quiet, almost withdrawn, and he clings to Marcus like he's a lifeline. Something's going on there," Scott said softly, his brow creasing in thought.

"Okay, I'll look into it and get back to you."

"Great. Well, I've got to finish unpacking, and prepare for other drop-ins. I'll call you tomorrow. Email me what you find." Scott swung his feet to the floor and stood.

"Scott—"

"I'm fine, Grace. Tomorrow." Scott ended the call before she could say anything else. He didn't really want to have that conversation right now.

He raised his arms high above his head and paused mid-stretch when Will came into the living room. The other man had changed into a pair of loose-fitting navy sweatpants and a white wife beater that clung to every muscle and curve of his torso. Trying to swallow past the sudden lump in his throat, Scott lowered his arms and forced a smile to his lips. "You all unpacked?" He tried to be casual, but even to his own ears his voice sounded a little strained.

"Yeah." Will flopped down onto one of the sofas, stretching his legs out and settling himself against the cushions. "I used the top two drawers and one half of the wardrobe, the rest is yours." He folded his arms behind his head and sighed. "I heard voices, who were you talking to?"

"Grace," Scott replied, bending to pick up his suitcase. "She's going to look into Brent, Marcus, and Todd." He paused in the doorway and gazed down at Will. "What did you make of Todd? Did he seem a little, I dunno, *off* to you?"

Raising himself up on his elbows, Will nodded. "Yeah, very clingy, a little agitated, like he couldn't wait to get away. I got the impression that if Marcus had let his hand go, he would have been out the door like a shot." Will's stomach grumbled loudly and Scott chuckled as the younger man said, "Dinner time? What do you want to eat? Chinese?"

"Chinese sounds good," Scott replied, heading toward the staircase. "Just get a selection. I'm going to take a shower and unpack. Call me when it gets here."

"Go ahead, Princess. Make sure you don't leave your tiara where I'll step on it."

Scott ignored Will's chuckling at his own joke and took the stairs two at a time. By the time he'd reached the bedroom, he couldn't help the twitching of his own lips. Maybe living with Will *'I'm a prima-donna'* Harrison wasn't going to be as bad as he'd feared.

****

Will brushed his teeth and studied his reflection in the mirror above the sink. This was going to be awkward. *Understatement much, William?* He rinsed his mouth and patted his lips with a towel, squaring his shoulders. *Jesus, Harrison, you'd think you'd never got into bed with a guy before.* He'd been in bed with plenty of guys, well, maybe not *plenty* but certainly enough. But none of them had been Scott *'My Shorts are so tight*

I squeak when I walk' Turner. He heard the creak of a drawer being opened, and glancing up, he could see Scott through a crack in the not quite shut bathroom door. *Jesus Christ!*

Will's lips dropped open and his tongue stuck to the roof of his suddenly dry mouth. He couldn't tear his eyes away from the sight of Scott sliding his sweatpants down over his hips and kicking them off. Neither could he stop staring at the curve of Scott's rounded ass in tight-fitting, black briefs, or the way the muscles in Scott's back rippled beneath the skin as he pulled the wife beater he'd been wearing over his head and tossed it on top of his discarded pants. When Scott turned toward the bed, Will took a step back and his head collided with the corner of the heated towel rail on the wall. The outline of Scott's cock was clearly defined beneath the cotton fabric of his underwear, and Will found his tongue involuntarily snaking out to moisten his lips.

Gazing up at his reflection, Will noted the flush in his cheeks and shook his head in the hope that the memory of Scott's almost naked body, gorgeous, muscled, tanned, *Oh shut the fuck up!* body would fall out of his ears. "Get a grip," he muttered at his reflection. "This is Turner we're talking about. Not only is he an asshole, he's a straight asshole." He reached up and turned off the light, feeling much better when he didn't have to look in his eyes anymore, then took a deep breath before walking out into the room and closing the door behind him.

Will noted that Scott had already claimed the right side of the bed, not that it mattered much to him; he pretty much slept in the middle anyway. He hadn't even realized he was hovering until Scott's voice broke through his internal monologue.

"Are you gonna stand there all night?" Scott asked his head tilted to one side as he watched Will shift from one foot to the other beside the bed. "I promise I won't take advantage of you."

"You wish," Will scoffed, the tension leaving his shoulders at Scott's jibe. He lifted the duvet and slid into bed. "You're too short for me." He rolled over onto his side and stretched, luxuriating in the feel of the cool cotton sheets against his bare legs and trying to ignore Scott *'Don't I smell good?'* Turner beside him. "I need to set up the study tomorrow—make it look like I'm writing in there, just in case anyone wants to see the master at work. I suspect we'll get more visitors tomorrow."

"Uh-huh. I get the feeling these people wouldn't even know how to spell personal bubble, never mind respect it," Scott agreed, settling back against the pillows. "Gracie's going to email me with anything she comes up with. I'm definitely curious to see what she finds on Todd. Brent seems harmless enough." Will snorted loudly in the quiet of the room. "What's so funny?"

"I might be wrong, but I get this strange feeling that, if Brent Miller got you alone in a room," Will countered, keeping his back to the other man, "the last thing he'd be is harmless." He grinned at Scott's derisive snort and reached out to turn off the light, plunging the room into darkness. "Night, sweetie."

"Fuck you."

V

Scott was hot. Too hot. Why was he so hot? His eyes fluttered open as he was pulled from unconsciousness by the niggling sense that he was going to spontaneously combust. He could feel sweat pooling on his lower back and across the nape of his neck. Scott groaned low in his throat as he slowly woke up, vaguely registering in the dim recesses of his mind, that he had a hard on. *Perfect!* Stretching out his leg, he froze. *Fuck!*

He'd just discovered why he was so hot. He was being spooned by two hundred pounds of Will Harrison. *God fucking hates me, that's what it is,* he thought desperately to himself, *is this some kind of test? I suck at tests.*

Certain there was enough heat radiating from Will to keep a small town toasty through the winter, Scott tried to ease his body away from the softly snoring man beside him. He wondered if the asshole was actually awake and yanking his chain, because every time he moved away from Will, the other man followed him and snuggled against his back. The hair at the nape of his neck lifted with Will's even breaths and he closed his eyes tightly at the puffs of air on his skin. Sighing, he began the insurmountable task of getting out of bed without disturbing the man beside him.

Scott thought he'd made it, but just as he was about to slide free, Will's arm curled around his waist and pulled Scott close to his muscled chest. So close, that Scott could feel the ridges of Will's abs against his lower back. *This is so not fair,* Scott thought, scrubbing a hand over his face. *Just wake him up, Turner. Push him away and wake him up. It'll be fine. He'll be freaked out but you can laugh it off. Then you can go whack off in the shower and all will be right with the world again.*

Any plan of action flew straight out of his mind when Will moaned softly against the back of Scott's neck in his sleep. Then the hand on his stomach drifted lower and ghosted over his now painfully hard cock. *Jesus fuck!* Scott's hips involuntarily jerked toward Will's fingers and he tried to keep his breathing calm when Will's warm hand cupped his erection through his briefs. At that point, Scott decided that breathing was no longer a problem, because he was certain his heart had just stopped beating altogether. He desperately tried to ignore the part of his brain that told him to just lay back and enjoy the moment, gripping Will's wrist as gently as he could and lifting his arm.

Of course, just like a well written comedy of errors, Will chose that moment to open his eyes. "What are you doing?" His voice was thick and heavy with sleep, the words spoken into the soft skin between Scott's shoulder blades.

"Trying to get your hand off my cock," Scott replied conversationally.

"*Holy shit!*" Will breathed in horror, pulled his wrist from Scott's grasp and shuffled backwards across the bed. Scott tried not to analyze the sinking feeling in his stomach at Will's total and utter embarrassment as he muttered, "Jesus, Scott. I'm so sorry." Will sat up in bed and ran his fingers through his hair, and Scott levered himself up against the pillows and faced him. "Scott—"

Scott lifted a hand and silenced Will, who closed his mouth abruptly. "You know what." His lips curved into what he hoped was a friendly and reassuring smile. "Let's just clear our throats like manly men, talk about last night's game and forget about it." The poor guy looked horrified and he didn't want to freak him out even more, which is exactly what he was going to do if they spent another minute in the same bed. *Yeah,* his inner voice chuckled loudly in his ear.

Burying your fingers in that gorgeous blond hair and jumping on top of him would definitely freak him out.

"So—how about those Giants?" Will cleared his throat and grinned widely.

To Scott it looked like somewhere between a grin and a weird grimace, like Will had had a stroke. Rolling his eyes, Scott thanked God that his cock had calmed down enough for him to move and threw back the covers. Clambering out of bed, he crossed the room to the chest of drawers and pulled out some underwear and a clean pair of jeans. He ignored Will completely and padded into the en suite, closing the door behind him.

Leaning his back against the door, he breathed deeply, dragging much needed air into his lungs. "If I make it through this alive, it'll be a fucking miracle," he muttered, opening the cubicle door and turning on the shower. Turning to the toilet to relieve himself while the water warmed, Scott tried not to think about sleepy, brown eyes or the way Will's scent had surrounded him, all funky and warm. He groaned loudly as his traitorous cock hardened in his fingers and he reached out to flush the toilet. Stepping in under the cascading water, Scott could no longer fight the images dancing behind his eyes and curled his fingers around his rock hard shaft. When he came, he almost bit through his lip to stop himself from crying out Will's name as he emptied himself against the tiles, ribbons of hot white sliding down the wall.

He was so screwed.

****

As soon as the bathroom door closed behind Scott, Will flopped back onto the pillows, and threw his hands over his face. *Jesus Christ! I touched his dick!*

Someone kill me now! "Nice one, Harrison," he mumbled quietly to himself. "Way to go, excellent job of molesting the beautiful straight guy." He groaned low in his throat as his cock twitched beneath his sweatpants at the memory of Scott's sleep warm skin pressed against his. The way his hips seemed to fit snugly against the other man's ass as if they were meant to be there. The scent of the man, filling his nostrils, the sweet combination of the remnants of cologne and masculinity. The little river of drool on Scott's shoulder. *Oh Fuck! I drooled on him?* Will shook his head in dismay. *Never mind the drool, doofus. Aren't you forgetting that, one he's straight, and two, he thinks you are, too? Keep your shit together, Harrison, or the only thing you're gonna be blowing is your career.*

Will climbed out of bed and grabbed some clean clothes before heading for the guest bathroom down the hall. He locked the door and turned on the shower, stepping in and leaning his head on the cool tile, reveling in the feel of the water flowing over his shoulders and down his back. Will's hands definitely did not linger on his cock as he soaped his body and he definitely did not jerk off with the image of dark eyes and plump lips dancing behind his closed lids. Nor did a breathy, cut off "Sco—" fall from his lips when his orgasm pulsed from him in hot spurts against the tiles.

He was so screwed.

****

When Scott finally emerged from the shower, he dried himself with the soft white towel on the heated towel rail and pulled on his clean briefs. After he'd slipped his legs into the well worn jeans he'd left on the counter, he padded back into the now empty bedroom and scrabbled around in the drawer for a T-shirt. Grabbing his faded Led Zeppelin tee, he put it on and smoothed the material down his chest before slipping his bare feet into his battered hi-tops. He glanced at his reflection in the mirror above the chest of drawers and ran a hand through his dark, wavy hair. Squaring his shoulders, he took a deep breath and headed downstairs to the kitchen.

As he stepped off the last step, he heard voices, one of which was Will's. He wandered into the kitchen to find David Taylor, and another man, sitting at the table drinking coffee and eating breakfast. Will was at the stove, bacon and eggs sizzling away in a large pan as he chatted conversationally with their guests.

"Morning, Scott." David smiled, getting to his feet and enfolding Scott in a bear hug. "Hope you don't mind us landing on you this early in the morning."

Scott returned the hug and the smile and shook his head. "Of course not," he replied, sliding into one of the vacant chairs. "*Mi casa es su casa* as they say."

Thanking Will for the plate of bacon and eggs he put in front of him, David picked up a piece of bacon and nodded toward the other man at the table. "Scott, the idiot who is busy stuffing his face, is Erik Walker, the other designer of our little estate." He tapped Erik on the arm, drawing his attention away from the food in front of him. "Erik, swallow and welcome our new resident."

"Sorry, man," Erik mumbled, chewing quickly and washing it down with a mouthful of coffee. "But these eggs are fabulous, you must keep him chained to the stove." He grinned widely at Will, before turning his attention back to Scott. "Nice to finally meet you, Scott." He reached out and shook Scott's hand. "Damon was right."

"Don't tell me, the lips?"

"Well, they're how you got me." Will put a plate loaded with food in front of Scott and leaned down to him. "Mornin', babe," he said softly, kissing him with a teasing glint in his eye that only Scott could see.

"Mornin'," Scott replied, lifting a hand and brushing Will's bangs from his forehead in a gesture of affection. *Two can play at this game.* He swallowed down the chuckle that threatened to escape his throat at the surprise that flitted across Will's eyes and picked up his knife and fork. "Erik, tell us more about how you and Jay came up with the idea for Laurel Heights? Jay said something about an incident where you lived before?"

Smiling up at Will as he refilled the coffee cup in his hand, Erik nodded. "Thanks. Yeah, it's just like it is all over, I guess. We'd been living together for about six months in our first home when the letters started appearing in the mailbox. Pleasant little ditties telling us to get out. That they didn't want "our kind" living in their building. Then came the slashed tires, the dog shit on the wind shield." He picked up a piece of hot buttered toast and bit into it, chewing thoughtfully and washing it down with some coffee before continuing.

"We reported it to the police but there was little they could do. Then the action stepped up a pace. I was attacked in the underground parking lot of our apartment complex. Some homophobic asshole; worked me over real good. I don't really remember much, thank God." He smiled softly at David, who patted his arm reassuringly. "Anyway, when I finally got out of the hospital, Jay said he was sick of people trying to make us conform to their idea of "normal". That he wished we could live in a place where we could be ourselves, you know? Where we could be free to express who we are in any way we wanted to, without tongues wagging or fists flying." Laying his knife and fork on the now empty plate, Erik leaned back in the chair and rubbed his stomach contentedly. "The answer was staring us right in the face. Jay's an architect, I'm a designer, and we decided the only way to ensure that we found the place we were dreaming of, was to build it ourselves. And here we are."

"Wow," Will said, sliding into the chair beside Scott and beginning his own breakfast, while Scott tried to ignore the waft of the cologne that drifted into his airspace. "Did they ever catch the bastard who attacked you?"

Erik shook his head. "No. There weren't any witnesses and my brain was pretty much Swiss cheese after that. I still have trouble with my short term memory, but I've learned to work around it."

David curled a hand around Erik's neck and pulled his head down so he could lay a resounding kiss on his friend's cheek. "Thank God his head took the brunt of the attack; otherwise he'd have been in real trouble."

"You're a fucking comedian, Taylor," Erik snapped back, elbowing the other man in the side. "Anyway, enough about me. I want to know more about you guys. Come on, tell me your deepest, darkest secrets."

They chatted with the two men amiably, finding out that David was also a writer, but obviously a real one. He had been on the bestseller list with his series of detective novels, which both Will and Scott had read and enjoyed.

"So, guys," he said. "Saturday night. What can we expect for our first gathering?" Scott kept his tone as even as he could. He could tell by the way that Will tensed beside him that the man was not looking forward to it.

"Don't worry, guys," David smiled, stroking a reassuring hand down Will's forearm, a hand that lingered a little longer than necessary in Scott's opinion. "We'll break you in nice and easy. We thought we'd just get together and see where the mood takes us. Brent and I are hosting this month, so we'll expect you both at seven sharp."

"I think we all need to unwind after the last few weeks." Erik picked up his coffee and sipped at the steamy liquid.

Putting down his knife and fork, Will picked up his own cup and leaned back in his chair. "It must have been hard for you all. Losing two of the residents like that. I mean, the community seems so close knit."

"It *was* a terrible shock," Erik murmured, his eyes glistening as they filled with tears. "They were a lovely couple. I still can't quite believe that Cory would have—" He paused and downed the rest of his coffee, tipping the cup back and tilting his head. "But I guess you never really know what goes on behind closed doors."

Scott's eyes narrowed slightly as he caught the glance Erik shot David, a mere flick of the eyes, but it was there nonetheless. Something was definitely going on here. His gut instinct told him that Damon and Cal were right.

****

Half an hour and another cup of coffee later, Scott closed the front door behind the two men and wandered into the living room to turn on his laptop. As he expected, there were three documents in his inbox. Each one a report on the three men he had told Grace about yesterday. He printed them and stretched out on the sofa, resting his head on one arm and his feet on the other while he read through the details Grace had sent him.

"I'm going to set up the study in case one of our neighbors decides to have a poke about," Will said, sticking his head around the open door. "Did Gracie come up with anything interesting?"

"Maybe," Scott replied, scanning the page again. "Brent has a record. He was arrested eight years ago for common assault, but the charges were dropped by his partner, David Taylor. He and David have been together for ten years and lived in Laurel Heights for five. The club does very well and Brent pays his taxes on time. Apart from the assault, which was obviously a domestic, nothing leaps out at me and screams murderer."

"What about Marcus and Todd?" Will put down the box of books he was holding on the arm of the sofa next to Scott's feet.

"Even less interesting. Marcus discovered Todd singing in a bar three years ago. They've been together ever since, and Marcus has helped build Todd's career. Which doesn't seem to have done his own much harm either. They've been living here for two years, and neither of them have any priors beyond a couple of parking fines."

"This whole set up is seriously nuts," Will said, raking his fingers through his blond hair. "Any one of these men could be a killer and I have absolutely no idea who. They all seem like Mr All-American. I can't imagine any one of them popping those two boys."

"I guess we'll get to see a different side to them on Saturday," Scott said, his gaze lifting from the paper in his hands to lock with Will's. He tried not to smile at the flush that warmed the other man's cheeks at his words.

"About that," Will said, clearing his throat and sitting down on the sofa opposite Scott's. "How are we going to get out of it?"

"Unless we find and arrest the shooter before Saturday, I don't think we can." Scott shrugged, leaning forward and putting his elbows on his knees. "I assume you're really asking how far we go with this charade."

"Well, yeah, to be honest." Will fiddled with his watch strap. "I mean, in the academy they said that one day every officer might have to take one for the team—but I always thought they were talking about bullets."

Scott chuckled in response to Will's phrasing. "Well, if we're being honest, here. I don't have the answer, Will. I guess that's one of those play it by ear situations." He lifted the laptop onto his knees and opened a new message to send Grace the details they'd learned on David and Erik over breakfast. At Will's heavy sigh, he couldn't resist adding, "But when you consider where your hand was this morning, I think you'll be able to hold your own—if you'll pardon the pun."

"Oh come on, that's just... just…" Will stood and picked up the box of books, glaring down at Scott in indignation. "You *suck*," he ground out, slamming the living room door on Scott's laughter.

****

He cried out as fingers grabbed at his hair, pulling him across the floor. "Please, don't, please. I won't do it again, I promise." He didn't know what he'd done, but he would promise anything, do anything, for the pain to stop.

"Damn straight you won't," was the gruff response. "I know you went over there. Did you think I wouldn't find out—that you could hide it from me?"

"I was with the others, I was just being neighborly." He whimpered, pain sparking through his kidney at the kick to his lower back, and he automatically curled in on himself.

Covering his mouth with his arm, he bit into his sleeve to stop the cry falling from his lips, knowing that if he cried out, it would be *so* much worse.

"Did he *fuck* you?" The words were punctuated with more kicks to his lower back, the muscle in his thigh, and a heavier one to his right buttock. "Couldn't you wait until tonight? Did you sink your teeth into those muscles? Let him open you up and fuck you right there in front of everyone like the whore you are? Did you think you could get away with it?"

"I didn't. I swear. He never touched me, baby— please you have to believe me. I'll do anything."

It was the same mantra, repeated over and over for every sin *He* thought had been committed, for every wrong that *He* believed to have been done. There was one last vicious kick and then the sound of his heavy breathing as he brought himself under control. The storm was over—for now.

The man on the floor tried not to flinch from the hand held out to him and he was pulled to his feet. Strong arms enfolded around him and warm hands soothed and rubbed small circles into his abused flesh, the voice in his ear soft and remorseful.

"I'm sorry, baby. I love you so much; I just get a little crazy. Follow my lead tonight. I'm in the mood for a little three way." His hands moved down over rounded buttocks as he pressed his lips to a fluttering pulse.

"Now." He pushed at the shoulders of the man in his arms, forcing him to his knees with a firm and warning grip. "How about you make it up to me?"

****

"Hey, it's me."

"Will? Are you okay?" Julie's voice was immediately concerned by the lackluster tone of her partner's voice.

"Not really." He sighed, running his fingers through his hair. He was out in the garden, pacing up and down the patio, his cell pressed to his ear. Looking up, he saw Scott at the kitchen window waving a coffee cup and he nodded, flashing him a bright smile. A smile that disappeared the moment Scott turned away.

They had settled into a sort of tolerable routine over the last few days. Both knowing that they had to keep up the pretense almost twenty-four/seven, in case one of their 'in your face every single minute of the day' neighbors came to call. They'd spent quite a bit of time with Damon and Cal, building a more detailed picture of the men who lived in the community. Also they'd braved the daily drop-ins by one or more of their neighbors with ease and surprising grace on Scott's part, Will had to concede. He'd never really expected Scott to be as easy going as he appeared to be. It was a side to the man that he had never seen in their work environment.

The sleeping arrangements had remained the same, except after that first night, when Will had insisted on putting pillows down the center of the bed. He did *not* want a repeat of their first morning. No matter how intriguing the idea, he admitted to himself grudgingly.

"Okay, talk to me," Julie hissed. "I'm in the bedroom and no one will hear me. What's going on? You sound weird."

"I'm sorry to call you on your day off. I know you don't get to spend much time with the kids as it is. Tell Chad I'll get him a beer when this is all over." Will sighed, slumping down into one of the chairs around the patio set and closing his eyes.

"He'll expect a case and a round of Guitar Hero, you know that, Harrison. Now don't make me come down there, what's going on in that moronic head of yours?"

Will could hear the smile in her voice but couldn't summon up one of his own. "Today's Saturday," he mumbled into the handset. "I can't do this, Jules."

"What do you mean? I thought everything was okay. Grace seemed to think you and Scott had called a truce."

"Ha! Is that what he called it?" Will huffed out a joyless laugh. "Julie, I have no idea what's going to happen tonight. There've been hints at partner swapping and such, but I don't have a clue what they're actually expecting us to do. What if he has to kiss another guy in front of me?"

"I'm confused. Don't you mean what if you have to kiss another guy in front of him?"

"That's what I said," Will snapped heatedly. "Aren't you listening to me?"

"Yes, I am listening, and no, that's not what you said," Julie drawled sarcastically. "I repeat: what the hell is going on with you?"

"I don't fucking know, all right!" Will sighed and changed hands, pressing the handset to his other ear, his gaze following Scott as the other man filled the coffee pot at the window. *God, how can the asshole be so calm? He's driving me fucking crazy!* "Fucking Turner is an asshole, that's what's wrong with me. You should see him, Jules. He's been walking around the house, all dressed and everything. Just walking—can you believe it? The nerve of the guy!"

Will's words tumbled over one another as he spoke, now that he had begun, unable to stop. "Oh, and don't get me started on the smell. The man has the audacity to wear this cologne that smells really good and I mean *really* good. And don't think I don't know why he's walking around in the clothes and smelling the smell, because I do. I know exactly what he's trying to do."

"Will, honey, you're not making any sense. I assume we're talking about Turner?"

Will grunted in reply.

"Let me get this straight. You think Scott is wearing clothes and smelling good because?"

Will listened to her pause and grumbled beneath his breath, knowing that she expected him to finish the sentence. "Because he wants to drive me crazy. It's totally obvious. It's been his one goal ever since I joined the department. He wants to drive me completely fucking cuckoo!" Will slapped a hand to his forehead and gave a half-hearted chuckle. "I'm losing it, aren't I?"

"Honestly? Yes, you've tripped over the line from insane to totally batshit crazy. I know you're nervous about tonight, baby, and you know what to do if anything gets out of hand. Tell 'em you've got crabs, or shoot the fucking lot of 'em, Turner included."

Will's chuckle was more genuine this time at the teasing note in her voice.

"Listen," she said, her voice softening. "You're both excellent cops, and whether you refuse to believe it or not, you work well together. Just follow each other's lead. We need to find out who killed those boys. I know you, Will. I *know* you can do this."

"Jules, my career is everything to me. You know that, too." Will took a deep breath to steady himself and let it out slowly. "What if I get turned on? He'll know I'm gay and I'll lose it all."

"Will, at the end of the day you're playing a part. You know how to play a part, hell, you've been playing one for years. And so what if you *do* get turned on? It's a physical response, nothing more. You don't have to explain anything beyond that. You can do this. He's probably just as worried about this as you are, with more cause, because at least you've kissed a guy before. Just work together."

Julie's voice sounded so confident that he could pull this off that, for a split second, he actually thought he could too. For a split second. Sighing, he rubbed a hand over his face. "Thanks for letting me unload."

"Hey, what else are partners for? Oh, and Will? About the clothes and the smelling?"

Will cleared his throat; glad she couldn't see the flush in his cheeks. "Yeah?"

"You need serious help, dude. Seriously."

The line went dead as Julie hung up and he choked back a feeble laugh. He had a feeling she was right. Looking up as the back door opened and Scott approached him with a mug of coffee in each hand, Will tried to smile.

"Here." Scott held out the cup in his left hand, his brow furrowing in concern. "You okay?"

"Yeah, I'm good." Will tried to sound nonchalant as he took the cup from Scott's fingers and sipped at the desperately needed caffeine fix.

"Sure you are." Scott's voice was heavy with sarcasm. "You're freaking out about tonight, aren't you?" Scott swallowed a mouthful of his own drink, and rolled his eyes at the pained expression on Will's face in answer.

"Okay," Scott put his mug of steaming coffee down on the table and plucked Will's out of his hand, standing it next to the other. "Look, man. We're two straight guys about to go to our first gay gang bang."

Will's eyes widened in panic when Scott nudged his knees together and sat astride his thighs. "What are you doing?" His voice sounded like he'd been sucking on helium and he tried not to lean into Scott's fingers as they stroked his hair back from his forehead.

"We're no closer to getting any information to break this case. It's obvious these gatherings have something to do with what happened to Jon and Cory. We ain't getting out of tonight, Harrison, so—" Scott continued to thread his fingers through his hair and Will tried to swallow past the lump in his throat. "We need to suck it up and get comfortable with the whole touching business, right now." Scott took a deep breath, picked up Will's hands and put them on his own hips. "Close your eyes," he said, his tone matter of fact as he cupped Will's cheek with the hand that wasn't buried in short, blond locks.

"Scott—"

"Close your fucking eyes, Will. I'm going to kiss you, and you're going to kiss me back, you got it?"

"Why are you yelling at me?" Will huffed, momentarily forgetting he had one hundred and eighty pounds of Turner on his lap.

"Because you're freaking out! One touch from someone tonight is going to have you running for the hills and you'll blow our cover wide open. I am *not* ending my career as a beat cop. I've worked long and hard and made sacrifices to get to where I am, and I'm not going to let you ruin it. Now fucking kiss me!" Scott hissed out through clenched teeth. In one swift move, Scott leaned down and captured Will's lips with his in a brief kiss. Pulling back, their mouths parting with a soft snick, he looked into Will's eyes. "Okay?" Will nodded, dumbfounded.

The first thought that crossed Will's mind was how soft Scott's lips were. But then he didn't have much time to consider anything else, because Scott put more pressure behind the kiss. The tip of the other man's tongue tentatively requested entrance to his mouth, and his lips parted of their own volition. When Scott's tongue slid into his mouth and gently caressed his, all other thoughts fled from his mind other than: *Feels. So. Good.*

Will's fingers curled into the denim of Scott's jeans when the man's fingers gripped tighter into his hair, making delicious heat unfurl in his belly. He couldn't stop himself from pulling Scott in closer, and felt, rather than heard, the other man's whimper as he ran his hands up the length of Scott's back. He loved the way the muscles rippled beneath his touch and any blood still left in his brain, rapidly headed south. The tongue sliding sensuously around his mouth tasted of coffee and he licked the bitter remnants away until all he could taste was Scott. He liked it. Wanted more of it. All of it.

Will's hands searched beneath the hem of Scott's T-shirt of their own volition, desperately wanting to feel the warmth of bare flesh against his skin. Which was when Scott broke the kiss, quickly pushed himself off Will's lap and grabbed his coffee. Will stared up at him, his breath panting through his parted lips.

"Okay," Scott cleared his throat and nodded at Will. "I think we can manage kissing." He motioned to the back door. "I'm gonna go see if Grace has come up with anything new."

Will couldn't trust himself to speak, so he acknowledged Scott's intentions with a lift of his chin and picked up his coffee. He watched Scott walk back into the house from beneath lowered lashes, and when the man had disappeared into the house, he put the cup down and ran shaking fingers through his hair. When had this stopped being an act? When had he developed the hots for Scott *'I'm so straight I sleep standing up'* Turner? Will pushed at the hard length of his cock and groaned as the sense memory of Scott's ass on his thighs washed over him. *Fuck—this is so not good!*

****

Scott closed the living room door behind him and leaned against the wood. "*Fuck!*" The expletive was hissed through clenched teeth and his trembling hand palmed his cock. *What the fuck are you doing?* He admonished himself internally. Hoping to God that Will hadn't felt him hardening in his pants during their kiss, he all but threw himself down onto the sofa in front of the laptop. He stabbed at the keys in his frustration. It had started out as a simple experiment to see if Will could get through an average kiss without screaming and running for the hills. But he hadn't counted on Will's lips being even sweeter than he had ever imagined them to be, or that all that thick, blond hair would feel so wonderful against his fingers. As for when Will's fingers had scrabbled at the hem of his tee, *Jesus!* He'd thought he was going to cream his pants like a teenager. Stupid fucking Will *'My thighs are so hard I can crack walnuts'* Harrison. They were supposed to attend their first gathering at David and Brent's in two hours. How the fuck was *he* going to make it through now? How was he going to be able to see other men touching, or kissing Will, without drawing his gun and screaming, *Mine!* He groaned and scrubbed his hands over his face. *This is so not good!*

****

"Well, I guess this is it," Scott muttered as they crossed the street to David and Brent's house. The night air was balmy and they were both dressed to suit the weather, in casual button down shirts and loose fitting shorts. They could clearly see the others through the big bay window beside the front door as they approached; Jay and Erik lounging on one of the sofas, with Marcus and a smiling Todd settled on another.

"I guess so," Will replied, his tone a lot calmer than Scott would have expected it to be.

Will suddenly paused in mid-step and grabbed Scott's hand. Gazing at him in question, Scott waited for the other man to speak. Since their kiss that afternoon, they hadn't really spoken to each other and the air between them had been heavy and cloying.

"Scott," Will began, pulling Scott to a stop and turning to face him. "I just want you to know that anything that goes on behind those doors tonight, stays behind those doors. We're partners, and we're in this together. I've got your back and I know you've got mine."

Scott's eyes widened in surprise at Will's heartfelt reassurance, but his smile was genuinely grateful. "Thanks, Will. I know we haven't always gotten along as well as we could have, but you know that I won't let anything happen to you in there. Well," he teased, nudging Will's foot with his own, "nothing you don't *want* to happen anyway."

"You couldn't resist it, could you?" Will shook his head slowly at Scott's remark and a smile curved his lips as they continued across the street.

Scott didn't even realize Will hadn't dropped his hand until they reached the door. Will's fingers in his were warm and reassuring, and as the other man pressed the buzzer on the door, he was struck by a sudden realization. He didn't want those hands on anyone but him. *Jesus, I need a drink.*

The front door was opened by David, who coaxed them into the hall and closed the front door behind them. "Hey, guys," David said brightly.

Something dark unfurled deep in Scott's gut as David walked toward Will with obvious intent and leaned up to press a soft kiss to Will's mouth. He forced a smile to his lips and bit back the urge to punch David there and then. If anyone should be kissing Will, it was him. *Get a grip, Turner!* He didn't have time to get a grip on anything because Brent moved suddenly into his line of vision and curled a hand around his neck. Pulling Scott down, Brent forced his lips open in a wet, dirty kiss. As Brent's tongue invaded his mouth and licked at his, he tried to remember to respond. Hopefully, his hesitation would be misinterpreted as nervousness.

"Brent," Jay called from the kitchen doorway. "Put him down. You'll get your chance. At least wait until the poor boy has sat down."

Obviously reluctant to break the kiss, Brent pulled back slowly, scraping his teeth on Scott's lower lip as he did so. "As long as I get first dibs," he drawled, lifting his hand and collecting the moisture on Scott's lips with his thumb, then sucking it into his mouth in an obvious display of possession.

Jay wandered out from the kitchen with some glasses on a tray and a large bottle of scotch. "You know hosts always get first dibs," he chuckled, smiling at Scott and Will. "Hey, guys, welcome."

"Hey, is that scotch I spy? On the rocks please, dude," Will said casually. Too casually for Scott's liking since David's hand was still on Will's ass. He allowed Will to lead him into the front room and took a seat next to him on one of the empty sofas. He started at the brush of Will's lips against his ear as he murmured, "I think this could be your lucky night."

Turning his head, Scott lightly captured Will's lips, clinging to his mouth slightly longer than was perhaps necessary for show. "Jealous?"

"You wish," Will shot back with a grin, before turning his attention to Jay and the glass he held out to him. "Thanks." He took a sip of the amber liquid and Scott chuckled as Will coughed indelicately the moment the whiskey hit the back of his throat.

"You're welcome," Jay replied, leaning down to kiss Will square on the mouth, before turning to do the same to Scott. "We're glad to have you both with us."

"Some of us more than others," Erik drawled, throwing a piece of ice at Brent's head.

"Fuck off, Erik," Brent chuckled, his gaze locked on Scott. "I can't help it if I'm a little more obvious than the rest of you. You can't tell me that you *don't* want a piece of that delicious ass, too."

"Maybe," Erik smiled at Scott and dropped him a wink. "But I prefer not to scare all the life out of my men before I've gotten anywhere near their cock."

"Oh, believe me," Will laughed, looping his arm around Scott's shoulders and pulling him closer. Scott could tell the whiskey had already started to mellow Will out, so he went with it, leaning against his side. "It would take more than a little tonsil hockey to scare Scott."

"Yeah, I have to look at Will's face every day, so I don't scare easy." Scott grinned, squeezing Will's thigh as a ripple of laughter at their banter echoed around the room. *Okay, this isn't so bad. We can do this.*

Envying Will the scotch humming happily through his bloodstream, Scott narrowed his gaze as Marcus and Todd rose from their seats, crossed the room to where he and Scott were sitting and leaned down to kiss them. He watched as Todd practically stole the breath from Will's lungs, thrusting his tongue deep into Will's mouth. Scott saw the almost imperceptible hesitation on Will's part before he began to respond to Todd's kiss, but then he was looking for it, he doubted if Todd even noticed. Then his attention was taken by Marcus's lips sliding sweetly against his, and searching fingers sliding between the buttons of his shirt, brushing against his skin. Marcus's kiss was warm and soft, the press of his tongue at Scott's lower lip gentle and coaxing. As Scott returned the pressure, stroking his own tongue across Marcus's teeth, he gasped as the other man was pulled away from him by Will. He watched, his chest rising and falling as Will kissed the big man, nibbling at Marcus's lips. The sight of Will's tongue retreating back into his own mouth as the kiss ended, had Scott already hardening in his pants.

"Okay, guys, now we've all said our hellos." Jay lifted his face for Marcus's kiss before continuing. "Scott, Will, tonight is about enjoying yourself, each other, and those around you. You don't have to do anything you don't want to, take things at your own pace." Scott was amazed at how Jay simply continued with his spiel even though Marcus was pressing open-mouthed kisses to the nape of Jay's neck. "Above all, this evening is about pleasure. No one is forced in our circle. No one is made to feel less than they are and whatever happens between you is simply that, between you. Where you indulge is up to you, whether it is here with others around you to watch and join in, or if you prefer, you can retire to one of the rooms in private. It is your decision and your choice." He leaned into Marcus's mouth as Erik's hand slid up his thigh and caressed the bulge in his pants. "Mmm—on that note, gentleman, let the pleasure begin."

Scott didn't miss the slight shake of Will's hand as he quickly poured himself another scotch and drank it in one. But then again, considering the almost ravenous look on David's face as he watched him, Scott couldn't really blame Will for needing more Dutch courage. *Fuck! Here we go*, Scott thought to himself when Brent dropped to his knees and crawled across the carpet toward him. Brent's intent was obvious as he licked his lips and Scott found himself transfixed by the movement of Brent's tongue. At the gasp falling from Will's lips, Scott shifted his gaze and watched David tug Will's hair so that his head fell onto the back of the sofa. He saw Will's uncertainty in the nervous smile he bestowed upon the man leaning over him and then

David pressed his lips to the tanned column of Will's throat, sucking gently on Will's Adam's apple. Trying desperately to turn his attention back to Brent, he wished he could close his ears to the whimpering moans emanating from Will's throat, but he couldn't. All he could do was wish he was the one responsible.

In his peripheral vision, Scott could see Will's hand twitching against his thigh as David mapped out the skin of his partner's throat with his lips. He wanted to grab hold of David's hair and yank him off Will, the desire to do so almost outweighing the reason they were there. *Do something, Turner, he must be freaking out!* Hissing a mental 'Shut up' to his inner voice, Scott slowly reached out his hand and placed it on Will's thigh, trying to kid himself that he was showing Will his support. *More like marking your territory! Why don't you just pee on him and be done with it?*

Scott was distracted from the irritating chuckle of his own subconscious by Brent shouldering his knees apart and settling himself between them. *Oh shit*, he thought, watching the path of Brent's seeking fingers up his leg as they paused to knead the muscles in his thighs. His fingers tightened involuntarily on Will's leg as Brent undid the last three buttons on his shirt and pressed his lips to Scott's stomach.

Crawling up Scott's body, Brent raised himself high on his knees and pressed his lips to Scott's ear. He licked at the sensitive lobe and whispered huskily, "I want to take you upstairs and then I want to just *take* you. You are so fucking beautiful. I want to bury myself inside you, make you scream." He bent his head and pressed his lips to Scott's throat. "Can I?"

Swallowing down the tingling in his belly that Brent's silky tones conjured up, Scott lifted his hands to cup Brent's face and kissed him slowly, shaking his head in regretful decline. "Not tonight," he replied, "but the wait will make it all the sweeter." He glanced at Will and wondered when David had moved around to sit astride Will's muscled thighs. Scanning the room, he saw Jay and Erik wander out of the room, with Marcus in tow and Todd sprawled out on the couch with his head in Damon's lap, his fingers entwined with Cal's. The couple were kissing and touching each other tenderly, while Damon's fingers slowly feathered through Todd's hair.

Scott caught Damon's eye and desperately hoped that the man got the message he was trying to convey. He had no idea if he had been successful, because Brent suddenly hooked his hands behind Scott's knees and yanked him forward on the couch. Scott almost fell off the soft cushions and onto the carpet but was saved by Brent leaning over him, guiding Scott's legs around his waist. Brent attacked his mouth again, the man's tongue delving deep and mapping out the inside in sharp stabs. Scott had to admit, Brent may be slightly over the top and creepy, but he was a fantastic kisser. He kept his own eyes open as Brent devoured his lips and glanced over at Will, who seemed to be lost in the kiss that David and he were exchanging. Trying to ignore the flare of jealousy that roiled in his gut, Scott let his eyes drift shut and allowed himself to respond fully to Brent. *Harrison looks like he's enjoying himself—why can't you?* Brent's warm hands slid more of his buttons free and he groaned low in his throat as they trailed across his skin. Scott could feel the heat of Will's thigh pressed up against his side and he tried to concentrate on that warmth seeping through to his skin while Brent kissed him, the pressure of the other man's lips and hands becoming more and more insistent.

****

Will moaned under the expert assault of David's tongue. The man's kisses, combined with the way he rolled his hips, had Will hardening in his pants and involuntarily grinding his erection into David's ass in his lap. He gasped into the kiss when David's fingers found his nipples beneath his shirt and he curled his fingers into the firm globes of the other man's ass, pulling him closer. He could hear Scott and Brent beside him, and tried to block out the sound of Scott's whimpering moans. He wanted to be the reason his partner made those sounds. *Fucking Turner. This is his fault. Why couldn't I find a nice homo? Why does the one guy I want have to be straight?* With two glasses of scotch buzzing through him, Will wanted to feel something other than lonely. Opening his mouth wide under the heated kiss David was giving him, he took the hint when David lifted his hands and put them to the buttons on his shirt. Will's shaking fingers dealt with the buttons on David's shirt swiftly, and he slid his hands up the other man's smooth, tanned chest and eased the shirt off his shoulders, letting the material drop to the floor.

"May I cut in?"

Brent tore his mouth from Scott's nipple to gaze up at Cal looming over the pair. Will watched as Brent's gaze traveled over Cal's broad, ebony chest, as he took the beautiful man's hand, let him pull him to his feet, and guide him to the sofa Erik, Jay, and Marcus had vacated. "David?" Cal nodded toward Todd and Damon. "Todd's waiting for you, baby."

Will followed the direction of David's gaze and his eyes widened at the sight of Todd, his jeans around his ankles as Damon ravaged his mouth. He started when David leaned toward Scott while still rolling his hips into Will's and captured Scott's lips, biting down gently on the full lower one before releasing him.

David moved back to Will and kissed his swollen lips softly, before sliding off his lap and crossing the room to where Todd lay, moaning quietly in ecstasy. Within seconds, Will was rock hard as he watched David drop to his knees beside Todd and lap at the other man's erection through his boxers. But there was something else that caught his eye—there were dark purple bruises along David's lower back. Bruises that disappeared beneath the waistband of his jeans. Before he had time to ponder where they had come from, Damon padded toward them and held out his hands.

"I guess that makes you two all mine," Damon smiled as the two men took his outstretched fingers and stood up. "Let's go somewhere a little more private," he said softly, glancing at Brent and Cal who had joined the two men on the sofa.

Will glanced over his shoulder as he followed Scott and Damon from the room and his breath caught in his throat. Brent was fumbling with the belt on Cal's jeans and David's mouth was firmly sealed around Todd's bare flesh, his dark head bobbing up and down.

"Come on," Damon said leading them up the stairs. "We'll go into the guest room; sounds like the others are in the master. Who wants to bottom?" He chuckled openly at the two men and opened the last door in the long hallway.

Will avoided Scott's gaze as the other man closed the door behind them and ran a smoothing hand through his hair. Thankfully, it appeared Scott was avoiding his gaze just as much, which suited him fine.

"Thanks for that," Scott said gruffly to Damon as he sank onto the edge of the mattress.

"You're welcome," Damon said, smiling as he sat cross-legged in the middle of the bed. He gazed between the two of them, his eyes narrowing thoughtfully. "I'm surprised you didn't call Uncle earlier. Brent was determined to get into those glorious pants of yours." He threw Will a teasing look. "Although you didn't seem to be having too bad a time with David." He snorted as Will blushed and flopped down into the armchair in the corner of the room.

"Don't be embarrassed, Will. I've had David, he's fantastic. The things that boy can do with his tongue. Anyway—" He looked from one to the other. "How's it going? Have you any leads yet?"

Scott shook his head. "We've been getting profiles drawn up on each of them. But at the moment, it could be anyone." He grinned wryly. "Hell it could even be me. All these guys seem to be pretty law abiding citizens. Apart from a domestic situation with David and Brent. Do you know if that still goes on? I noticed some bruising to David's back. Looked a bit like boot print and fresh too. Has David ever mentioned abuse to you?"

Damon shook his head. "Never." His eyes widening in what appeared to be genuine surprise as far as Will could tell. "Brent's an arrogant ass, but he's never come across as the violent type. David's a pretty sporty guy and he's always at the gym. Maybe it happened there. I'm sorry, but it's hard for me to believe that Brent would do that."

"Maybe we need to look into that assault charge on Brent a little more closely. I noticed the bruising, too. It didn't look like anything you'd get at the gym," Will said softly, noting Scott's acknowledgement. "So, how long have we got to stay up here?" He had the sudden urge to wash David's scent off him. *Why? Cause it's not Scott's?*

"Well, longer than the five minutes it probably takes you, from start to finish," Scott drawled.

"Very funny. You're becoming a regular comedian, Turner. You should be on the stage," Will countered, anger beginning to fizz in his belly. Seriously? The asshole was gonna bait him now? "I could always ask Brent if he wants to come up and finish what he started."

Scott narrowed his eyes at the sarcasm in Will's voice. "Well it would probably take him longer than you. Brent doesn't strike me as the two pumps and a squirt kind of guy."

Will glared at Scott and opened his mouth, closing it again before he said something he was going to regret. Pushing himself out of the chair, he cleared his throat and nodded at Damon. "I think I've gotten just about all I can out of our first gathering," he said, his tone flat and devoid of emotion. He quickly undid the buttons on his shirt and pulled it open, undoing the belt on his jeans and leaving it hanging.

"What the fuck are you doing?" Scott snarled, his disbelieving gaze following Will's movements.

"We're supposed to have just had sex, moron," Will hissed at Scott, reaching up and ruffling his fingers through his blond hair, making the soft strands stand up in disarray. "Thanks for the rescue, Damon." He threw a disparaging look at Scott and opened the door, shutting it behind him.

Ignoring the writhing bodies in the living room, Will opened the front door and strode down the path. He didn't even acknowledge Scott, although he heard the door close and the other man's footsteps behind him. *Fucking, Turner. Who the fuck does he think he is?* Will fished in his pocket for the door key and winced as the fabric tightened across his cock. He was still at half mast and he pulled at the crotch of his shorts in thinly veiled frustration as he stabbed the key into the lock.

"What's up, Harrison?" Scott said as he came up behind him. "Feeling a little tense? I'm sure David wouldn't mind picking up where you left off. Don't mind me." Sarcasm dripped from every word and he abruptly pushed past Will as the lock turned and the door swung back on its hinges.

Will saw red. He shut and locked the front door and toed off his shoes in the hall, stomping into the kitchen after Scott. "What the fuck is that supposed to mean?"

"I saw you," Scott retorted, filling a glass from the faucet and downing it in one. He wiped his mouth with the back of his hand and tossed the glass into the dishwasher, closing the door with a slam. "You were practically fucking David right there in front of me."

"What?" Will yelled in disbelief. "Me? What about *you*? I thought you were gonna hump Brent's leg right there in the hall as soon as we got through the door!" He crowded Scott up against the sink. "Where the hell do you get off? You're driving me crazy. You fucking hypocrite!"

"I'm driving you crazy? I sat right beside you. I saw you. His hands were all over you, Will." Scott jutted his chin out angrily. "Is that why you're so pissed off? Because you liked it? Did he turn you on? Did you want him?"

"Stop it," Will said, a note of definite warning in his voice. He was hanging on to his temper by the skin of his teeth and if Turner didn't back off right now, he couldn't be held responsible for his actions.

"You did, didn't you?" Scott spat. "Did you want him to *blow* you?"

"Scott!" His name was ground through Will's teeth, but the clear warning in his voice was obviously not going to deter Scott, as the other man closed the tiny gap between their bodies and pressed his thighs against Will's.

"Did you want to fuck him?"

"I'm warning you, Turner. That's enough!"

"Why, what are you gonna do hotshot?" Scott taunted. "You gonna arrest me? You—"

Before he even knew he was going to do it, Will pressed his lips to Scott's in a hard brutal kiss. Anything to stop the words falling from his lips. *What the fuck am I doing?* Will grunted as Scott pushed him away and he watched him lift a hand to his own lips, as he gazed at Will in stunned amazement.

Will felt immediately contrite as Scott stared at him, and he ran a hand through his blond hair. "Sco—" It was Will's turn to have the words stolen from his mouth as Scott grabbed hold of his shirt and yanked him forward, crashing their mouths together. He moaned into Scott's mouth, as the warm wetness of the other man's tongue forced his lips apart and sucked Will's tongue into his mouth. "Fuck," he groaned, when Scott broke the kiss to slide his lips along Will's jaw and down the side of his throat, nipping at the fluttering pulse he found there. "What are we doing?" He all but ripped off the buttons of Scott's shirt with shaking fingers, desperate to feel the skin beneath. As Scott's shirt fell to the floor and Will felt the warmth of smooth skin against his hands, he suddenly didn't care about anything beyond *want, him, now!*

"You smell so good, Turner," he growled against Scott's throat. His hands curved around Scott's hips and slid beneath the waistband of the shorts the man wore. He brought their mouths back together, licking a path across Scott's teeth and lapping at his tongue, as his hands searched further. "So fucking hot," he mumbled against the lips he was nibbling at as his fingers slipped past the waistband of Scott's briefs and the firm globes of the man's ass filled his palms. Gripping the rounded flesh in his hands, he pulled Scott closer still and rolled his hips against the erection that threatened to burst from Scott's zipper. "*Yes*," he hissed, rolling his hips again and swallowing the whimper that crept up Scott's mouth before it could leave his lips. "You like that? Is that what you wanted Brent to do?" He winced when Scott bit down on his lower lip and he kissed his apology into Scott's throat. He'd probably deserved that.

Turning Scott around, Will began to walk the man backwards out of the kitchen, their lips never apart longer than to take their next breath. Scott's hands seemed to be everywhere all at once and Will thought he'd come on the spot when the sinful tongue that lapped at his, changed tack and zeroed in on the sensitive spot behind his ear. "Fuck!" Will's growl was almost feral as he urged Scott up the stairs, amazed that they didn't injure themselves on the way to the bedroom. He managed to kick the door open and lower Scott to the mattress, pulling back to yank his shirt over his head, not even bothering with the buttons. Leaning on his hands, he bent his head to lick his way back into Scott's panting mouth.

The feel of Scott's chest against his was intoxicating, he couldn't get enough. And his mouth, *God,* his mouth. Will knew that even if he spent the rest of his life attached at the lips with Scott Turner, it still wouldn't be long enough. He whimpered as Scott's fingers found his nipples and teased the flat discs until they stood proudly against his chest. Fumbling with the button on Scott's shorts, he knew he should stop this. Knew that the situation they'd found themselves in had heightened every look, every touch and he would have to face the music in the morning—but he didn't care. He couldn't stop if his life had depended on it. Will needed to taste every inch of Scott. Needed to lose himself in the man writhing beneath him. Of course, he knew it was wrong—even as he hooked his fingers into the waistband of Scott's shorts and briefs—even as he slid them slowly down muscled thighs and onto the floor. Of course it was wrong—even as he dealt quickly with the rest of his clothes and covered Scott's body with his own—even as he pushed Scott's hands above his head and held him down. Even then he knew it was wrong.

Scott's back arched into the first thrust of Will's hard shaft against his steadily leaking cock, and Will gave a half-strangled cry. He couldn't remember having felt anything as intense as the feel of Scott's body moving with his. He bent his head and lapped at the man's nipples, lavishing on them the same dedicated attention as Scott had his, all the while not stopping in the rolling of his hips. He could feel the whimpering that rumbled in Scott's chest vibrating against his skin as he lapped at the puckered flesh.

"Will—" Scott breathed.

Will lifted his head and gazed into Scott's lust-blown gaze. "Don't tell me to stop," he groaned. "Please Scott—don't tell me to stop."

"Don't," Scott rasped. "Don't want you to stop." He lifted his head and captured Will's lips again.

Will groaned into Scott's mouth, their tongues matching the frantic thrusting of their hips. He was coming undone and he was coming undone fast. Heat spiraled out to all his nerve endings, setting them on fire. Scott felt so good. Their fingers were entwined, the sheen of sweat glistened between them as they strived for their release, together. "Oh God," Will whimpered, breaking the kiss and holding Scott's gaze. The taut thighs wrapped around his flanks tightened their grip and he knew that Scott was close. Could tell by the panting gasps falling from Scott's lips as he stared up at him. "I want to see you come," he breathed, rutting against Scott, pre-come from both their cocks easing the slip and slide of velvety skin against velvety skin, never breaking the punishing rhythm he had established.

"*Yes*, make me come." Scott cried out, his back arching as Will's hips snapped against his once, twice and then he came, spilling between them, hot spurts pulsing from his cock and splattering onto his chest.

Will didn't think he had ever seen anything as hot as Scott Turner pumping hot, white streams across his skin, and the sight sent him over the edge. "*Fuck… Scott…oh God… Scott!*" Will's seed shot across Scott's stomach in thick, hot bursts, his hips jerking uncontrollably as his orgasm slammed through him.

He collapsed on top of Scott, practically boneless in the aftershocks of his orgasm. His grip on Scott's hands loosened and he felt shaking fingers feather gently through his hair. When he was certain his heart wasn't going to jump out of his chest, Will rolled off Scott and blinked up at the ceiling. He glanced over at the man beside him and saw the sheen of sweat and come on Scott's tanned skin, and his stomach bottomed out, as the magnitude of what he had done washed over him.

Will ran his hands through his hair and gripped the soft strands as Scott got up off the bed and padded, bare-assed and beautiful to the bathroom. What had he done? What had he allowed to happen? My God, he'd instigated it. Scott may have wound him up, but he was the one who flicked the switch. He'd been so jealous at the sight of Scott making out with Brent and the other man's hands gliding over that soft skin that he'd lost control. It was his fault. Christ, Scott must be mortified. How could he ever look at him again, without remembering how that beautiful body felt against his? He closed his eyes tightly. *Fuck! I'll have to leave the force! I'll have to leave the country!* The guilt was overwhelming.

Will's eyes opened in surprise when a damp towel was thrown onto his stomach and Scott slid beneath the duvet on his side of the bed. He noted the way the other man couldn't even look him in the eye and groaned inwardly. *I should say something. What the fuck can I say? How the hell am I going to find anything to justify what we did? What I did?* Wiping the towel across his stomach, he tossed it to the floor and slipped under the duvet. *Say something, Harrison, you heartless shit!* Will closed his eyes against the inner voice screaming in his ear and hissed back. *I'm working up to it!* Moistening his lips, he turned and took a deep breath.

"Scott—"

"Go to sleep, Will," Scott cut him off before he could begin.

Will closed his eyes in despair. The poor guy couldn't even speak to him. How the fuck was he going to make this right? He lay rigid beside Scott until he heard the man's breathing finally even out and he knew he was asleep. Only then did he allow himself to drift. Sighing, he settled down against the pillow and pulled the duvet up around his shoulders.

His last conscious thought before the sandman caught up with him, was that they would need to tell Julie and Grace about the bruising to David's back.

VI

Strains of Nickelback's "If Today Was Your Last Day" filtered through the blanket of sleep Scott was wrapped in and he reached out blindly toward the nightstand, feeling for his cell phone. "Hello?"

"Scott? Why are you still asleep? It's ten-thirty," Grace's voice trilled down the line.

"Because it's Sunday, you know, the day of rest? Besides, I was up late last night," he yawned, still not bothering to open his eyes.

"Really?" Grace said teasingly. "How *up* are we talking?"

"I don't kiss and tell, Cassidy." Scott stretched and then rubbed a fist into his eye. "What do you want?"

"I've got some information for you. Cory reserved three bus tickets to Phoenix for the day *after* the shootings." Grace sounded very pleased with herself.

"Okay," Scott drew out the word, forcing one eye open slowly. "That doesn't mean anything. Defense will just say they booked a vacation, had an argument the night before they were due to leave, and wound up dead. "

"They booked *three* tickets, Scott," Grace pointed out. "Why would two boys whose fathers own private jets, go on vacation by Greyhound? And who was the *third* ticket for? Something's not right here."

While he listened to Grace's voice, Scott slowly stretched out his foot and encountered nothing but cool sheets. He heaved a grateful sigh. Will had obviously gotten up earlier without disturbing him. Sitting up, he ran a hand through his bed head and arranged the sheet in his naked lap. "All right, Gracie. Check and see if they were booked into any of the hotels in Phoenix, maybe we can track down the other traveler."

"I'll get right on it. Are you going to tell me what happened last night or not? You've got that cagey tone in your voice."

"I don't even know how to do a cagey tone," Scott snorted. "How do you think this shit up?" Scott shook his head in amazement, even though she couldn't see him.

"Scott."

"I am not discussing this with you, Gracie. Just," he sighed, a little too heavily, "just leave it."

"Scott?" Now she sounded concerned. "What happened? They didn't force you did they?"

"No, no, nothing like that," Scott rolled his eyes, wishing she didn't know him so goddamn well. "I just don't wanna talk about it." He flopped back onto the pillows and hoped she would let it go. Fat chance.

"Crap, did something happen between you and Will?"

"Grac—"

"Jesus, Scott."

He knew that tone. He could imagine her right now, sitting at her desk, phone in hand, wearing that look she got on her face whenever she was pissed at and worried about him at the same time.

"What did you do?"

"Why do you automatically assume it was something *I* did?" His voice rose an octave. "He started it." *Way to go, Turner! Very mature.*

"Scott, please. Don't do this to yourself. That road doesn't lead anywhere good."

Scott closed his eyes and ran a hand over his face. "Don't you think I know that? Don't I feel shitty enough without you confirming how stupid I am?" He *really* didn't want to have this conversation right now. "I've got to go. Look into the hotels and let me know what you find." Scott hung up on the sound of her protests, promising himself that he would call her back later and apologize. Putting his cell back on the nightstand, he folded his arms beneath his head and stretched out his legs against the coolness of the sheets.

He was glad that Will had already vacated the bed, because he had absolutely no idea what to say to him. *Why should you say anything? As you told Gracie, he's the one who started it.* Rolling his eyes at the tiny little voice whispering in his ear, he murmured, "Shut up, you're not helping."

Of course he had to say something—but what? What could he possibly say to make what had happened last night okay? Will had already been half hard when they got back to the house. Not that Scott blamed him for that. The guy would have had to have been in a coma, or dead, *not* to have had a reaction to the moves David had made on him. Hadn't he reacted to Brent's expertise in exactly the same manner? He rubbed a hand over the stubble on his chin and groaned aloud. *He started it, Scott.* "No he fucking didn't," he mumbled. "I did." Scott shook his head. He'd told Will that he had his back. But instead of trying to be supportive and reassuring him that Brent had gotten him hard too, what had he done instead? Oh yeah—he'd been so jealous at the sight of David kissing where he wanted to kiss, of touching where he wanted to touch, that he'd hounded Will before the guy even had a chance to catch his breath. *Smooth, Scott, real smooth. If the poor guy can't trust you—who can he trust?*

Turning his head to search for his cell on the nightstand, Scott's gaze fell on the shorts he'd worn last night. A moan crept up his throat as he was hit by the sense memory of Will's fingers unbuttoning them and yanking them off in their haste to feel naked skin against naked skin. Everything about it had felt right.

The way Will's tongue had felt in his mouth—the touch of his fingers on smooth skin—the way their shafts had slid against each other, tipping them over the edge. Everything had just felt *right*. Until their seed was drying on their sweat-slick skin and they were brought back to reality with a heavy thud. The way the light had gone out in Will's eyes when he realized what they'd done. The way he'd rolled off Scott at double speed, as if he could no longer bear to touch him once he had come to his senses.

How the fuck was he supposed to brush it all under the carpet now that he knew how Will felt in his arms, against his body, in his mouth. How? How the fuck was he supposed to make it through this assignment without blowing his cover, or his career?

How—? His inner monologue was cut off by the sound of footfalls on the stairs and Scott tried to swallow past the lump in his throat as Will walked into the bedroom. The man was bare-chested in loose fitting navy sweatpants that clung to his lean hips as he padded toward the bed, with a steaming mug of coffee in each hand.

"Morning," he said quietly, holding out one of the cups.

"Morning." Scott sat up against the pillows and took the cup from Will's outstretched fingers. Sipping at the coffee, he sighed as it slid down his throat, the heat of the liquid warming and expanding in his chest. He glanced at Will out of the corner of his eye as the big man sat on the bed and leaned back against his own pillows. There was only a small gap between them, but to Scott the chasm was bigger than the Grand Canyon. He took another sip of coffee to moisten his suddenly dry mouth. How was he supposed to say something profound when all he wanted to do was rip off those sweatpants with his teeth? When he wanted to feel that smooth skin all sweat slicked and sticky against his?

When all he wanted to do was wrap his legs around those lean hips and lose himself.

"I'm sorry—"

"I'm sorry—"

Will looked at Scott and shook his head slowly. "You have nothing to be sorry for. It was my fault."

"No," Scott replied, running a hand through his tousled hair. "I goaded you into it. It was me. I'm so sorry, Will."

"Look," Will began, turning to face Scott. "Everything was major league weird last night and we just got caught up in it and carried away. Why don't we chalk it up to experience and move on, okay? We're supposed to be working a case here, so let's do what we came here to do."

Scott nodded his agreement. If only it were that easy. He squared his shoulders. "Okay, let's just move on and concentrate on the case. Speaking of which," he put his coffee cup down on the nightstand, "Grace called. Cory reserved three tickets to Phoenix for the day after he and Jon died. She and Jules are going through all the hotels in Phoenix to find out which one they were booked into and maybe unearth who the third ticket was for."

Will frowned. "Three tickets?" He gave a low chuckle. "I can't say I envy the girls trying to track down that information. Talk about needle in a haystack."

"Hey guys!"

"What the fuck?" Scott's gaze flew to the bedroom doorway at the sound of Marcus's voice floating up the stairs. "How did they get in?"

"Shit, dude," Will cursed, quickly putting the mug down on the nightstand. "I left the patio doors open in the kitchen. They're coming up!"

Scott told himself that he was thinking on his feet and that this was the only thing he could come up with at short notice—at least that's what he would tell himself later to justify his actions. Reaching out, he curled his fingers around the back of Will's neck and yanked the other man toward him. He just had time to see startled surprise in deep brown eyes before he captured Will's lips with his own.

What the fuck are you doing now? Scott ignored his own subconscious and closed his eyes, winding his arms around Will's neck. He was unable to stop the groan that crept up his throat when, after his initial gasp, Will's lips moved against his, kissing him back. He slid his tongue out to meet Will's when he felt the tentative touch of the other man's, pressing his body closer to Will's and burying his fingers in the soft strands of blond hair. When Will's fingers unconsciously skimmed across one of Scott's nipples, he gasped into the other man's mouth and arched his back, needing that teasing touch again.

"Shit!" The expletive came from the doorway, followed by several chuckles.

The two men broke apart and Will turned so that he was back against the pillows, his cheeks flushed. "Um, morning," he said breathlessly.

Scott scrubbed a hand over his face and double checked that the sheet was still covering his modesty. "Hey, guys," he said lamely, his gaze flitting between Brent, Todd, and Marcus. "Sorry, we didn't hear the doorbell." In his peripheral vision, he could see Will's chest rising and falling with each of the harsh breaths he took, and he quickly suppressed the urge to tell the other men to fuck off so he could finish what he'd started.

"Didn't you two get enough last night?" Marcus drawled, his eyes lingering on Will's muscled chest.

"Don't mind us." Brent grinned, his gaze roaming over Scott lasciviously. "Carry on," he said suggestively. "Pretend we're not even here."

Marcus elbowed his friend in the ribs and laughed when Brent grunted. "You must forgive Brent, as you may have already discovered, he's a sleaze. We'll wait downstairs while you two get dressed. But don't be long, we're dying to know what you thought of last night. Come on, guys."

"Before I forget," Todd added, rolling his eyes at Marcus manhandling a reluctant Brent down the stairs. "Scott, could you have another look at my laptop? I can't access my emails and it's driving me nuts."

"Sure thing," Scott tried to smile as casually as he could. "I thought we fixed that last week, but I'll have another look when I come down, did you bring it with you?"

"Yeah, it's downstairs in the living room."

"No problem." Scott glanced at Will, who was now breathing more regularly. "Give us five minutes and we'll be down. Mine's black no sugar."

"And mine is white with three," Will said, grinning as the smaller man left the doorway and they listened to him making his way down the stairs. "Jesus Christ," he hissed. "Doesn't anyone knock anymore?"

"What the hell is wrong with these people?" Scott grumbled as he tried not to watch the way the soft fabric of Will's sweatpants stretched across the curve of his firm ass as he stood up. Scott bit his lower lip and gave a mental shake of his head. *Get a grip, Turner!* Judging the distance from the bed to the dresser, Scott came to the conclusion that the time for modesty was long gone. It wasn't as if Will hadn't already seen him naked. He threw back the covers, climbed out of bed and padded in his bare feet to the dresser to open a drawer and take out some boxers. Bending and giving

Will a bird's eye view of his ass, he slipped his feet into the underwear and pulled them up, before grabbing a pair of faded gray sweatpants and a white wife beater.

When he'd dressed, he turned to find Will pulling a black wife beater on, his back to Scott. He bit harder at his lip, tasting the copper of blood as his gaze followed the ripple of muscles as Will pulled the material over his head and smoothed it down his chest. At the sound of his name being called, his gaze flew up to meet Will's—the expression on the other man's face making it clear that his name had been said more than once.

"What?"

"I said, are you ready?"

Scott cleared his throat and slipped his feet into his hi-tops. "Yeah, let's go."

"Hey, guys," Will said, smiling brightly as he bounded into the kitchen with Scott behind him.

Scott took the mug that Marcus held out to him, slid into the only vacant chair around the table, and tried to ignore the graceful way Will crossed his legs at the ankle as he leaned against the counter top. *Come on! Now you think he's graceful? When did your balls drop off, Turner?*

"Dude." Marcus grinned at Will and held out his hand, encouraging him to take it. "You're making the place look untidy, come, sit."

"If you insist." Will grinned in reply and slipped his hand into Marcus's, letting the other man guide him onto his lap.

Scott quirked an eyebrow at Will as he perched on the other man's knees. He tried to ignore the arm that Marcus looped around Will's waist, but the sight of his tanned fingers resting casually against Will's stomach lit a flame of jealousy deep in his belly. He wished one of the men would suddenly jump up and declare he knew who the killer was, just like Miss Marple in an Agatha Christie novel, so they could slap on the cuffs and get the hell out of Dodge. Will chose that exact moment to catch his gaze and Scott's gut tightened. He knew that there was no way Will could have not noticed the jealousy written all over his face.

He was so screwed.

"So," Todd said with a smile, "we all want to know. How was your first gathering?"

"It was very… interesting," Scott drawled, dragging his gaze from Will's and trying to concentrate on the other men around the table. But the confusion in Will's eyes was making it difficult. "We didn't know what to expect, so we arrived with a very open mind, didn't we, babe?"

"We enjoyed it," Will replied quietly.

"We enjoyed *you*," Brent said, his tone laced with insinuation. "Not as much as we'd have liked, but there's always next time." He turned his gaze on Scott. "Maybe next time, you won't say no."

Scott simply smiled at Brent and turned his attention back to his coffee. *Maybe if you'd said yes, last night would never have happened. You wouldn't be trying to convince yourself that it was the strength of the coffee that was making your guts churn.* The vicious little voice in his ear laughed derisively. *Will looks real comfortable on Marcus's lap. I bet Marcus is as hard as nails with that gorgeous ass on his cock. Bet he's wishing he could bend him over right now. Lick him open and fuck—*"Shut *up*!"

"You okay, Scott?" Will's voice broke through the fog of jealousy that currently surrounded Scott's brain.

Shit! Had he said that aloud? "What?"

Will frowned at him but didn't embellish, simply saying, "Brent was saying that Todd's singing at the club tonight."

"Fantastic, I can't wait to hear you sing, Todd," Scott replied, smiling brightly at the other man. He quickly downed the rest of his coffee and stood up, padding over to the sink and rinsing his mug. As he stood there, gathering himself, he hissed in a breath when Will's shoulder brushed against his. Glancing up, he caught the other man's gaze—contemplative and uncertain—and immediately looked back down at the water flowing into the mug. Was that a shudder he felt flow through Will when they touched? What the fuck was going on here? He'd seen confusion on Will's face. He was sure of it. But what did it mean? He turned away from the sink without looking at the man beside him again, turning his attention to Todd. "Hey." he put his hand on the man's shoulder. "You want to show me that laptop?"

Todd nodded and got up to follow Scott into the living room, leaving Will with the others discussing the coming evening. "I don't know what's wrong with it," he said, dropping down onto the sofa beside Scott. "I can't access my emails and it keeps freezing up on me."

"If what I did last week didn't fix the problem, I think we're going to have to reload your shit again, dude." Scott opened up the laptop where it sat on the coffee table and turned it on. Grabbing a piece of paper and a pen from his backpack on the floor next to the sofa, he turned to Todd. "Give me your login and password and I'll see what I can do. If I have to reload, I'll back everything up onto disc first."

"There are some files on there, you know, personal files. Would you be able to recover everything?"

"I should be able to. Don't worry about it," Scott smiled reassuringly, his gaze narrowing slightly in confusion as Todd looked over his shoulder toward the door to check there was no one there and they weren't being overheard.

"Thing is, I don't want them falling into the wrong hands. It's just pictures and stuff," his gaze became cloudy, "from home."

"I'll be very discreet, Todd. Seriously." Scott watched Todd wrestle with his decision and then scribble down the details that Scott needed. "I'll go through everything, back it all up and reset it. It should work fine after that." Putting the pen and paper on top of the laptop keyboard, he leaned back against the cushions and studied the striking man beside him. Todd obviously wasn't good with strangers at first, because over the last week he had come out of his shell on the few visits he had made to the house with Marcus. "It must be an amazing feeling, singing to a crowd of people. I don't know how you do it. I'd be scared shitless."

Todd chuckled softly, his cheeks flushing. "I've been doing it for years and I never get used to it. It's always overwhelming until I'm a few bars into the first song, then," he shrugged, "all the nervousness just fades away and I become this different person. I feel like I can do anything when I sing."

Scott nodded and reached out his hand to squeeze the other man's shoulder. "Did Jon and Cory watch you play?" He kept his tone soft.

Todd's shoulders immediately tensed at the names and he hung his head. He huffed out a laugh. "Yeah, Jon was my number one flag waver, never missed a gig, no matter where it was. Benefits of having a plane at your disposal." His smile didn't quite reach his eyes. "If you could keep what I said about the laptop, you know, between us, I'd be grateful." He moved closer so that their knees touched and he reached to smooth long fingers down Scott's forearm.

Gazing deeply into Scott's eyes he moistened his lips nervously. "*Really* grateful."

Scott's gaze widened at the obvious intent in the other man's eyes, and the touch on his skin. "Todd," he shook his head slowly, and stilled the movement of Todd's fingers. "You really don't—"

"It's okay," Todd assured him. "Marcus suggested it. I've been monopolizing your time a bit with this stupid laptop, and it's only fair you get something in return. Or, maybe Will if... you... don't like me."

"Of course I like you," Scott said softly, loosely entwining his fingers with Todd's. "But you don't have to offer yourself to me in payment. If we ever did get together," he said softly, "it would be because we both wanted it. Not because you were working off some debt." Anger unfurled in his gut, hot, heavy, and directed at Marcus. How *dare* he treat the man he was supposed to love, this way? Who the *fuck* did he think he was pimping Todd out like he was some kind of hooker. Scott noted the play of several emotions across Todd's face at his words. He tried to pin them down, confusion, relief, *fear?* That had alarm bells clanging in the part of his brain labeled "cop". Why would Todd be afraid?

"Thanks, Scott." Todd tilted his head slightly as he studied him. "You remind me a little of Cory. He was one of the good guys, too."

"All fixed?" A deep voice had them looking up to see Marcus leaning on the door jamb.

Scott forced a smile on his face and closed the lid of Todd's laptop. "Not yet. But I'm hoping to have it up and running in a few days. Then you can see if you can beat my score on WoW," he added, turning his head to wink at Todd as if they had been having a totally different conversation.

"You are going down, dude," Todd's smile was grateful.

"We'd better go, babe," Marcus said, a loving smile on his face. "We need to get some rehearsal time at the club."

Scott stood as Todd rose from the couch and moved into the circle of Marcus's arms, lifting his chin for his partner's kiss. He worried at the inside of his lip with his teeth. They appeared to be the image of the perfect couple. But were they? He glanced at Will as he and Brent came into the room and tried to contain the shiver that flowed down his spine at the warmth of Will's arm as it casually slipped around his waist and pulled him close. Unable to find a good enough reason not to, he automatically leaned into Will as their visitors offered friendly kisses and hugs of farewell. Scott tried to turn his cheek for Brent's kiss, but the man grasped his chin and held him steady so he could bring their mouths together and kiss Scott thoroughly. He gave Brent what he hoped passed for a genuine smile as he broke the kiss.

"See you tonight," Brent drawled, reaching up to kiss Will swiftly on the mouth. It was a barely there press of lips, serving to let the two men know where his desire lay.

"For God's sake, dude," Marcus griped, shaking his head at Brent and grabbing his elbow. "You have no shame." He rolled his eyes at Will and Scott and guided an unremorseful Brent and a chuckling Todd out of the room. Moments later the heavy front door slammed behind them.

"Ow, dude," Scott griped, pulling at the fingers digging painfully into his side. "You're hurting me." He turned to look up at Will when he'd dropped his arm from around him, and his stomach flip-flopped at the way the other man was staring, transfixed, at his mouth. Lifting his hand, Scott had every intention of wiping the beads of moisture from his lips, a reminder of Brent's kiss. An astonished gasp fell from his lips as Will beat him to it. The pad of Will's thumb moved over his mouth, his gaze following the movement. *What is he doing? Is it possible to come just from someone staring at your mouth?*

Scott didn't have time for any other semi-coherent thoughts, because Will bent his head and kissed him. It wasn't a heated kiss—it wasn't aggressive—or a mark of possession. It was tender, soft, and he felt it everywhere. Even his toes curled in his hi tops. When Will pulled back, Scott stared at him in confusion. "Will?" The other man didn't reply, simply released Scott and walked out of the room, pausing in the doorway at Scott's, "What—?"

He turned and gazed into Scott's confused brown eyes. "When you lick your lips, I don't want you to taste him."

Scott touched his fingers to his lips and sank back onto the couch as Will closed the living room door behind him. "Oh, no," he hissed sarcastically. "Not confusing, not confusing at all."

VII

Will stared at the blank screen on the desk. *What the fuck were you thinking?* He ignored inner Will and scrubbed a hand over his face. The truth was he couldn't answer anyway. All he'd been thinking about was hot, ugly jealousy washing over him in waves every time Brent looked at Scott. Jesus, he'd barely waited until the door had closed before he was kissing Brent's taste from his partner's lips, wanting Scott to taste only him. Let's face it, he hadn't really been thinking, period.

He'd kind of zoned out after Brent had revealed that Scott had turned him down last night. He couldn't believe it. Scott said no to Brent? Was that why he'd let Will do what he'd done? Because Brent had gotten him so turned on? Because he needed release? Sighing heavily, he groaned at his own stupidity. He'd thought that maybe, just maybe, a tiny piece of Scott had wanted him last night. *Dumbass! You were just there is all.* The thought crept into his head, unwanted and unasked for and he brushed it aside. What did it matter to him, anyway? Scott Turner was an asshole, wasn't he? A week ago he couldn't stand the guy for Christ's sake. Hated everything he represented—the atypical heterosexual male. And now what—he couldn't bear the thought or sight of another man's hands on him?

"Get a fucking grip, Will," he hissed through gritted teeth, his voice low and angry in the quiet of the room. "What the fuck has that asshole done to me? I've got gaydar like everybody else. I don't make a play for the straight ones. What's the point? I'm not an idiot."

Oh, for God's sake. You want him. You know you do. Stop lying to yourself and figure out what you're going to do about it!

He knew exactly what he was going to do about it. He needed a drink—a lot of drinks. Maybe that would drive the sound of Scott whimpering *"Don't want you to stop"* from echoing around his head.

Half an hour of moping later, unable to ignore the rumbling in his stomach, Will wandered into the kitchen to make some lunch. Opening the huge fridge, he scanned the contents and settled on the makings of a chicken and cheese sandwich. He picked up the packet of cooked chicken and peeled back the already open seal. Taking a sniff he shrugged and quickly deemed it edible, tossing it onto the counter and then hunting for the cheese. With the large unopened block in his hand, he threw a bag of mixed salad to join the chicken and grabbed the mayonnaise, nudging the door closed with his shoulder. In the bread bin there was half of a long baguette, and he remembered that he'd gotten the munchies yesterday afternoon and eaten the rest of the bread. Of course, in the build up to the gathering, he'd forgotten to replace it. The half baguette would have to do.

Pulling open the cupboard door directly above him, he reached up to take out a plate and paused. He rolled his eyes and took down a second and placed them both on the counter. What was he going to do? He couldn't ignore the guy. He was just being polite, nothing more. Will cut the baguette in half, made a slice down the center of each and thickly spread the mayonnaise. Quickly tossing in the chicken and grating some cheese over the top, he squeezed some salad leaves into the overflowing sandwich and squashed it together.

Will looked quite satisfied with his creation and placed the sandwiches on the two plates. Turning back to the fridge, he pulled out two bottles of the fancy Colorado microbrew Scott had insisted they buy, and slipped one in each armpit for ease of carriage. He picked up the plates and headed for the living room, trying to ignore the flutter of anxiety in the pit of his stomach.

Taking a deep breath, Will pushed open the living room door and walked through it. "I thought you might be hungry," he said conversationally, putting the plates down on the coffee table. Glancing up at Scott when he received no response, he reached out a hand to him in concern. Scott was sitting cross-legged on the couch, gazing in stunned horror at the screen of Todd's laptop. "Scott? Dude, what's wrong?" The other man said nothing, simply turned the laptop around so that Will could see the image on the screen. It took a few moments for Will's brain to process what his eyes were seeing because, quite honestly, he couldn't believe it—didn't want to believe it. "My God," he murmured, sinking onto the couch next to Scott.

In the first image, Todd was on the bed. His hands bound behind him. There was a man Will didn't recognize fucking him, and another stranger with his cock shoved into Todd's mouth. His gaze darkened when Scott clicked on the arrow to activate the slide show of the contents of the file they were looking at. There were hundreds of pictures. Some of Todd with other men. Some of him on his own, bruising obvious on most parts of his body, but never his face. Never where it would show. Some were posed, some had obviously been taken during some act of degradation, but there was one thing that was identical in every shot. The fear, panic, and pain in Todd's blue eyes as the tears rolled down his cheeks. It was obvious he had been forced to participate in these acts. Forced to accept the abuse.

"Where's my gun?" Will's voice was heavy with barely controlled anger.

"What?"

"I'm going across the street to shoot Marcus." He made to stand and was pulled back to the sofa by Scott's hand on his arm.

"Don't be stupid," Scott said in a small sad voice. "What would that achieve?"

Will huffed out a joyless laugh. "It would make me feel a whole lot fucking better." He ran a shaking hand through his blond hair. "*How*?" The word was spat from his lips. "How could he do that? He's supposed to make Todd feel safe, loved, cherished. Not violate him, and make him," he waved at the screen, "make him. How the fuck does someone do that to the person he's supposed to love?"

"I don't know." Scott leaned his head back against the cushions and put both his hands over his face. "What he said to me earlier makes a hell of a lot more sense now."

Will slammed down the lid on the laptop as the screen was filled with an image of Todd, face down on the bed, all life gone from his eyes as his own hands held his ass cheeks apart. Obviously being given instructions by Marcus so he could take the picture. *Fucking bastard!* He turned to face Scott. "What do you mean what he said to you earlier?"

Scott grabbed the beer from the coffee table and opened it, taking a low draw before answering. "He offered himself to me as payment for fixing his laptop. He said Marcus had suggested that I should get a little *something* for my trouble. And he said if I didn't like him, *you* could have him."

Will shook his head slowly in disbelief. "Guess you really can't go on first impressions, can you? I would have pegged Marcus as one of the good guys. Brent is definitely a sleaze, but at least he doesn't try to hide it behind a smooth veneer."

"I think you've made your feelings about Brent perfectly clear," Scott mumbled sarcastically.

Will ignored the remark and continued. "I guess that would explain why Todd clings to Marcus like he's a life preserver. They always say that for some bizarre reason you gravitate toward your abuser, trying desperately to make them happy so they don't do it again." He sighed heavily. "What do we do now?"

"We make a copy and send it to Grace and Julie. See if they can get anything off the pictures." He groaned and slipped a blank disc into the drive, transferring the pictures. "How am I supposed to listen to him sing now? Now that I've seen these?"

"We don't have a choice," Will murmured, standing up. "We're supposed to be at the club for seven thirty. Todd goes on at eight. I don't know about you, but I don't really have the stomach for Laurel Heights right now. I need a drink."

Scott nodded in agreement and raised a questioning eyebrow at Will. "Shall we go into town early and get some dinner first? I can order a cab for five o'clock and we can go find a restaurant. I don't think too much alcohol is a good idea, though. I don't want you going all Dirty Harry on Marcus's ass. It wouldn't look good to Hall if I have to arrest *you*, now would it?"

Will scoffed, appreciating Scott's attempt to try to lighten the moment. "I'm too well dressed to be Dirty Harry. I see myself more as the McGarrett to your Danno. I'm the strong silent type, while you're the short one that gets to do all the grunt work."

"Ouch, my sides are hurting."

Chuckling to himself, Will picked up his sandwich, which he suddenly had no appetite for and padded back to the kitchen to toss it into the trash. Running some warm water, he rinsed the plate, dried it, and then put it back in the cupboard. He leaned against the sink and closed his eyes as the images he had seen on the screen replayed behind his lids. More disturbing was the sense memory of Scott writhing beneath him, full lips parted, navy gaze darkened to almost black in his desire.

****

Scott followed Will and the waitress to their table. He'd been unsurprised when they'd ended up at BLT Steak on Main Street. He wouldn't have expected anything less from Will '*Just wipe its ass and stick it on the plate'* Harrison.

The young woman led them to a table by the window and took their drinks order once they were seated. Scott scanned the room, taking in the brown and leather décor and the long yellow dinette seating that took up one wall, brown suede cushions laid on the plastic for people to sit against. Although it looked very modern and effective, Scott was rather glad they had a table with two leather backed chairs at it. He didn't think the restaurant's version of a booth would suit someone of his stature, even less someone of Will's.

Taking the menu that Will held out to him, Scott scanned the contents and glanced across the table at his partner. "Are we getting starters, or just going straight for the main?"

Will shrugged and studied his own menu. "I'm hungry enough to just go straight to the meat," he drawled, jabbing his finger at a picture of a huge porterhouse steak. "I'm having that!"

Scott snorted and shook his head at the childlike glee on Will's face. "What a shocker. Are you going to let them actually shoot the thing before they put it on your plate, or do you still want it to be mooing?" Scott smiled up at the waitress as she put two bottles of Corona on the table. "Do you have anything that's rarer than rare?"

"Um... raw?" The pretty young woman raised her eyebrows and glanced at Will. "I'm guessing you like it bloody, sir."

"Ignore my uncultured friend," Will replied, glancing back down at the menu. "I'm ready to order. Scott?"

"I'll have the rack of lamb," Scott replied, handing the menu to the waitress. "With mashed potatoes and green beans, please."

Scribbling down his order on her notepad, she turned her attention to Will. "And for you, sir?"

"I'll have the Porterhouse, please. Mashed potatoes, onion rings, green beans, and," Will tapped his chin as he scanned the menu one more time, "a mixed salad."

"And I'm assuming you want your steak rare?" She grinned at Will as he nodded his head and handed her the menu. "It won't be too long, gentleman. Would you like any more drinks?"

Will lifted his bottle to his lips and downed it in four large swallows. Handing the bottle to the rather stunned young woman, he nodded. "Two more, thanks."

"Easy there, cowboy," Scott said, watching Will from beneath lowered lashes. "I ain't carrying your heavy ass into a cab." He didn't like the way Will was already knocking back the beer. He was just as upset as Will about their findings today, but they had to remain professional. They couldn't let their personal feelings damage the case.

"You don't like me very much, do you?"

The tone of Will's voice was tinged with something... regret? Scott gazed across the table at him and was unable to stop his biting response. "You've had my dick in your hand. I think it's safe to say I don't exactly hate you." A flush immediately filled Will's cheeks at his remark and he wished he could take the words back. Heaving a sigh, he ran a hand through his hair. "I'm sorry. That was uncalled for. I get sarcastic when I'm nervous."

Their waitress reappeared with two more beers and set them down, tossing them a brief smile as she hurried off to another table. "So," Scott began when they were alone again. "What do you want to talk about?" He rolled his eyes at Will's shrug. "Why don't you tell me about yourself? Apart from the obvious, like you were seconded eight months ago, and you have a girlfriend named Amanda. I guess I don't know that much about you."

"Wow," Will drawled, putting the second bottle of beer to his lips. "That's the first time you've ever asked anything about me."

"I don't remember you bombarding *me* with questions either," Scott replied, picking up one of the bread rolls from the basket in the middle of the table and tearing off a piece. He took his knife and buttered the piece in his hand and popped it into his mouth, savoring the creaminess of the butter and the softness of the fresh bread. Chasing the crumbs on his lower lip with the tip of his tongue, he glanced up and felt the sharp stab of desire warm his belly as Will's gaze followed the movement. The knife he was holding slipped from his suddenly numb fingers and clattered onto the side plate, causing Will to blink and look away.

Will cleared his throat and took another sip of his beer before answering. "You're not exactly a closed book, Scott."

Raising an eyebrow, Scott tore off another piece of bread and popped it, unbuttered this time, into his mouth. "Oh, really? I tell you what—" He paused as the waitress approached the table with two plates laden with food. Smiling up at her as she placed the rack of lamb and assorted vegetables in front of him, then chuckled out loud at the sheer size of the steak she put in front of Will. When the waitress had wished them bon appétit and had resumed her duties elsewhere, Scott cut into his rack of lamb and continued where he had left off. "You tell me what you *think* you know about *me,* and I'll tell you what I *think* I know about *you.*"

"All right." Will cut himself off a good sized chunk of almost blood red steak and chewed thoughtfully, picking up his beer and washing it down. "You have an ego the size of the Grand Canyon. You think you've seen everything, done everything. You waltz into the office most days with a hangover and ribald stories about your latest conquest, causing most of the girls in admin to snivel because it wasn't them." He grinned widely. "How am I doing?"

"Nice," Scott replied, waving his fork in a circular motion. "Keep going."

"You have very little respect for the rule book. Spend far too much time in front of the mirror and you're probably banging Cassidy." He chuckled at the look on Scott's face. "But," Will conceded grudgingly. "I've seen you harangue a three hundred pound man into confessing, without giving an inch. Then watched you comfort the family of a victim with more compassion than I would ever have thought you could summon up." He took another swig of beer. "In short, you irritate me like no one I've ever come across. But you *are* one of the best cops I've ever worked with." Will scooped up some mashed potato and forked it into his mouth. "And you're a fantastic kisser." He chuckled heartily when Scott snorted beer through his nose at that last remark.

Scott wiped his nose on his napkin, grateful that he hadn't dribbled the beer down his dress shirt and narrowed his eyes. "Okay," he dragged out the word, his gaze roaming over Will's face, taking in every detail. "You walked into the department, with your breezy attitude and your big cheesy grin and I knew I was going to want to kill you inside of ten minutes. I was wrong."

"You were?"

"Yeah," Scott smiled, mixing his green beans with his potato. "It was more like five. You're so *likeable*, Will. With your stories of home, the little white picket fence, and the girlfriend. I don't know, maybe that's why you irritate the fuck out of me. You have everything sewn up."

"How do you mean?"

"You're good at your job. You're well liked and respected by your peers, and at the end of the day you have someone to go home to. Isn't that what everyone wants?" Scott leaned back in his chair and sipped at his beer. "I admit I thought you were so anal that you squeaked when you walked—but I remember the day I saw a different side of you, one who was willing to throw away the rule book at a moment's notice. Do you remember the day the four of us were on our way back to the station, and we got cut off by the fire trucks blocking the road because of that pile up? The one with the little girl stuck in the back seat of the crushed car?" He waited for Will's affirmation before continuing.

"As soon as they told us what the holdup was, you... you didn't hesitate, man. You just got right out of the car, waving your badge at anyone who wouldn't let you through. You crawled into the back of that car as far as you could get and held her little hand. What was she, about eight?" Another nod. "I don't think I've ever told you how impressive you were, Will. The way you talked to her about anything and everything you could think of, taking her mind off what the FD guys were doing. She was in so much pain, not to mention scared out of her mind. Hell, so was I.

"I remember the guys kept trying to get you out, but you wouldn't leave her. She was hanging on by the skin of her teeth and you kept her calm so they could do their stuff and get her out. Hell, I'd have just gone in all guns blazing, yelling and barking orders, but you... all you could think about was her.

"You're a good cop, Will, and a good man." He dropped him a wink. "But you're nowhere near as good a kisser as I am." Will guffawed loudly at that and Scott joined in, their laughter drawing the attention of other diners.

Will pushed his plate away and brushed a hand across his eyes. "I guess you really can't go by first impressions, can you?" Avoiding Scott's gaze, he picked up the dessert menu. "What are you having?"

Scott rubbed a hand over his stomach and shook his head. "I don't think I have any room for dessert. And I'm surprised you have any either," he said, raising his eyebrows and looking down at Will's empty plate. "You've just eaten half a dead cow." He sighed at the pout on the other man's face. "Seriously? Is that supposed to work on me? 'Cause it's not." *Yeah, right. You have not gone all weak in the knees and gooey over that tempting bottom lip?* The lip was forced out even more and Scott snorted inelegantly when Will actually batted his eyelashes. He swallowed as he hardened in his pants, images of what he'd like to do to those lips bouncing around his mind. "Oh, for God's sake, don't look at me like that," he complained, grabbing the desert menu. "We'll order dessert."

"Yay," Will said, actually bouncing up and down in his chair. "I want the chocolate cheesecake, with the chocolate sauce, and the chocolate curls."

Scott couldn't help but smile at Will's enthusiasm and rolled his eyes in apology at the waitress as she began to clear their plates. "You'll have to excuse his drooling, but I think he's ready for dessert."

She laughed heartily. "Don't worry, sir. Most people have that reaction to the chocolate cheesecake. Shall I put you down for two slices?"

Scott shook his head and handed her the menu. "Just one. I'm watching my figure."

The two of them sat in what passed for almost companionable silence for the next ten minutes, until the waitress brought Will's dessert over to the table and set the plate down in front of him. With a bright "Enjoy" the woman walked away and Scott glanced over at Will. He suppressed a giggle at the expression on the other man's face. Will was staring down at the cheesecake in front of him, with a reverent look in his eyes and Scott couldn't help but tease, "You want me to leave you two alone?"

"Huh?" Will's slightly glassy gaze met Scott's.

"I feel a little awkward; you two are obviously having a moment here."

"Very funny," Will drawled, picking up his dessert fork and waving it at Scott. "Were you born in a barn? Don't you know that with cheesecake, especially *chocolate* cheesecake, anticipation is all part of the experience?"

"It's cake, doofus. You eat it."

"Pay attention, Grasshopper," Will said in a ridiculous impression of a Chinese accent. "You will learn much from me."

"There's something seriously wrong with you," Scott mumbled, picking up his beer and taking a healthy swig. The ice cold liquid slipped down his throat like nectar, fizzing into his bloodstream. He leaned back in his chair and yawned, as though watching Will fawn over his cheesecake had no effect on him whatsoever. *Oh, come on. Why is he doing this to me?* Scott tried to ignore the way Will broke off a forkful of cheesecake and followed the path with appreciative eyes, between his plate and his mouth. *Jesus!* The moment Will's lips closed around the dessert and pulled it into his mouth, Scott was fucked. Will emitted an erotic moan that had Scott going from zero to sixty in three seconds flat. The way the other man licked at the chocolate sauce that dripped down his chin was sinful, and Scott couldn't help but imagine what that tongue would look like licking at the come dripping down his shaft. *For God's sake, Turner. Pull yourself together, man!* He shifted in his seat, trying to discreetly adjust his now painfully hard cock without touching it. Concerned that even the ghosting of his fingers across his erection would have him exploding in his pants like a teenager. *Fucking asshole is doing it on purpose!*

"Come on, Harrison. Todd's going to be on soon and we have a half an hour cab ride into the city."

"What?" Will looked up from his dessert, his expression confused. "You can't rush this, you know."

Clearing his throat, Scott pulled his wallet out of his pocket and threw some bills down on the table. He had a feeling his waitress was going to be very happy about her tip. "Just shovel it in for God's sake. We're working a case, not pandering to your sweet tooth. I'll go get a cab."

Scott grabbed his jacket from the back of his chair and quickly shrugged into it, ignoring his partner's questioning gaze. Turning on his heels, he strode from the restaurant. Once outside, he breathed in the cool night air as he waited for Will. His heart was racing and his nerves endings were on fire. He was unable to believe that Will had got him so hard just from eating a piece of cake. This shit was ridiculous. Scott shook his head to clear it of thoughts that bounced around his head. Thoughts of skipping the club and bundling Will into a cab and taking him home—of laying him out on the mattress, all honey-toned skin and muscles rippling beneath him. Of exploring acres of skin with his tongue. Of—

"Are you okay?"

Will's concerned tone had Scott closing his eyes as the sound washed over him. Scott knew from experience that The Rose had a back room and, if he had the chance to get away from Will, he was going to visit it. He needed release. Needed to find comfort any way he could, and try to forget whose arms he really wanted to be in.

Scott lifted his hand and waved down a passing cab, pulling his jacket closer around his body as the car stopped at the curb. "I'm fine, let's go."

****

Ignoring the glares and heartfelt complaints that were thrown at them from the men in the line, Scott and Will waited while the bouncer checked their names on the VIP list and lifted the velvet rope from across the doorway. "Go on in, gentlemen," he said brightly. "Mr Miller and his group are expecting you. They're in the VIP booth at the back of the club." He guided them in through the doors and motioned to the girl seated behind the glass petition of the reception desk. "Polly, these gentlemen are in Mr Miller's party."

Scott and Will flashed smiles in response to the wink the beautiful redhead dropped them and as she raised her hand in acknowledgement and waved them toward the heavy black curtain.

The Rose was one of the top clubs in New York and, although Scott had been there before, he let Will lead the way. Pushing through the curtain, they walked along a low lit corridor that opened out onto the main room of the club. The dance floor was the size of a large gym; the walls lined with comfortable booths for the patrons to relax in during breaks from the dance floor. The DJ's stage at one end of the room was immense, with two large cages containing scantily clad young men, gyrating to the music. Curving staircases stood at the four corners of the room, lights built into the handrails and steps, guiding the way to the upper level where more private booths were situated. The rule of the house being that you could get to know each other in the private booths, and partake in some heavy petting—but for anything more than that, you headed to the back room. Even though it wasn't quite eight o'clock yet, the floor was already covered with writhing bodies pressed up close, the scent of lust in the air, as the bass beat in time with the dancers racing hearts.

Scott's thighs tingled with the pounding of the music as they made their way across the floor to the booths. He felt more than one hand trail over the curve of his ass between the door and their destination, but he ignored them, keeping his gaze on Will's back as he followed him. He could see Jay, head and shoulders above the crowd, his arm draped around Erik as he laughed at something the other man said to him. Jay spied them and Scott acknowledged him with a wave of his hand, reaching out and curling his fingers into the hem of Will's shirt so that they weren't parted. He kept his gaze as impassive as he could when Will turned at the pull on his clothing and simply held onto Scott's hand, and then continued to push through the sea of bodies.

"Hey, guys." Erik grinned, when they reached them, and leaned in for a kiss on the cheek. "Glad you could make it."

"Todd's on soon," Cal said from his position in Damon's arms on the booth's leather seat.

"Looking forward to it," Scott replied, accepting the two beers that Jay held out to him and handing one to Will.

"Where's everyone else?" Will asked, leaning against the handrail and crossing his ankles.

Damon and Cal got up from the couch and stood beside the two men. "Todd and Marcus are in the dressing room and David and Brent disappeared upstairs to the office for a little," Damon grinned and waggled his eyebrows suggestively, "alone time."

"What do you think of the club? Insane isn't it?" Cal hugged Damon from behind and rested his chin on his boyfriend's shoulder.

Scott nodded, stepping back when someone pushed past him. His breath hitched in his throat when he collided with Will's solid chest and his attempt to lurch forward again, upset his balance. *Fuck!* He waited for the ground to come rushing up to meet him, but it didn't as he was hauled back against Will, a strong arm around his waist steadying him. His head dropped back onto Will's shoulder as if his neck muscles had suddenly lost all control, his cheek against the warmth of the other man's tanned throat. He was unable to prevent the shiver that prickled up his spine when Will's deep, rich voice murmured into the shell of his ear, "You okay?" *I was fine until you put your big, muscular arms around me and then breathed all over me.* Scott nodded and attempted to step away, but Will obviously had other ideas as his hold tightened. Sighing, Scott let Will take his weight and lifted the bottle in his hand to his lips, and the other he placed over the top of Will's, swallowing when Will entwined their fingers.

For everyone else around them, the display would look like a normal couple showing their affection. For Scott, the feel of Will's heart beating against his back, the other man's crotch against the crack of his ass, and his warm breath against his hair— it was torture. He had a feeling it was going to be a long night.

"We're out of champagne!" Jay wrapped his arm around Erik's neck and kissed him soundly on the cheek. "How many should I get? Two, three?"

"Three!" Damon shouted, waving his empty champagne glass at Jay. "It's got bubbles." He giggled, sliding his hands up Cal's forearms. "I like bubbles."

Cal grinned down at his boyfriend, his face open and adoring. "I think you've already had way too many bubbles."

"Bubbles are wonderful," Damon insisted, his voice already slurred. He reached out a hand and gently punched Will on the arm. "Don't you agree? Back me up here. I mean," he ticked them off on his fingers like a list, "you've got, Bubble Wrap, Bubblicious, bubble hats, blowing bubbles." He smiled wistfully. "I love blowing bubbles, they're foamy. And there's chocolate that has bubbles in it and, of course," he waved his champagne glass, spilling some on the floor, "bubbles in champagne that go right up your nose and make it all fizzy."

Scott laughed raucously as he watched Damon. The guy was obviously three sheets to the wind and judging from Cal's fond smile, this over the top version of Damon was one he was well acquainted with. "Bubble hats?" he queried, feeling Will's laugh rumble against his back.

"They're the hats with the balls on the top."

"Damon, those are *bobble* hats." Will chuckled, sipping at his own drink.

The realization of his mistake slowly crossed Damon's face and he giggled uncontrollably for several minutes—much to the other men's amusement. He finally got himself under control and wagged a finger at Will. "Okay, I'll give you that one. But they *should* be called bubble hats. Maybe there's a gap in the market— I could make a fortune." He slapped a hand to his forehead. "I almost forgot *bubble baths!* You have to let me have that one, there is nothing like a long, hot bubble bath."

"Baby, we're gay, but even we're not *that* gay." Cal gave Damon a sloppy kiss on the cheek and joined in the other men's laughter, before grabbing Damon's hand and pulling him onto the dance floor.

Scott gulped down the rest of his beer. They were alone. His gaze searched for Erik and found him in animated conversation with a stocky man in a black suit. Will's nearness was driving Scott insane. He had to get away. He couldn't think when Will was this close. The man's scent filled his nostrils and in his peripheral vision he could see the pulse beating in Will's throat. He had this primal instinctive urge to press his lips against Will's neck and feel his life fluttering against his tongue. *God! I've got to get out of here!* Thankfully he didn't have to worry about making a fool of himself, because Will chose that moment to loosen his hold and mutter gruffly, "I need the bathroom."

"Okay." Scott forced down the ridiculous feeling of disappointment that flowed through him at being out of Will's arms. *For Christ's sake, a moment ago you wanted him to let you go!* He watched Will weave his way through the crowd and sighed, running a shaking hand through his dark hair.

"It's nice to see."

Scott started when he felt warm breath fan across his ear and he turned to gaze into Erik's slightly glassy eyes. He'd obviously had quite a lot of champagne too. "Hey," he said, his lips curving into a smile. "What's nice?"

"The way you look at him." Erik dropped a wet sloppy kiss to Scott's forehead. "The love you have for him is written all over your face." Erik was distracted by someone coming over for a hug, so his arm dropped from around Scott's shoulders and he turned away.

Scott's stomach bottomed out, and his jaw dropped open. *No, no, no, no, no! Holy fuck!* He wanted to shout at Erik and demand he take it back. *No, I can't be! That's not what this is—is it?* Grace had been right. Except he wasn't just setting himself up for a fall, he was nose-diving off a cliff into the abyss. *But when? How?* It had crept up on him so quietly over the last eight months of bickering and disguised glances that he hadn't even noticed. Scott Turner was in love with Will *'white picket fence and happy ever after'* Harrison. Only he wasn't going to be *Scott's* happy ever after, would *never* be Scott's happy ever after. Scott sighed, swallowing the rest of his beer in his despair. What the fuck was he going to do, now?

****

Will did need the bathroom, but that wasn't the main reason he had for getting the hell away from Scott Turner. The feel of the other man's lean, but muscled frame pressed up against him, had had him hardening in his pants with every shift of weight. *Then why didn't you let him go when you righted him?* He mentally grabbed his inner voice and slapped duct tape on its mouth, fed up with its constant interference. Obviously he liked torturing himself with what he couldn't have, that's why he hadn't let Scott go. He'd only meant to keep him from falling, but when that firm ass had fit so snugly against him, he couldn't seem to come up with a good enough reason to let him go. They had an audience for crying out loud, how would it have looked to the others if he'd let Scott fall flat on his face, or not shown any affection? Their cover could be blown.

"Pathetic, Harrison," he mumbled aloud and made his way down the long corridor, following the signs for the bathrooms. As he lifted his hand to push open the bathroom door, he heard the sound of raised voices coming from farther down the corridor. He ignored the glare thrown at him by the man pushing past him to get into the bathroom, and inched his way along the wall and saw that the dressing room door was open. Coming from inside he could hear Todd's voice, high pitched and pleading.

"I didn't tell him anything. He just thinks they're pictures of home; he won't even look at them. *Please*, baby."

"How could you be so *stupid?*"

Will flinched at the meaty sound of flesh upon flesh.

"Why do you make me do these things? You bring them on yourself."

The voice was gruff and filled with menace, but with all the commotion of men coming in and out of the bathroom, Will couldn't quite make out everything. Marcus must be standing farther away from the door.

"Please, don't. I'll be good. I'll do whatever you want. I won't go over there again. I promise."

"Did you offer yourself to him like I told you to?"

"Yes, but he didn't want me."

"That's because you're *nothing*. Why would he want a useless little whore like you? You're *nothing* without me. What are you?"

"Nothing," Todd whimpered. "*Nothing.*"

"That's right and don't you ever forget it. Now get on your knees, we only have a few minutes. Oh, and Todd? Make it good, you don't want me to be angry, do you?"

Will walked into the bathroom and joined the line for the urinals. Anger pulsed through him. *Fucking bastard.* He wanted to grab hold of Marcus White and beat him down. Wanted to make him whimper as he had just made Todd. Wanted to have him cowering before him, as Todd must have been in that dressing room. Wanted to—

"Will, you're here! Todd's going to be stoked. Where's Scott?"

Will's head snapped up as if it were on a spring, staring in stunned silence as the man who had called his name closed the stall door behind him and walked over to the sinks where he soaped and rinsed his hands. "*Marcus?*" he said incredulously. "I thought you were in the dressing room with Todd."

"I was, but I get nervous for him when he's performing," Marcus said, grimacing. "You'll always find me in the bathroom before a gig. I threw up on stage in Portland once." He chuckled, sticking his hands under the dryer. "Todd gets nervous enough without worrying about my weak stomach. It's ridiculous really. I mean, I'm fine as soon as he sings that first note, but it's all the build up before hand." He checked his hands were dry and padded over to give Will a hug. "I keep telling Brent to put more bathrooms in this place. The line is always horrendous, which is why I closet myself in here for half an hour before a gig, otherwise I'd embarrass myself." He grinned widely, his blue eyes sparkling, and slapped Will on the shoulder. "Anyway, I'd better get back to him. Now is about the time he usually decides he can't go on. I'll see you out there."

Will nodded, forced a smile on his face and watched the big man stroll out of the bathroom, unable to believe what he was seeing. Marcus had been in the bathroom for at least the last half an hour? He ran a hand through his hair and shuffled forward as the line moved. A million other thoughts pin-balled around his head, but only one was lit up like a flashing neon sign.

If Marcus had been in the bathroom—who the fuck had been in with Todd?

VIII

Scott glanced up and watched Will walk toward the booth through the sea of writhing bodies. He frowned at the unreadable expression on the man's face and stood when Will paused on the dance floor and beckoned to him. Putting his drink down on the table, Scott ignored Jay's leer and made his way down the steps and onto the dance floor. He weaved his way through dancing bodies until he came to a stop before Will. He couldn't stop the gasp that left his lips when Will slid warm hands around his waist, and pulled him against a hard, muscled chest. Scott ran his hands up Will's chest and wound his arms around the column of his neck, burying his fingers in the soft waves of blond hair. He noted for the first time, the flush on Will's cheeks. "What's wrong?"

Will pressed his lips to Scott's ear and began moving his hips to the pounding beat of the music, swaying against his lean body. "When I was looking for the bathroom, I heard raised voices from the dressing room, so I eavesdropped. I heard who I thought was Marcus telling Todd how he was nothing and a whore, and asking if he'd offered himself to *him*—which I assume was you—and then I heard Todd being hit."

"And?" Scott raised his eyebrows, trying to concentrate on the sound of Will's voice and not the warmth of Will's breath on his skin. "Wait a minute, who you *thought* was Marcus?"

"I ducked into the bathroom and Marcus came out of one of the stalls. He told me that he locks himself in there for half an hour before each show, 'cause he gets sick to his stomach with nerves. It wasn't *him*, Scott. He's *not* the one abusing Todd," Will hissed, his hands moving slowly up Scott's back, kneading the muscles beneath the skin.

"What?" Scott pulled back and gazed into Will's eyes in stunned amazement. He tried desperately not to give in to the shudder that coursed through him as Will's fingers retraced their path down his back, his thumbs dipping below Scott's waistband and resting on the belt holding up his pants. *Focus, Turner, focus, Goddammit!* "Then who the fuck was it?"

"I don't know," Will replied, his tone frustrated and angry. "I couldn't make out the voice, there was too much noise behind me in the corridor, and whoever it was must have been farther away from the door than Todd."

"Will?" Scott gasped, when Will's fingers slipped over the curve of his ass, bringing them closer. His hips involuntarily jerked against Will's. "What are you doing?"

"Brent's watching us," Will said softly.

It was a pitiful excuse, he knew, but the warmth of Scott's skin was searing against his cheek and he needed to touch, to taste. He'd beat himself up about it later. Fueled by the beer pleasantly speeding through his blood stream, he lowered his head and flicked his tongue out against the pulse fluttering in Scott's throat. He hummed at the vibration of the other man's low moan against his lips when he sealed them over soft skin. Long fingers curled into his shoulders, holding on, and Will could have sworn he felt the thickening length of Scott's shaft against his thigh. The tap on his shoulder had him inwardly cursing and he reluctantly lifted his head, annoyance clear on his face as he glanced up at Brent.

"Come on, you two, enough of that." Brent leaned in close to be heard over the music. "They're about to announce Todd." Brent leered at Scott and ran a blatant hand over his ass. Will felt a curl of satisfaction in his gut when Brent's eyes widened, knowing the other man wasn't prepared for the iron grip Will had on his fingers. "What are you doing?"

"Brent, you're a nice guy." Will shrugged nonchalantly and kept his tone even and conversational. "And I get that you want to fuck Scott's tight little ass. Can't say I blame you, because being inside here, burying yourself hard and deep, where it's hot and wet, it's like nothing you've ever felt before." He smoothed his other hand over the swell of Scott's ass, ignoring the total disbelief on his partner's face. "And who knows, maybe at one of the gatherings you'll get your chance. But, out here, in the real world," he tightened his grip on Brent's fingers, satisfaction tightening his gut at the wince the other man couldn't hold back, "his ass, and everything else he has, belongs to *me*. So, unless you want to lose your hand, or your tongue, it's probably a good idea if you keep them to yourself. Do we *understand* each other?"

Brent's gaze narrowed slightly, his only show of anger, and he nodded. "I think you've made yourself perfectly clear." He rubbed his fingers when Will dropped them and smiled apologetically at Scott. "I'm sorry. I tend to get a little carried away."

"No harm done," Scott replied, sliding his arm around Will and rubbing his nose against the big man's cheek. "Will, let's go find a seat to watch Todd. Come on, baby." Scott guided Will over to the booth and pushed him down onto the couch, sitting next to him and leaning into his side. "What the fuck are you doing?"

"I need a drink." Will ignored Scott's question and leaned forward to grab one of the champagne bottles from the table and put it to his lips. Tipping his head back, he let the wine bubble and fizz over his tongue then glide down his throat, the dryness expanding in his chest and hitting his stomach with a satisfying sigh. Will rested his head against the cushions and closed his eyes.

He didn't know how he had managed to keep from beating Brent to a bloody pulp when he'd put his hands on Scott—again. Who the fuck did the guy think he was? He'd looked through him as though he wasn't even there and just fawned all over Scott. Touching him with those slimy, sleazy hands of his.

Chugging back more champagne, Will could see Scott keep glancing at him, but he kept his gaze firmly on the stage area as they waited for Todd to come out. He knew Scott was confused—how could he not know? He knew the other man wanted answers, but what was he supposed to say? That the sight of another man putting his hands on Scott had anger so white hot burning in his belly it took all of his training not to just punch him in the face? That hearing Todd's abuse first hand had left him sick to his stomach? That every fiber of his being had told him to run into that room and stop what was happening? Or knowing that he had to stay on the job left Todd open to more abuse. How the fuck was he supposed to forgive himself for that?

"We've got a real treat tonight!" Will's gaze found the DJ at the mike, and the lights stopped flashing, changing to give the room a muted ambience with the sole spotlight on the stage. "The Rose is proud to present, singing live especially for you—Todd Campbell!"

Staring at the stage, Will watched Todd walk out with his guitar and climb up onto the stool. There was a soft, slightly nervous smile on the man's lips and Will swallowed hard. How many times had Todd smiled like that after he had been dealt a punch? He wondered where the bruises were tonight. Where they wouldn't show, obviously. But he must have bruising, regular bruising. How the fuck did he explain that to Marcus? *Unless Marcus is in on it! Fuck!* He took another swig of champagne and closed his eyes, letting the sound of Todd's voice wash over him as he introduced the first song.

"Hey everybody thanks for coming out tonight. I want to thank Brent for letting me come back and sing for you, so let's get started." Todd put his guitar strap around his neck and strummed a few chords as he got comfortable. "I would like to dedicate the first song to a couple of friends of mine, who are no longer with us. Cory and Jon."

Todd's voice rang sweet and clear around the hushed club and Will opened his eyes a fraction to study Scott from beneath lowered lashes. The other man's body was half turned in the seat and the warmth of his back pressed into Will's arm. He decided there and then that he could stare at Scott's profile all day. That he would never tire of looking at the way his dark hair swept back from his forehead and curled around his collar. That he could probably spend the rest of his life counting the streaks of red that the low lighting behind the booth picked out in the dark waves. Scott must have felt the weight of Will's gaze, because he turned his head and stared back at him through lowered lashes.

Will had no idea what motivated Scott's next move, he only knew that he was more than happy for his partner to reach out and take his hand and pull him closer. He allowed Scott to guide his hand around Scott's waist and he lowered his head against the man's shoulder, keeping their fingers entwined while they listened to Todd sing. Will sighed and rubbed his cheek on the soft cotton it laid against, closing his eyes when Scott tilted his head and rested it against Will's. The mixed signals he was getting from Scott were driving him crazy, but right now, he didn't care. He just wanted to listen to Todd sing, breathe in Scott's scent, and revel in the warmth of his lean frame pressed up close.

Forty-five minutes later, the entire clientele clapped, whistled, and whooped Todd off the stage. He was slapped on the back and hands were held out to him from every direction as Will watched him make his way across the floor to the booth and Marcus. Todd was immediately enfolded in Marcus's arms, and the big man pulled him in close and murmured in his ear. Will obviously couldn't hear what was being said, but he could guess it was words of congratulations and adoration from the happiness on Todd's face.

Who had been in the dressing room with Todd? Who thought they had the right to do that to the other man? Was Marcus allowing it to happen? Will ran a hand through his hair. He couldn't believe that. Not looking at the two of them together now. There was no way that Marcus would stand by and let someone hurt Todd. He was sure of it.

Sighing, Will eased away from Scott and stood. He slipped his hand along Todd's back, turned the smaller man to face him and pulled him into a hug. "That was great, Todd. You're the man, dude." He started when Scott sidled up beside him and hugged both him and Todd, adding his own congratulations.

Will could feel the champagne buzz through his veins, knowing there was no way he could sit next to Scott and pretend to be the perfect couple. Not for one more minute. He needed to get out. His cock was half-hard in his pants and the yearning for release curled tightly in his gut. He needed to get as far away from that navy gaze and dark soft hair as he could. *Now!*

"Excuse me, guys," he said, his voice gruff as he pulled away and stepped back. "I'll be right back."

****

Scott's gaze followed Will's path across the dance floor, lingering on the sway of Will's lean hips and the rippling of taut muscles beneath the tight-fitting shirt. Heat flowed through him and he changed his stance as he hardened, hoping no one would see. *"Shit,"* he hissed quietly, picking up the champagne bottle Will had put down and taking a long swig. He wrinkled his nose as the bubbles fizzed and popped their way down his throat and he sank back down onto the seating he had occupied with Will.

Scottee, you got some esplainin' to doooo. Ignoring the pathetic Ricky Ricardo imitation of his inner voice, Scott swigged another mouthful. What could he explain? That he'd been affected by Todd's sweet rendition of the first song? That it had resonated deep within him, and he'd been overwhelmed by the sudden need to have Will as close as possible? To feel their bodies pressed against each other? To lose himself in the comfort of the other man's scent as it washed over him?

It was blatantly obvious that he had not only stepped over the line, he'd got down on his hands and knees and scrubbed it out, because the moment Todd had stopped singing, Will hadn't been able to get away fast enough.

Scott forced his lips into a smile as David slid into the booth beside him. "Hey."

"Hey yourself, did you enjoy the show?" David leaned in a little closer and put his hand on Scott's forearm. "Brent told me what happened on the dance floor." He held up his hand when Scott opened his mouth to respond. "I just wanted to apologize on Brent's behalf. He gets a little carried away sometimes and forgets there are boundaries to be adhered to. I'm so sorry if he upset you and Will. I've told him to rein it in."

"Honestly, Dave," Scott replied, patting the hand curled around his forearm. "It's fine, there was no harm done. I'm the one who should be apologizing. I don't know what's got into Will tonight. It's not like him to be so rude."

"I did notice he was a little off tonight." David ran a hand through his hair and gazed at Scott, a faint flush staining his cheeks.

"What?" Scott frowned at the expression on David's face. The man looked as though he wanted to say something, but was unsure as to whether he should. "David? What's wrong?" He didn't like the way David hesitated before replying.

"I know we haven't known each other that long, and it's really none of my business. Brent said I should leave it, but I don't know. Will doesn't really strike me as the type and I know he's had a lot to drink—"

"Dave, just spit it out," Scott said, anxious butterflies beginning to take wing in his stomach.

David pressed his lips to Scott's ear. "I saw Will going into the back room."

"You're kidding, right?" Scott snorted, downing another mouthful of champagne. He chuckled softly until the expression on David's face sent the fizzy wine back into his throat in a hiss of acid. "You're *not* kidding." Putting down the bottle, he tried to force a natural looking smile to his lips, but it felt wrong, and judging by the concern in David's gaze, the smile obviously looked wrong, too. He stood and laid a hand on David's shoulder. "I'd better go rescue the asshole before he does something stupid. Thanks, David. I appreciate it. Would you make our apologies to everyone? I'm going to take the idiot home before he embarrasses himself further."

Scott pushed his way through the crowd and headed for the back room. A gazillion thoughts pin-wheeled around his head and echoed off his skull. *How does he even know there* is *a back room? What the hell is he trying to do? Kill me? Make me kill him?* He strode purposefully toward the black curtain and pulled the material aside, letting it fall behind him as he entered the large room.

Most gay clubs had a room where you could fulfill your wildest dreams with any number of willing strangers, and The Rose was no exception. In the darkness, Scott scanned the space, squinting in the semi-darkness, his gaze searching for Will. There were bodies everywhere. Heated kisses were exchanged. Hands whispered across soft skin. Men on their knees as fingers wound in their hair and cocks thrust into their mouths. Couples lying on the banquettes lining the walls. Not just couples, three men or more, their limbs entangled, tongues sliding across naked flesh, their soft moans and whimpers echoing around the room. He stepped around men who moved into his path, smiling apologetically at the owners of hands that reached out for him—only interested in one man.

Then he saw him.

Scott froze, unable to believe his own eyes.

Will Harrison, *his* Will Harrison, leaned against the wall, his stance wide-legged to retain his balance. His eyes were closed and his head thrown back, exposing the tanned column of his throat. A beautiful black man kitten-licked Will's skin, drawing it into his mouth and scraping the flesh with his teeth.

But it didn't end there. Scott's stunned gaze followed the length of Will's body, pausing at a second man, with short spiky blond hair, running long fingers up and down Will's muscled, shirtless chest. The point of his tongue, lapping ferociously at one of Will's nipples.

As if that weren't enough for Scott's brain to process, a third man knelt before Will, and pressed wet, open-mouthed kisses to his flat belly, his tongue dipping in and swirling around his navel.

What the fuck was he doing? Was this *his* fault? Had *he* done this? Gotten Will all worked up with the touching and the mixed messages? Driven him to seek someone else to put out the fire *he* had started? Had—?

Scott suddenly found himself staring into deep, brown eyes. Eyes that had darkened to almost black in the low, muted lighting of the back room. He could see the lust burning in Will's gaze and it sent a jolt of desire straight to his cock. An involuntary gasp left his lips when Will smiled softly at him, stroked a hand over the back of the black man's head, then held the other out to Scott, the invitation clear in the curl of his fingers. *What the fuck are you doing, Turner?* His feet seemed to be ignoring every message from his brain, as they carried him closer to the four men.

He had no idea what he was doing when he slipped his fingers into Will's, but he allowed the other man to pull him in. The man paying close attention to Will's chest, moved around to Scott's other side and slid his hands beneath Scott's shirt, warming his skin. The movement pressed him into Will's side, his crotch grinding into the meat of Will's upper thigh. His breath hissed between his teeth at the delicious friction. Staring deep into Will's eyes, his gaze dropped to full lips when Will's hand curled around the back of his neck and drew him in until there was barely a breath between them—each man's exhalations being swallowed by the other.

The sound of Will's breathy "*Scott*" had the effect of a bucket of cold water being thrown over him. Scott blinked owlishly just as Will brought their mouths together. He had no idea what the hell was going on, in either Will's or his own head. But he knew for sure that this wasn't how he wanted the other man, not here. Not in the near dark in the sleazy back room, rushed and unsatisfactory, with God only knew how many men watching, and even participating. *Participating? Shit!*

Scott wrenched his mouth away from Will's ignoring the other man's groan, and grabbed hold of the fingers currently fumbling with the buttons on his partner's pants. He shrugged off the hands of the man behind him and threw him a heated glare over his shoulder. He turned his attention back to the black man who was now kissing Will and the man who was staring up at him in confused bewilderment.

"I'm sorry, guys," he said with a cold smile. "This one's mine."

The three men took one look at the thinly disguised anger in Scott's stance and raised their hands in submission, simply moving away and disappearing into the crowd of bodies around them.

Will's eyes opened slowly and his gaze locked on Scott's, confusion furrowing his brow. "What—?"

Scott glared at Will and the other man's mouth immediately snapped shut. Turning his attention back to Will's clothes, Scott quickly and deftly buckled Will's belt and buttoned his shirt. He didn't want to talk. Not here. Once Will's clothes were straightened, Scott grabbed his wrist and pulled him through the curtain and back into the club. He wound his way through the crowd of dancing men and tightened his hold on Will, not wanting to lose him. His frustration must have shown on his face, because neither of them were bothered by the other patrons as Scott fought their way to the exit.

Once they were outside in the cold night air, Scott caught the eye of one of the bouncers, who nodded without a word at his brief explanation and trotted out into the street to hail a cab. Throwing thanks over his shoulder, he bundled an extremely quiet and forlorn looking Will into the back seat and slid in beside him. After giving the driver the address, Scott leaned back against the head rest and looked out of the window. The tension in the back of the cab was palpable. He was afraid to speak. Afraid of what might come flying out of his mouth if he didn't get his emotions under control. *What emotions, Scottee? Anger, jealousy, desire, and dare I say it, betrayal?* Scott ran a hand through his hair and closed his eyes against the voice echoing around his head. *Yes, betrayal.* But what gave him the right to feel betrayed? Will hadn't cheated on him. They weren't a couple for Christ's sake. For crying out loud, if Will had cheated on anyone in this whole stupid mess, it was his girlfriend. Not *him*. He resumed his staring out of the window and watched the buildings whizz by as the cab took them out of the city.

****

The cab driver pulled up to the gates of Laurel Heights and Scott leaned out of the window to press the security code into the pad. The gates whirred into life, opening inwards and the driver steered the cab to a stop outside number four. Leaning over the passenger seat, Scott handed the cab driver the fare and then opened his door. He strode around to the other side, yanked Will's door open and grabbed a handful of his shirt to haul him out with. Slamming the door behind the other man, he pushed him up the path to the front door. He wrestled with the lock, his own champagne consumption fueling his anger. Finally the key turned and he shoved a morose looking Will over the threshold, kicking the door shut and then slamming the lock home.

Throwing his keys onto the hall table, Scott crowded up behind Will and urged him forward. "Get upstairs," he ground out through clenched teeth, pushing the other man up the stairs to the master bedroom, and into the en suite. Pulling open the glass door, he set the shower to cold and shoved Will under the spray, fully clothed.

"What the fuck?" Will sputtered, cursing loudly and shaking water from his eyes.

"Maybe that'll cool you off!" Scott threw a towel at him and stormed into the bedroom, leaving Will to stare at him, wide-eyed and open-mouthed. Toeing off his shoes, he paced up and down the plush carpet, muttering to himself. A few minutes later, Will padded out into the bedroom with a towel secured around his waist, obviously having shed his wet clothes where he stood and leaving them in a heap on the bathroom floor. *Which he'll fucking expect me to pick up in the morning!* Scott stopped pacing when he drew level with Will, and jabbed him in the chest with a pointed finger. "Are you going to tell me what the fuck you're doing?"

"None of your fucking business," Will shot back, rubbing his hair with another towel that he held in his hand. "Who *are* you, my *mother*?"

Ignoring the petulant glare Will threw him, Scott bit back the desire to slap him stupid and ground out, "What were you trying to prove?"

"I wasn't trying to *prove* anything! I would have thought that what I was doing was obvious," Will spat. "I was trying to get off."

"In the back room of a gay club?" Scott's gaze was incredulous.

"What does it matter where? And you didn't seem to mind the show."

"Don't be an asshole!" Scott felt a flush of warmth in his cheeks as an image of Will beckoning to him flashed across his mind. "What the hell is wrong with you? We're on a job! This isn't you! For God's sake *talk* to me, Will. I don't understand what's going on in that moronic head of yours!" He gasped and almost took a step back when Will's gaze hardened and he moved toward him.

"You want to know what's going on in my head? You sure about that, Scott?" Will practically snarled the words as he approached Scott with purpose in each step. "Okay, I'll tell you. *You! You're* in my fucking head! I've tried to get you out, but I can't. You're everywhere I turn. Under my skin." Will crowded into Scott's space, his voice rising with every word. "I can *smell* you on me. Can't scrub your scent clean. Can't stop *wanting* you. Believe me, I've tried, but I can't."

Scott watched in bemused amazement as Will walked backwards and sank down onto the edge of the bed. *What? Can't stop wanting me? Under his skin? What?*

"Stupid dumb. Harrison. Breaks the golden rule and falls for the straight guy." He lifted his gaze to Scott's, a frown on his forehead. "And I'm *so* sorry about the other night. I couldn't help myself. I needed you so bad, and when you kissed me back—" He hung his head and tossed the towel he held in his hands to the floor. "So go on, have a good laugh. Go back to the station and tell everyone the secret's out. Macho Will Harrison is a big fat homo."

"A week in Laurel Heights and you think you're gay?" Scott wanted to take the words back as soon as he saw the hurt and frustration in Will's eyes. Hurt and frustration he had seen in the mirror a million times.

"Don't be a jerk, not *now*," Will pleaded, his shoulders slumping in defeat as if all the fight suddenly left him. "You may as well know it all. I came out when I was eighteen. But I experienced firsthand how gay cops are treated, when the other cadets in my class forced one of my classmates out within three weeks of starting at the academy. He told me, just before he left, not to let them know, or they'd steal my dream too. So I shut my mouth and came up with this whole other Will Harrison. The one with Amanda, pretty little dark haired girl, engaged, building the perfect life together. Not that anyone ever met her, and nor would they, since she's the girl who came with the photo frame. There is no *Amanda!* Never has been. I became the cop everybody thought I should be, so I could get to where I wanted to go." He sighed heavily and huffed out a joyless laugh. "Then came Laurel Heights. How nuts is this, huh? A gay man who pretends to be straight, having to pretend to be gay? When we find the shooter, I'm going to be giving him an extra kick in the pants, just from me."

"Will—"

"Look, can we just be kind and rewind? I'd appreciate it if you could forget that I threw myself at you. Oh, and the part where you saw me in the back room of The Rose with two men, it would be cool if you could kind of gloss over that one, too."

"Three."

"What?"

"It was three men," Scott said softly. *Shut up, Scott! Why are you still talking?*

"Thanks for that," Will said, his tone derisive. "I guess I'll go sleep in the other room."

Scott was dumbfounded—couldn't believe what he was hearing. Will Harrison was gay? *His* Will Harrison, was gay? A fully fledged member of the queer club? Had a badge and a lifetime membership? Had been there, done that, and bought the T-shirt? He never had a clue. How the hell had he never had a clue? He seriously needed to get his gaydar checked. He— *Snap out of it, Turner! Say something for God's sake!*

Taking in the dejected slump of Will's shoulders and the way he was drawing circles with his big toe on the carpet, his heart ached in his chest for the man before him. He dropped to his knees and shuffled across the carpet. Placing his hands on Will's thighs, his fingers curled into the soft cotton of the towel covering the other man's modesty. His touch had the forlorn brown gaze meeting his. He never thought he'd be saying these words, not to another cop and certainly not to Will Harrison, but Scott moistened his lips, took a deep breath and said softly.

"Matt Logan." He ignored Will's frown and plowed on, afraid if he stopped he wouldn't be able to get it all out. "He was my first, when I was seventeen—in the back of his dad's Camaro. It was black and his dad had it custom painted with flames along each side.

154

If I said it *wasn't* that car that had a lot to do with how attractive Matt Logan was, I'd be lying.

"I came from a strict Catholic family, which in itself wasn't the problem. The problem was the fact that my father was the biggest bigot in the state. It wasn't just gays. Hell, Paul Turner hated everybody, blacks, Hispanics, Puerto Ricans, the Irish, but he had a special dislike for what he liked to call ass-loving abominations of God. Being a cop was all I ever wanted. My dad was so proud, you know. I was the first Turner to graduate and he couldn't tell enough people I'd been accepted into the academy. Until he found out, by accident ironically, that I was one of the ass-loving abominations, and he never spoke to me again." He ignored the pity in Will's eyes. He'd emotionally buried Paul Turner a long time ago.

"When I entered the academy, I knew, almost from day one, that I couldn't be me and be a cop, 'cause the bigoted assholes wouldn't let me. So I built another Scott Turner, just like you did. One who likes his women blonde and built. Who likes to brag about what a man's man he is." He lifted one of his hands from Will's cotton covered thigh and cautiously stroked a finger across a high cheekbone. His smile was gentle as he added, "One who most definitely wouldn't fall for Will *'I'm so straight I sleep with a poker up my ass'* Harrison."

"Are you fucking with me?" Will said, his gaze wide and confused. "I couldn't stand it if you were fucking with me—"

Scott cut off the flow of words from Will's mouth with the press of his lips. "Will," he dropped his voice an octave and actually felt the big man shudder under his hands. "You have no *idea* how badly I want to *fuck* with you."

"Are you sure? We—"

Scott pressed his fingers over Will's lips and then replaced them with his mouth. "Will?" He closed his eyes as Will's breath sent chills across his skin.

"Uh-huh?"

"Stop talking."

"Okay."

****

Will parted his lips readily beneath Scott's when he brought their mouths back together. He would take the time to process Scott's confession later. Right now all he could think about was the way Scott *'Oh thank God, he's gay!'* Turner was devouring his mouth. A low groan escaped his lips as Scott broke the kiss long enough for them to draw breath, and he took his chance to take control. Reaching up, he grasped a handful of dark hair and pulled lightly to angle Scott's head just where he wanted it. Scott tried to move in to kiss Will again but he held the man steady, allowing him to get close, but not quite close enough.

"So impatient," he teased softly. "You're the bottom, remember?"

"Fuck that," Scott hissed, his hands moving up Will's muscled arms and curling into the soft strands of blond lying against his neck.

"Uh-uh, I'm going to fuck *you*." The whimper that fell from Scott's lips had Will going from half-mast to diamond cutter so fast that for a moment he felt light-headed. Leaning in, he trailed the tip of his tongue along the soft flesh of Scott's lower lip in light stabs, ignoring the moans of complaint from the other man. Pulling back when Scott tried to deepen the kiss. "So needy," he murmured, "so fucking hot, so fucking beautiful."

"Will, stop teasing," Scott pleaded, pulling on the back of his neck, trying to bring them closer. "Come on, man."

Will was unable to resist the need in Scott's gaze and the temptation to tease evaporated. He slanted his mouth over Scott's in a heated kiss, reveling in the feel of soft lips readily parting beneath his, tongues colliding in a display of desire and need. The slide of Scott's tongue against his sent a shiver down his spine, his toes curling against the pile of the carpet as if to ground himself. He'd been kissed before, a thousand times, but he'd never felt anything like this. Had never been so turned on by the mere press of another's mouth on his. Even though they had kissed, and more, the other night, this felt different. Now there were no barriers, no secrets, and no lies. Only want, need, and each other.

Grasping Scott's forearms, Will hauled him high up onto his knees, pulling him into the cradle created by his open thighs. He slid his hands across Scott's firmly muscled chest and popped the top button on the black shirt the man wore. Keeping his gaze locked with the smoldering darkness of Scott's, his fingers stopped at the second button and his lips curved in a teasing smile. "How much do you like this shirt?"

"It's not my favorite," Scott rasped, his breath quickening.

"Good to know," Will murmured curling his fingers into the cotton and ripping it open in one swift movement. The remaining buttons popped off, leaving Scott's chest bared to his gaze. Pushing the tattered fabric off the other man's shoulders and letting it fall to the floor, Will couldn't help the smile of smug satisfaction as Scott's entire body jerked toward him. "When I dreamed of this moment," he said softly, reaching out and trailing his finger around the flat disc of Scott's nipple. He teased the sensitive flesh into hardness with the scrape of his blunt nail and blew against the puckered nub. "I wanted it to be perfect, wanted to go so slow, to tease you and make you beg me for release. But—"

Scott nodded in understanding and eased himself to his feet, urging Will back onto the bed. "Don't need slow," he said urgency in his voice "We can do slow later."

Will shuffled back into the middle of the bed and raised himself onto his knees. His gaze never leaving Scott's face, he reached down and slipped his thumbs beneath the edge of the towel covering his arousal, and pulled, tossing it to the carpet. "Naked," he ground out. "*Now*." He watched as Scott practically tore open his pants and pushed them and his briefs down his legs, stepping out of them and toeing off his socks at the same time.

Crooking his finger, he let his gaze travel wantonly over Scott's body as the man crawled up the bed on his knees toward him. Scott's dark hair fell in disarray around his face, the victim of Will's fingers. His cheeks were flushed and his navy eyes had darkened to the point that it was impossible to tell where the pupil ended and the color began. The length of Scott's hard shaft bobbed proudly against his belly, leaving behind a sticky trail of pre-come where it touched his skin, and Will licked his lips. Oh, God, how he wanted to taste, but that would come later.

He reached out and yanked Scott up against his body, crashing their mouths together, again and again. Mumbling between biting, tongue-teasing kisses, "Need you… so bad… so fucking *hot*, baby." Will slid his hands down Scott's back and palmed the firm globes of that perfect ass, pulling him even closer, their cocks rubbing tantalizingly together. "On all fours," he instructed, his voice low and commanding, smiling again when Scott whimpered and immediately did as he was told. He filed the observation that Scott obviously liked being ordered around, and concentrated on not creaming there and then at the sight of Scott presenting his ass so eagerly.

Pressing wet, open-mouthed kisses up the length of Scott's spine, he leaned over him and wrenched open the drawer of the nightstand. The drawer and its contents fell onto the floor in his haste and he cursed, bending over the edge of the bed to grab the lube and a condom.

"Eager much, William?" Scott's tease was emitted on a soft chuckle.

"Laugh it up, baby," Will replied, opening the lube with a click and leaning down to bite down on the soft flesh of Scott's shoulder. "Let's see if you're still laughing when I'm buried balls deep inside you." He actually felt Scott's entire body shudder against him at his words. Peppering the smooth skin of Scott's neck and shoulders with kisses, he lubed up his fingers quickly. He nudged Scott's ankles a little farther apart and bit into the fleshy part of his right buttock, smiling at the man's yelp. "I'm going to fuck you so hard," he said in a hushed voice, circling the puckered skin of Scott's hole, pushing inside in one swift move. He soothed his tongue over the spot where he had sunk his teeth and moved his digit in and out, sliding in another finger as soon as the muscle began to give.

"*Fuck, Will!*" Scott cried out, falling to his elbows on the mattress and dropping his head into his hands. "Yes… come on… do that again!"

Will pressed hard on the nerves inside Scott's channel and groaned when his cock began to weep steadily at the sounds Scott was making. They were the hottest sounds he had ever heard. Knowing that he was responsible for them, sent shockwaves of heat throughout his body. Scraping his nail across that sweet spot one more time, he pulled his fingers free. Ignoring the grumbled complaint from the quivering man beneath him, Will ripped open the condom with his teeth and slid the thin latex sheath down his length. He bit his lower lip, almost drawing blood as he lubed his cock, groaning when his fingers passed over the sensitive head.

"Wider," he grunted, smoothing his hands over Scott's lower back and positioning the crown against the loosened hole as Scott spread his legs on command. "Good boy... so fucking good." Will pushed in, his gaze widening as he watched the thick mushroom-ridged head of his cock slip past the rim and inside Scott. *Fuck, he's so tight!* It was as though his shaft was in a vice. Scott's chest was heaving with the effort to breathe deeply and concentrate on letting him in, and Will stroked his hands slowly across soft skin in encouraging circles. But this obviously wasn't enough for the other man. "*Scott!*" Will gasped out the name and held onto lean hips, when Scott pushed back against him, trying to take him in faster.

Scott reached behind him and dug his fingers into the fleshy part of Will's thigh. "So fucking big, Will." He panted. "Come on... fuck me... just do it."

Will didn't need to be asked twice. Gripping Scott's hips, he slammed into the willing body shaking beneath him and their cries mingled as his balls slapped into Scott's. He gripped the base of his cock and closed his eyes, feeling Scott's ass contract around him. "I'm driving the bus, dude," he ground out, administering a playful slap to the globe before him.

"*Yes!*"

"Like it rough, huh?" Will pulled out until the head of his cock stretched Scott's rim. "You want this cock? Want me to plow that tight ass, Turner?"

Scott lifted his head and turned to meet Will's smoldering gaze. "Do you ever shut the fuck up?"

Will slammed back in so hard that Scott moved up the bed, fingers clutching at the cotton of the sheets, his whimper echoing in Will's ears. *He wants it rough, I can do rough.* He could feel the sweat pooling in the hollow of his throat as he set up a punishing rhythm, hard and deep into the dark wet heat of Scott's channel. The only sounds echoing around the room were their breathy moans and heated grunts. Every few strokes, Will slapped Scott again. Not hard, but enough to leave a red handprint on his skin. The animalistic groans that came from Scott only fueled his desire and urged him on. His fingers slipped as he tried to get a purchase on Scott's sweat-slick skin and they scrabbled against soft flesh, momentarily interrupting his rhythm.

Leaning forward and reaching around Scott's chest, he hauled the other man up so that his back was against Will's chest and he was practically sitting on his lap. Wrapping one of Scott's arms around the back of his own neck, Will thrust deep. The incoherent mumblings that began to fall from Scott's lips at the change in angle told his addled brain that he was hitting the right spot on every stroke.

Scott met every thrust with one of his own and Will's control was slipping away. He couldn't hold on any longer. Yet being inside Scott, engulfed by Scott, *surrounded* by Scott, felt so fan-fucking-tastic that he didn't want it to ever end. Unfortunately, he wasn't Superman and that wasn't going to happen. His balls ached they were so tight to his body and he was sure he could feel them in the back of his throat. The telltale tingling of his release crept up his spine and his thighs began to shake in anticipation.

Thrusting as deep as he could into Scott, he ran one hand down the length of slippery skin and curled his fingers around the weeping thickness of Scott's cock. He groaned as the pre-come wet his hand, easing the movement of his fist. His hips didn't stop as he began to jerk Scott in long, twisting pulls, taking his entire length in time with his thrusts.

"Will... fuck, man... harder..."

Will moved his hand up to just fist the head of Scott's cock and was rewarded with an erotic cry that vibrated against his chest. "Come on, Scott," he gasped, his eyes closing tight as he tried to hang on to the orgasm that was rushing through him at a rate of knots. "I'm so…" he grunted harshly, "close, man… come on, and come for me, baby."

"Will!"

"That's it, man, oh, fuck!"

"*Yes!*"

"Scott! I'm coming!" Will's release pulsed through him like the waves pounding on the rocks on the shore. Hot bursts of seed filled the condom as he came harder than he'd thought possible. "*Scott!*" His groan was hoarse and fucked out as the other man came with a cry and spilled over his fingers, the warmth pumping over his skin, mirrored by the slip and slide of his own release against his cock in Scott's channel.

He held Scott, both arms wrapped around the man's broad chest, his face buried in the damp skin of Scott's neck. Will didn't know how long they stayed that way, with Scott's arm still looped around his neck, fingers stroking through the hair at Will's nape, but he was more than happy to continue with the pose. Until he felt Scott's insistent stroking change to tapping and then pulling. "Ouch," he mumbled into the soft skin his mouth lay against.

"Will, I gotta move, dude," Scott murmured, turning his head to press a kiss to Will's forehead. "My legs are asleep."

Mumbling his apologies, Will eased Scott back down onto all fours so he could withdraw his still, unbelievably, half-hard cock. He couldn't help the shit-eating grin on his face as he watched Scott pad slowly on shaking legs to the bathroom to get something to clean them up with. Sighing contentedly, he rolled onto his back on the mattress and stripped off the condom, tying it securely and tossing it into the trashcan by the bed, to be dealt with later. He glanced over at Scott as he returned to the bedroom with a damp cloth, and giggled as the other man wiped his cock and hand free of all traces of come. Rolling his eyes against the twitch of Scott's lips, he grabbed a muscled forearm and pulled Scott back down beside him.

Suddenly unsure, he gazed at Scott where he lay smiling on the pillow and a frown creased his brow. "Is this where we talk about sports again?" He hated the way the words sounded like a plea, but he needed to know if this was going to go the same way as the other night.

Scott nodded, his face impassive and unreadable. "I think we should," he said quietly.

Will's stomach hit his shoes or at least it would have if he hadn't been naked. He'd thought that—fuck it he hadn't been thinking at all, let's face it. Starting when Scott's fingers curled around the back of his neck, his gaze widened.

"Or you could just shut the fuck up and kiss me."

"You're such an asshole," Will ground out before bending his head to wipe that teasing smirk off Scott's face. "I wonder if they'll give me my own cell," he panted through parted lips when Scott finally let him up for enough air to draw breath.

"Huh?"

"When I shoot you."

"You can't shoot me for being an asshole," Scott replied, swallowing a yawn. "It's un-American."

"How the fuck did you slip under my finely tuned gaydar, man?" Will chuckled drawing figure eights with a lazy finger around Scott's nipples. He smiled at the way Scott arched into his touch and he pulled his lower lip into his mouth when the darkening navy gaze met his.

"The same way you slipped under mine," Scott replied, a frown creasing his brow. "Although the girlfriend didn't help. Hey, didn't I speak to her on the phone, when she called the office?"

Will grinned widely and nodded, scratching his fingernails over the hardening nubs of Scott's nipples. "My sister, Amy."

"I should arrest you for deceiving a police officer."

"You gonna cuff me?"

****

Scott shuddered at the images those words evoked and he stroked his fingers across the firm muscles of Will's flat belly. "Do I need to?" He kept his voice low and followed the line of pale hair that lead to crisper hairs around Will's cock. "Is this where you want the cuffs?" He circled the soft crown of the rapidly hardening flesh with his forefinger and moaned as Will's hips involuntarily jerked toward him. Opening his mouth when Will brought their lips together, he kitten licked at Will's tongue as the other man mapped out every ridge and curve of his mouth.

Scott's fingers left Will's cock and feathered through soft tendrils of blond hair, holding Will in place, as they kissed, hard and dirty. He'd never been kissed the way Will kissed him. Had never felt a connection as deeply. It was almost as if Will was trying to taste his very soul. As if he were the last drink of water in the driest of deserts and he was the only one who could assuage Will's thirst. He wanted it to go on forever.

Scott's moan of complaint when Will broke the kiss, soon turned to a gasp of anticipation when the other man slid down his body. The teasing kisses that Will pressed across his belly had Scott's cock twitching with every touch. As he looked down the length of his body, he arched off the bed when Will's tongue dipped into his navel and swirled around, sucking the flesh into his mouth. "Fuck... *Jesus, Will*!" He couldn't prevent the groan of Will's name when he stroked Scott's cock in a curled fist before lowering his mouth over the crown and sucking him down to the root. "Oh—my—*God*!" Scott buried one hand in Will's hair and curled the other in the sheet beneath him. The sensation of being inside Will's mouth was almost too much. He had to hold on to something to keep himself from floating clear off the bed. The right amount of suction, the right amount of tongue, and the right amount of pace. *How does he know exactly how I like it?*

"Look at me."

Will's voice was husky and deep as he released Scott's cock to issue the order. The sparks that the command sent coursing through his body, had Scott's balls drawing themselves up tight, searching for release. Forcing his eyes open, he looked down his body and watched Will's tongue work his cock. Their gazes locked as the other man pressed his tongue in the slit and slid down, time and time again, burying his nose in the curls of hair at the base. His pace quickening.

"Oh, God. Right... there," Scott moaned breathlessly, when the flat of Will's tongue caressed the nerves just under the head in quick hard swipes. "Don't stop... fuck... so good... don't stop!" He was panting heavily, desperately trying to drag air into his lungs as his orgasm began to spiral low in his spine, rushing forward. "Suck it... take that cock, baby... oh, shit... Will, Will!" Scott frantically batted at Will's head, any coherent thoughts impossible as with one more stab at his slit, Will pulled off and he was shooting hot streams of essence onto the fingers the other man had wrapped around his cock. His hips thrust mindlessly as Will jerked him through his orgasm.

Holy fucking shit! Not particularly succinct, but it was the best he could come up with as his entire body seemed to pulse in the aftershocks of his orgasm, with every beat of his heart. *That was—*

"*Fuck!*" Without warning, Will maneuvered himself and slid back inside of Scott's well fucked hole. *When did he put another condom on?* His breath fell from his lips in harsh gasps as Will rolled his hips in gentle waves inside him, slow and deep.

"So good, baby," Will groaned, not faltering in his steady pace. "The way you taste… un-fucking believable. Hot… sweet."

Scott cried out at the end of each word as they were punctuated with deep thrusts into his channel. "Will… I'm on fucking fire…" He tried to encourage Will to pick up the pace, the slow drags over his prostate driving him insane. His cock was, unbelievably, hardening valiantly against his thigh and he wasn't sure he could come again, but he wasn't sure he was going to get a choice. "You feel so good… inside me." He reached up to drag Will's face down to his, lifting his head from the pillow so he could suck on the other man's mouth, drawing his tongue into his mouth and lapping at the muscle, swallowing Will's moans. He felt totally strung out, his nerve endings lighting up and sending sparks up his spine and straight to his cock.

"*Scott*, so good… so hot, so wet… pulling me in." Will buried his face in Scott's neck as his hips began to roll harder.

"Jesus, *Will!*" Scott couldn't have stopped himself from crying out at every thrust if his life depended on it. Will filled him completely, he felt him everywhere. He felt so connected to Will at that moment, moving in perfect sync with him, that he was unsure where he ended and his lover began. Scott's fingers instinctively reached for his own cock, matching his strokes on his flesh with the push and pull of Will's length in his ass. "*Yes,*" he hissed, whining when Will slapped his hand away. "Will—" He bit down on his lower lip as Will's thrusts picked up pace.

"No," Will ground out, his tone commanding. "Don't... touch yourself. I want you to come... on my cock... hear you scream... my name."

"Fuck!" Scott's neck arched on the pillow as Will angled his hips and thrust even deeper, hitting that wonderful spot that sent bursts of pleasure to his brain. He'd never come on any man's cock before. Never had an orgasm without his cock being jerked to completion. Never—until Will Harrison. His orgasm hit him almost without warning, his eyes rolling back in his head as it rushed forward, Will panting words of encouragement in his ear.

"Come on, man, let it go. Do it. Come for me. Come... around me!"

"Fuck! *Will*!" Scott's third orgasm pulsed through him and he spurted in weak bursts across his own belly, his ass clamping down on Will's cock. He trembled beneath Will, his entire body shaking as the other man thrust twice more and stilled, their bodies pressed hard together as Will's hot seed filled the condom, his cock pulsing and Scott whimpering at every throb in his ass.

"Jesus," he panted, his head dropping onto the sweat slick skin of Scott's neck as he collapsed on top of him.

Scott wrapped his arms and his legs tightly around Will's body and held on. He wanted to freeze this moment. Stay here forever In each other's arms, away from the rest of the world. Hissing softly when Will reached down to hold onto the condom and withdraw from him, he tangled his fingers in Will's hair and lifted his head, pressing their lips together. "Stay with me," he murmured, completely boneless and sated, on the verge of sleep already.

Will kissed his jaw softly. "I'll be back."

Scott watched Will pad into the bathroom through lowered lashes, smiling as the other man wobbled slightly on shaky legs. His gaze followed the way the muscles bunched and moved beneath Will's skin and his cock twitched pathetically against his thigh. Chuckling softly to himself at the ridiculous notion of being able to get it up again, he accepted the damp towel Will handed him as he climbed back into bed beside him.

Wiping the cloth across his belly and over his hyper sensitive cock, he hissed and mumbled beneath his breath, glancing up at Will when the other man prodded him. "I said, I think you broke it."

Will laughed boisterously and plucked the towel from Scott's fingers, tossing it in the direction of the bathroom. Pulling the covers up and over both of them, Will slid his arm around Scott's waist, and spooned up behind him. "I hope not." He yawned, pressing a kiss to the nape of Scott's neck. "I have big plans for him."

"Oh, really?"

"Yes, *really* but not tonight, hot stuff. I couldn't even raise a smile right now."

Scott chuckled and rubbed his cheek on Will's bicep, turning his head to drop a kiss to the sweat dampened skin. "That was fucking amazing, Harrison." He sighed contentedly, unable to believe the way the evening had played out. That it had taken this case to make them realize their need for each other. "I can't believe we wasted so much time."

Will pulled him even closer and tightened his hold. "Ssssh, it's okay, baby. We won't waste any more."

Scott listened to the soft sound of Will's even breathing and slowly drifted off to sleep in the circle of Will *'I'm gay, but sssh, don't tell anyone'* Harrison's arms.

****

"Todd?" Marcus's voice drifted through the bathroom door. "You okay in there?"

Todd froze, not opening his eyes when he heard the shower door open and Marcus step in behind him. Crossing his arms across his midriff, he let his partner pull him close, leaning against Marcus's solid chest. "Hey," he murmured, resting his head on the other man's shoulder, his lips curving at the brush of warm lips against his temple.

"You've been in here so long, I thought I may as well join you." Marcus chuckled, tightening his hold.

Todd was unable to prevent the involuntary cry of pain that fell from his lips and bounced off the tile. He cursed inwardly, knowing that he had to lie to Marcus, yet again as the other man turned him and gazed down at him.

"Baby? What's wrong?"

"It's nothing, honest," Todd said, flinching at the look on Marcus's face when he uncrossed Todd's arms and took in the large bruise on his right flank. "You know how accident prone I am."

"Did I do that?" Marcus's voice was filled with concern and the despair in his gaze was palpable as he reached out and gently brushed his fingers against Todd's bruised skin.

Todd knew he was talking about the hot and heavy session they'd had last night. Marcus had been away for two days signing up a new band, and naturally they'd missed each other. Marcus had barely made it through the front door before Todd had lunged for him. Needing Marcus's arms around him again, his lips on his, taking away the feel of other arms and other lips that had touched him while Marcus had been gone. Todd shook his head as he remembered Marcus lifting him up at one point and slamming him against the wall in his haste to get inside him. He knew Marcus was appalled by the thought that he had marked him. "I didn't complain at the time, did I? It's nothing, babe—really." He wound his arms around Marcus's neck and pulled him down for a hot and dirty kiss of half need and half distraction.

He was disgusted with himself for letting Marcus think, even for a nano-second, that he was responsible for the bruise, but Todd didn't know what else to do. He had already had to lie about how he got the bruising on his lower back and thigh. With a forced laugh, he'd explained to Marcus how he'd taken a tumble down the stairs after tripping over his guitar case.

Todd sighed as Marcus's lips left his and trailed across his cheek to pull the sensitive skin of his earlobe into his mouth. He sank against Marcus, his arms tight around the other man's waist. With his head tilted back under the spray, he hoped that the tears on his face would go unnoticed beneath the cascading water. When Marcus whimpered, "I love you," into his ear, he bit back the sob that threatened to escape his throat.

He wanted to tell Marcus everything. Tell him how *sorry* he was, how *afraid* he was, beg him to make it stop. But he couldn't—didn't dare. *He'd* said he would hurt Marcus. Todd couldn't put him in danger. Hadn't Cory and Jon already paid the ultimate price for trying to help him? Todd closed his eyes against the weight of his guilt, fear, and despair, feeling it pressing down on him.

He couldn't lose Marcus; he was the only good thing in his life. He'd rather die. There was nothing he could do. *He* was right. Todd was used goods. He was nothing. If Marcus ever found out what he'd done—what he'd *allowed* to happen. He didn't want to think about the look on Marcus's face if *He* told him the truth. Didn't want to think about watching the love fade from his eyes when he realized exactly what Todd was—a useless whore. Todd pressed his body closer to Marcus, as if he were attempting to crawl inside him, where he would be safe, protected. *He* couldn't touch him here.

"Do you *really* have to go away again tomorrow?" He wiped away the beads of water clinging to Marcus's handsome face.

Marcus nodded his smile rueful. "But it's only one night, babe, I promise. After tomorrow I've cleared my schedule for two whole weeks. I'm going to take you away to a quiet beach somewhere and spoil you." He kissed Todd softly. "Sipping margaritas by the pool, making love on the sand… what, you don't like the idea of margaritas?"

"The margaritas are fine, it's the thought of picking sand out of my ass that's not too appealing," Todd said, his tone teasing. "How about a big bed with crisp white sheets, and French doors that open onto a secluded veranda?"

"I love the way you think." Marcus grinned and captured Todd's lips again. "Seriously though, you'll be all right while I'm away, won't you? I'm sure the guys will make sure you don't spend more than a minute alone. You'll be perfectly safe."

"Of course," Todd replied, burying his face in the crook of Marcus's neck, not wanting him to see the fear on his face that uncurled in his gut. *Safe?*

He didn't think he'd ever be safe again.

IX

Will stretched languidly as he slowly threw off the blanket of sleep he was wrapped in. He felt boneless, sated and would be more than happy to never leave this bed for the rest of his life. Except for odd trips to the bathroom, and maybe to the kitchen for food, but apart from that Scott and he could do everything from bed, like John and Yoko. He rolled over and threw out an arm to wrap around his lover's warm body, immediately realizing there was one major flaw in his so far brilliant plan—he was alone.

Raising himself on his elbow, he gazed around the room through a sleepy haze. The shower was silent, so Will surmised that Scott must be downstairs. *Wow, you should be a detective!* Ignoring the sarcasm of his inner voice, Will threw back the covers and climbed out of bed to pad naked to the chest of drawers. Pulling out a pair of well worn sweatpants, he pulled them on over his naked ass to go and search for Scott.

Will padded into the kitchen, his bare feet quiet on the tile, rubbing his fist into his eye, and yawning widely. He paused mid-step and almost choked on his own breath, not sure if his sleep fogged brain could process the messages his eyes were sending. Scott *'Would you look at the curve of that ass!'* Turner was standing at the sink, rinsing out the coffee pot—butt-naked.

After taking a few moments to study the way the muscles rolled beneath the smooth, honey-toned skin of Scott's back as he washed the pot, Will stepped up behind him and murmured, "I hope that water's not too hot." He couldn't contain the grin curving his lips when Scott dropped the glass pot into the bowl of water and almost left the ground, he'd started so violently.

"*Jesus!*" Scott turned and glared at Will, flicking foam from his soapy hands onto Will's bare chest. "You scared the shit out of me!"

Will chuckled as he reached out and pulled Scott into his arms, kissing him softly. "Sorry, couldn't resist it." Conforming his hands to the globes of Scott's ass, he raised a questioning eyebrow. "Not that I mind, but aren't you a little under-dressed?" He yelped when Scott slid still wet hands beneath the waistband of his sweats and gave his own ass the same treatment.

"If you ask me," Scott drawled, "you're a little *over*-dressed. Why aren't you still in bed?"

"Because I woke up and you'd left me all alone with no one to talk to." Will bit-kissed along Scott's jaw, the prickle of morning stubble teasing his lips, "No one to hold, no one to kiss—"

"I was coming back. I only came down to make coffee. I was going to bring it to you in bed."

"Really?" Will mumbled against Scott's neck as his lips continued their journey. "What about *after* the coffee?" He slid his tongue up Scott's skin and bit down gently on his earlobe. "More sleep?" His stomach tightened at the breathy moan he elicited from the sexy man in his arms. He didn't think he would ever tire of the sound of Scott's pleasure.

Will hissed through his teeth when Scott's hands left his ass and wound tightly in his hair, fingers pulling at the soft strands and yanking his lips from warm skin. He swallowed involuntarily at the way Scott's eyes had darkened so quickly, they were almost black. Delicious heat spiked in his gut and he hardened immediately, knowing in that single moment, that he would let Scott Turner do anything he wanted, for as long as he wanted. He tried to lean in to kiss him, but Scott was determined to tease just as he had last night—keeping him just a breath away from connecting. "Bastard," he mumbled, his fingers digging into the flesh of the man's buttocks.

"Be nice," Scott replied, licking out his tongue just far enough that it touched Will's lower lip.

"*Scott.*" The name was a breathy moan. Will was trembling in his hands. He wanted to be closer, but the grip Scott had on his hair prevented him from moving without sparks of pain flashing across his skull. "Upstairs—now!"

"Uh-huh." Scott shook his head and mumbled softly, "My turn."

Will groaned into Scott's open mouth as the other man closed that final infinitesimal chasm and brought their lips together, his tongue delving deep inside Will's mouth. He had no choice but to surrender all control to Scott as he plundered his lips, scraping his teeth over Will's tongue, drawing it into his mouth and suckling it as if he needed it to survive. Will ground his hips into Scott's already weeping cock and almost sobbed when the pressure was returned, igniting the flame of desire in his belly and turning it into a forest fire.

By the time Scott released his mouth, Will was not ashamed to admit that he was a babbling mess of incoherent need, and it took him a moment or two to register what the other man was doing. "Scott?" His question was moaned through parted lips as Scott turned him and walked him toward the kitchen table. "What—?"

"Ssssh, grip the table, baby. Show me that ass."

"*Jesus!*" Will hissed, doing as he was bid, laying his naked torso over the table, squawking at the coolness of the glass, and curling his fingers over the edge, presenting his ass to Scott. He gasped as Scott pulled his sweats down and helped him step out of them without uttering a word, before nudging his ankles apart with a bare foot. His legs were actually shaking with the anticipation of what Scott was going to do, nerves screaming out for his touch. *What's he doing? Oh, fuck!*

He's not—oh, fuck! Will cried out when his ass cheeks were gently pulled apart and he felt the first pass of the flat of Scott's tongue across his quivering hole.

He turned his face against his upper arm and bit down on his own flesh. It wasn't that he'd never been the bottom, but he'd never felt comfortable enough with anyone to allow them to rim him. With Scott's tongue stabbing and licking at his pulsing hole, he wondered what the hell he'd been thinking. His body felt as though it was burning up from the inside out. Every time Scott's tongue lapped at him, he moved on the table from the force of the shivers flowing up his spine. "Fuck... don't stop... dear *God*, don't stop!"

"Jesus, Will. You taste so good. I could eat this sweet ass all day."

Will took one hand off the table and curled it around his throbbing shaft. Pre-come dripped steadily from the slit, wetting his fingers as he spread it around the head and down his length. "Ungh, Scott... gonna come, man. You got me so fucking... *hard!*" He whimpered low in his throat when Scott withdrew his tongue and stood. "Scott? Come on, man... don't stop!"

"Easy, tiger."

It was only a matter of seconds, but to Will, they were the longest seconds of his life as he waited for Scott to do whatever the fuck he was doing and get back to the job in hand. He didn't have to wait long. "Holy shit!" He lifted his head off the table, his neck arching and the tendons chording as Scott's now slippery cock nestled between his ass cheeks. Will could do nothing but grunt out his pleasure as Scott began to thrust mercilessly between his cheeks, the thick length of his cock rubbing across his stimulated muscle. Rough fingers dug into his hips, hard enough to cause sparks of pain to flash over his skin, but Will didn't care. All he cared about were the sensations Scott was creating throughout his body, with his hands, his cock, and his desire.

Will closed his fingers around his shaft and began to jerk himself in time with Scott's thrusts between his cheeks. He vaguely wondered if his shaking legs would hold him up much longer as he raced toward his release. Needed it. Craved it. The combination of Scott's thickness across his throbbing hole and his own furious jerks on his cock had his toes curling against the tile beneath him as his orgasm swelled and washed over him in waves.

Warm, thick streaks of come spilled over his fingers and onto the floor under the table, some of it even splattering the underside of the table top itself. He moaned harshly with every pulse from his cock, Scott's shaft speeding up against his hole and then stiffening against him and shooting his load across Will's back.

"Fucking Christ, Turner," Will rasped, his throat raw and choked from the intensity of his orgasm, his chest heaving. He smiled lazily as he felt the swipe of a cloth across his lower back and the other man cleaned him of all remnants of their passion. "Mmmm," he mumbled, when Scott draped his body over Will's back where he lay, spread out on the table top, unable to move. "Where the fuck did you learn to do *that*?" The warm puffs of Scott's chuckle, stirred the hair at his nape.

"Biology class."

"Biology class?" Will countered, turning his head as Scott's lips feathered across his cheek. He wanted to stay like this forever. Okay, maybe not on the table, 'cause Scott was a heavy fucker and the glass was digging into his belly—but he was more than happy to have the other man on top of him for the rest of time. Scott chuckled again, warm and rich in Will's ear, sending a shiver down his spine.

"One of the seniors tutored me on a Wednesday afternoon."

"You dog," Will smiled, rubbing his cheek against Scott's and nudging him gently. "Dude, need oxygen." He couldn't resist rolling his ass back into Scott's sensitive cock and opened his eyes slowly at the man's expletive. "What's up, big—?" His tease froze on his tongue. "Oh, God!"

Both he and Scott gazed in horrified embarrassment at the stunned faces of Grace Cassidy and Julie Bates, and the far too interested leer of Jay Randall, staring back at them through the patio doors.

****

Scott was rooted to the spot, more precisely, rooted to Will's back. A million thoughts echoed around his head as Grace crossed her arms and raised an inquiring eyebrow. *How long had they been standing there? How much had they seen? How much hadn't they seen? How the fuck were they going to move without giving them another eyeful of the jewels? Oh my God, they've seen my sex face! Get a grip, Turner!* "We have to move," he hissed through clenched teeth, his gaze flitting around the kitchen to judge how far he was from grabbing the nearest dishtowel.

"How?" Will hissed back.

"Can't you reach your sweatpants, or—" Scott started at the bang that rattled the glass doors leading onto the garden.

"The time for modesty is over, assholes! Just go and find some pants!"

Scott flushed heatedly at the sarcasm dripping from Grace's voice and stood, immediately clasping one hand over his dick and grabbing Will's arm with the other. He hauled the other man upright and turned him quickly, shoving him out of the kitchen in front of him as Julie's "You don't have to cover up on my account, Turner" followed them from the room.

When they reached the bedroom, Scott sank onto the bed, his cheeks—both sets—burning with humiliation. He ran a hand through his dark hair and glanced at Will, who had collapsed beside him, and a frown creased his forehead. He noted the hand pressed to Will's side where he lay on the bed, the forearm flung over his eyes, and the shaking of his entire body. "Something funny, Harrison?" His tone was filled with derision as he stared at him. He kicked the big man when he didn't get an answer.

"Ow… can't breathe…" Will's laughter echoed around the room. "When I saw… them, I nearly shit… my pants!"

"You weren't wearing any," Scott said dryly, shaking his head in disbelief.

"I know! Neither… were you!"

Scott's lips twitched as Will broke into fresh peals of laughter, his chest heaving and tears leaking out from beneath his eyelashes and running into his hair. The twitch turned into a chuckle, then a snort, and then he collapsed beside Will on the bed and laughed boisterously. "How am I… s'posed to look at… them again?" His breath hiccupped from his lungs as he tried to drag more air in. "They've seen… my… my…" Scott couldn't finish the sentence; he just turned and buried his face into Will's shoulder.

"Your what?" Will nudged him with his nose. "Your what?"

"Sex… face!" Scott finally managed to get the words out between snorts.

"I know," Will guffawed, "mine too!"

"Could you two control yourselves long enough to come down?"

Scott's eyes widened when Grace's voice floated up the stairs. He managed to put a stopper on the bubbles of laughter still gurgling in his stomach and leaned over Will, planting his hands either side of his lover's head. Gazing down into Will's deep brown, laughter-filled eyes, he smiled softly. "I don't suppose we can stay up here forever?"

"It's funny you should say that," Will replied, feathering his fingers through Scott's dark hair. "I was—"

"Um, guys!" It was Jay's voice this time. "I'm going now. I'll see you in a couple of days; I've got to wine and dine potential clients in Stamford. Besides, your sister's hitting on me and it's freaking me out."

"See ya, Jay!" Will called out lifting his head and chasing Scott's mouth. "Hold on, how the hell did they get in?"

"They probably picked the goddamn lock!" Pressing a kiss to Will's lips, Scott eased himself off the bed and padded into the bathroom to run a sink of warm water. Dealing quickly with the now dry seed on his stomach, he rinsed the face cloth and returned to the bedroom. "Um… you don't seem worried that Julie saw you," he said, reaching out a hand to haul a still chuckling Will to his feet and turning him around.

"That's because Julie already knows about me. I told her when I was partnered with her, and I trust her implicitly," Will said, glancing over his shoulder. "I'm assuming Gracie knows about you?"

"Yeah. You can't keep anything from Gracie," Scott mumbled, unable to resist leaning in to nip at the curve of the other man's shoulder blade, Scott wiped Will clean and tossed the cloth into the hamper in the corner. "Come on then, gorgeous. Put some pants on, I think those girls have seen more than enough ass for one day."

****

Ten minutes, two pairs of sweatpants, and two tees later, the two men entered the kitchen to the smell of percolating coffee. Scott ignored Grace's smirk and felt his cheeks burn as he saw Julie on her haunches, scrubbing at the floor with a cloth and some Clorox. "Jules, let me do that," he said on a rush of breath and tried to grab the spray bottle out of her hand.

"Go away," she admonished, continuing with the task. "You think this is the first time I've cleaned up jizz off the kitchen floor? Or the bathroom floor? Or the hot tub? Or—"

Will held up his hands in horror. "Eww, Jules, come on… how can I look at Chad now?"

"Don't you dare 'eww' me," Julie complained. "You can *never* 'eww' me again, not after what I've just seen."

Scott banged his forehead against the cupboard before taking out four mugs. "I can't even begin to tell you how much I'm going to regret this," he sighed, "but come on… get it over with. Let us have it."

"I think Will's the one that got it."

Scott glared at Grace and held up his hands in supplication. "Okay, okay. You caught us having sex. We're *both* consenting *gay* adults. It's no big deal." He opened the cupboard to take out the sugar bowl. "Is there anything else you two want to add, or can we just put it behind us?"

"From where I was standing, it looked like a *very* big deal," Julie said, dropping Scott a wink.

"Mmm," Grace agreed with a nod of her head. "And you looked more than happy to be behind."

Scott took a step toward his partner and halted as Will's arms came around his waist and held onto him tightly. "You're lucky my gun's upstairs," he hissed, scowling at the two hysterical women. Allowing Will to guide him toward a kitchen chair, he sank down onto it and frowned in annoyance at the other man, whose shoulders were shaking, too. "For God's sake," he mumbled. "Grow up."

Turning his full attention back to the two women as Will dealt with the coffee, he leaned back in his chair, his gaze flitting from one to the other. "So… which one of you is my *sister*? And why were you hitting on the neighbor?" He stared pointedly at Grace. "As if I need to ask."

"I can't help it," Grace replied, tossing back her long blonde hair. "He's fucking gorgeous. I only suggested that maybe he hadn't met the right woman, *yet*."

"You have no shame." Scott shook his head in disbelief and took the mug of coffee Will handed to him. "And why are you both so unsurprised about the two of us?" He sipped slowly at the steaming liquid, wincing as it left scorch marks on its path down his throat. Watching Will walk back to pick up the other coffees, he couldn't help the way his gaze lingered on the swell of that ass beneath the cotton of the sweatpants the other man wore. Glancing back at Grace, he blushed again as she grinned widely.

Julie shrugged. "We're women."

"What my esteemed colleague, both in work and in gender, is trying to say," Grace embellished, "is that our gaydar is more finely tuned than even the queerest of queers."

Scott stared at the two of them, open-mouthed for several seconds before spluttering, "Bullshit! I can't believe we entrusted each of you with our deepest, darkest secret and you *told* each other!"

"Jules!" Will rasped.

"What?" Julie waved her hand between Grace and herself, repeating simply, "We're *women*. Have you any idea how goddamn excited I was when this assignment fell into your laps. You've been panting after Turner for months; you were just too stupid to see it."

"Exactly," Grace added. "And tall, dark, and stoic has been so dewy-eyed since you walked into the department that it's been like working with a fifteen-year-old girl."

Biting his tongue and rolling his eyes, Scott sighed heavily. "Can we get to the reason you're here?" He couldn't believe that Grace had betrayed his trust. Admittedly it was only to Julie, but that wasn't the point. Had she told anyone else? His gaze flew to Grace's and he let go of the breath he hadn't even known he'd been holding, as she met his gaze and shook her head. A wealth of meaning in the movement.

"We found out who the third ticket was for." Grace picked up her coffee and gave Scott a smug smile.

"Okay, I'll bite," Will said, sitting sideways in the chair beside Scott's and lifting his feet to rest them in Scott's lap. "Who?"

"Todd Campbell," Julie replied. "We searched through half of the hotels in Phoenix before we came up with a winner. Cory, Jon, and Todd were booked into the Armada Inn." She frowned at the two men when a glance passed between them. "What?"

Scott nudged Will's feet off his lap and strode down the hall to the living room, returning to the kitchen with the disc he had copied and his laptop. He turned it on and, after it whirred into life, inserted the disc into the drive. As the first photograph appeared, he hovered the pointer over the slideshow button and tapped the pad twice to start it. Turning the screen around, he and Will waited in silence while the girls watched the evidence of Todd's degradation roll by.

"Jesus Christ," Julie ground out. "Is it White?"

"No," Will said. "It's definitely not Marcus, unless he's in on it somehow—which I doubt very much. I've no idea how Todd explains the constant bruising he has, but we're both convinced Marcus doesn't know what's happening."

"How can he not know?" Julie replied, her tone aghast. "That's a lot of doors Todd would have had to bump into to be marked that badly."

Scott ran a hand through his hair and took another swallow of coffee. "I guess our next move is to see if we can get Todd to talk to us." He was beginning to see the pieces of the puzzle inside his mind. Now he needed to slot them into place. "If we look at this mess logically for a minute. Jon and Cory were close friends of Todd's, and I mean *close*—"

"You think there was anything going on there?" Grace questioned.

"I don't know." Scott rubbed at the back of his neck, feeling the beginnings of a headache at the base of his skull. "There's real affection in Todd when he talks about them, what little he *does* talk about them. But I couldn't say that there was anything sexual going on between the three of them. Not for certain." In his peripheral vision, he saw Will rise and pick up his chair. *Where's he going? What? Oh, ungh, that's good.* He briefly closed his eyes when he felt the pressure of Will's fingers on the back of his neck, kneading the tense muscles, having repositioned the chair behind him.

"You two are *so* cute," Julie crooned. "I think I'm actually having a moment here."

"Ignore them," Will instructed, continuing to massage. "Carry on… we don't know if there was anything sexual…"

Swallowing down the moan of pleasure-pain that threatened to escape his lips, Scott gathered his errant thoughts. "We've got two options here, as far as I see it. One, the three of them decided to take a vacation together in a little no-tell motel in deepest, darkest Phoenix—then Jon and Cory fought the night before they were due to leave and everything happened just as the police report said."

"And two?"

Scott unconsciously leaned back into Will's touch, feeling the tension leaving him and the throbbing at the base of his skull lessen. "And two, Jon and Cory found out what was happening to Todd and tried to do something about it—and they were stopped." His dark eyes narrowed as he reached behind him to still the movement of Will's fingers. "There's only one person who truly knows what's going on in Laurel Heights, and I hope he'll let us help him."

****

"Morning."

Todd looked up from where he was scrambling eggs on the stove top, as Marcus wandered into the kitchen, yawning widely. He grinned as his lover slipped warm arms around his waist and dropped a kiss onto his shoulder. "Good morning."

"You didn't have to get up and make me breakfast. You had a late night last night."

"Yes, I did," Todd replied, turning his head to brush his lips against Marcus's cheek. "I know you, White. You've got a four hour drive. If I don't feed you before you leave, you'll stop at the nearest candy store and fill the glove compartment with Hershey bars." Todd chuckled softly. "Besides, I seem to remember the late night was your fault. You kept me up."

"Well, *parts* of you were definitely up," Marcus drawled, sliding a hand into Todd's boxers.

Todd's hips jolted when the warmth of Marcus's palm rubbed at his cock. His length thickened and filled immediately under expert ministrations, and he groaned low in his throat. Reaching out, he turned off the heat under the eggs and pushed the pan to the back of the stove, then pressed his ass back against Marcus's hardness. He hooked a hand around the back of Marcus's neck to keep those soft lips pressed against his skin. "Don't start anything you don't have time to finish, White," he moaned, loving the feel of Marcus's fingers touching him just the way he loved to be touched. It had always amazed him, even from the very start, how Marcus seemed to be attuned to every need he had, almost before Todd felt them himself.

"Oh, I always have time to finish where you're concerned, Campbell," Marcus replied, turning Todd around and dropping to his knees. "I'm going to make sure you're thinking about me all night long while I'm gone."

Todd's stomach immediately tightened at the reminder that he would be alone tonight. For a brief blissful moment, he'd almost forgotten. "I'm always thinking about you, baby," he murmured softly. "Always." His eyes drifted shut as Marcus's soft lips swallowed down his engorged flesh.

Pushing all thoughts of *Him* from his mind, he concentrated on the man before him. This was Marcus, the man he loved more than life itself. The man who loved him back without question or condition. *He* didn't belong here.

An hour later, Todd leaned against the car and watched Marcus pack his overnight case into the trunk of his silver Prius.

"Hopefully, I can get the band I'm listening to tonight to sign to the label. They're so good, baby, you'll love them. In fact." Marcus leaned into the car and popped the CD from the stereo. "Here. Have a listen while I'm gone. I think they could be big. Not quite as big as you," he grinned, wrapping his arms around Todd's waist. "But they can make us a lot of money and then we can finally think about that ranch."

"Really?" Hope lit up Todd's gaze and he pressed his lips to Marcus's, reaching up to cup his face. "Just the two of us? No one else for miles around? I can't tell you how I long for that, Marc. No neighbors. No gatherings. Just you, me, and a roaring fire."

"Sounds like heaven," Marcus smiled, kissing Todd deeply. "I'll see you tomorrow, probably early evening, depending on traffic, but I'll try and make it home for dinner." He smiled and slid behind the wheel, closing the door behind him.

When Marcus had turned on the engine, Todd knocked on the window. He desperately grasped at reasons why Marcus couldn't go. Why he shouldn't leave. But he couldn't find any that didn't make him sound like a raving lunatic. Instead, he waited for the window to finish its downward journey and then leaned in to kiss Marcus again. A hard, deep, and dirty kiss that left both of them panting into each other's mouths when it was over.

"Wow," Marcus said, licking his lips. "What was that for?"

"Because I love you," Todd whispered. *Please don't leave me! He's watching us right now! I can't take it anymore! Please don't let him hurt me!* His gaze traveled over Marcus's face, memorizing every detail as if he was afraid he might not see it again.

"I love you, too." Marcus smiled adoringly and cupped Todd's face with his palm. "See you tomorrow."

Todd watched Marcus drive toward the gates and listened to the whirring of the motor as they opened. He lifted his own hand in return when Marcus waved out of the window one more time before driving through the gates and away up the street, the gates automatically closing behind him. "See ya," Todd sighed and glanced around the cul de sac, his eyes resting on one house in particular, before he wrapped his arms around his torso and hurried back into the house.

****

After Grace and Julie had raided Will's candy stash, Scott and Will shepherded the girls out of the front door and waved them off. They took with them the discs Scott had copied and promised to get the technical department to go through them with a fine toothed comb.

It was obvious to all of them that whoever was abusing Todd had had something to do with Cory and Jon's deaths. It had been agreed that Todd's safety was paramount and the two boys would speak to him, try and get him to open up—even if it meant blowing their cover.

Scott stood at the window in the living room, his re-filled coffee in his hand, gazing out at the splendor that was Laurel Heights. There was no denying that this was a beautiful place to live. The houses were majestic and opulent, the gardens carefully tended by a couple of handymen twice a week and to the outside eye it looked perfect. His jaw tightened at the thought of what went on behind those beautifully painted doors, wondered how long Todd had had to endure his humiliation. He gazed at Marcus and Todd's house, noting that Marcus's car had gone from the drive. *Does he know? Are we wrong? Is he letting this happen? God, I hope not.* Scott shook the thought from his head and downed his coffee.

He padded back down the hall and into the kitchen, pausing mid-step when he saw that the kitchen was empty—except for the T-shirt Will had been wearing lying on the cool, black tile of the floor. Putting his empty mug down on the table, Scott reached out and plucked the tee from the chair, unable to resist holding it up to his face and inhaling Will's scent. He smiled and folded the material, wondering when he had indeed turned into a fifteen-year-old girl, then froze in the task as he caught sight of the sweatpants that had been covering Will's gorgeous ass, hanging on the banister. Scott's smile widened as the tingle of anticipation bloomed inside his belly, spreading a thousand tiny sparks throughout his body.

"Okay, Harrison," he murmured softly. "I'll follow the breadcrumbs." With the tee still in his hands, Scott put his foot on the first stair and grabbed the sweatpants off the banister. Biting back the almost girlish giggle that threatened to escape him, he took the stairs two at a time, stopping at the bedroom door. On the handle hung Will's boxers. Shaking his head slowly, he removed them and opened the door, half expecting Will to be spread out on the bed, waiting for him. But the bed was empty. A tiny knot of disappointment tightened in his gut for a split second—for that was all it took for him to register the sound of the shower.

Licking his lips, Scott dropped the items of clothing onto the bed and hooked his thumbs into the waistband of his own sweatpants and briefs. He slid them down together and stepped out of them, tossing them and his tee on top of Will's. The other man's voice drifted into the room through the slightly ajar bathroom door as he began to hum, and Scott's cock filled at the sound of Will's rich, deep tone. Well… off key deep, rich tone… but damn sexy regardless of its inability to hold a note. He pushed slowly at the door and let his gaze wander over the vision that was Will Harrison, standing with his back to Scott, water running in rivulets down his skin. His cock went from *gotta have that* to *gotta have that NOW!* in about three seconds flat. The sight of Will, naked and beautiful in the shower, left him incapable of doing anything but staring at him, open-mouthed. Then Will turned and looked over his shoulder, a big shit-eating grin on his face as he raised a questioning eyebrow.

"Took you long enough."

"Traffic was a bitch," Scott replied, finding his voice and padding across the tile to open the cubicle door and step inside. He'd barely closed the glass partition behind him when Will's mouth was on his, stealing the very breath from his lungs and making his thighs tremble. "Wow," he murmured, his fingers carding through the damp tendrils of hair at Will's nape, as long arms encircled his waist and pulled him close. "Where did you learn to kiss like that?"

"Biology class."

"Oh, really? You had a tutor, too?" Scott groaned as Will's teeth nipped at his fluttering pulse. "Fuck, Will. I want you so bad. All I have to do is look at you and I could cut diamonds. No one has ever done that to me before."

"I can't think of anything else but you," Will gasped against Scott's skin. "You kissing me, fucking me, making me yours."

The words had Scott whimpering in his throat and he grabbed Will's hand, turning to push open the door of the shower, fully intending to drag the other man to bed and do exactly that: kiss him, fuck him, make him his. He gasped when Will's fingers closed over his and he turned to see blond hair dripping into Will's eyes as he shook his head. "I thought you—" His lips were crushed beneath Will's again as he was dragged back under the spray. When his kiss-swollen lips were finally released, he noted the condom and lube bottle that Will held in his hand.

"I'm always prepared." Will smiled, capturing Scott's lips again.

Scott's tongue delved deep into Will's mouth, grabbing the condom and lube and putting them on the soap dish hanging on the wall. With his now empty hands, he roughly skimmed Will's already hardening nipples, tweaking at them with his fingertips, reveling in the moans Will couldn't contain. "I want to be inside you," he rasped, dragging his mouth away from Will's and running his tongue around the whorl of his ear. "*Fucking you.*"

"*Yes!*" Will hissed. "Do it!"

"Easy there, cowboy," Scott soothed as Will stepped away from Scott and turned to plant his hand on the tiled wall, and spread his feet apart, giving Scott his ass. "I need to get you ready."

"No need." Will looked back at Scott, his eyes heavy-lidded and lust-blown. "I told you, I was a Boy Scout."

"You mean?" Scott's eyes widened and his cock got even harder, something he wouldn't have thought possible. That Will had been in the shower, opening up that tight ass for him, fucking himself with his own fingers, head thrown back as he slid one in up to the knuckle, and then another, and another—getting himself ready. Scott pressed his hand to the base of his cock, to stop the orgasm that threatened to pulse from him at the images skittering across the surface of his mind. "*Jesus*, Will!" The other man's name was a whimper on Scott's tongue. "You're gonna kill me, man."

"Scott?"

"Yeah?"

"Stop talking."

"Okay." Scott pressed his body up close behind Will and curled his fingers around Will's throat, tilting the man's head so that he could bring their mouths back together. He hadn't been lying when he'd said that no one had done this to him before. Never before had he felt the desire, no, scratch that, the *need* for anyone, that he felt for Will. Never had his heart even come close to being touched by one of the nameless, faceless conquests he had resigned himself to. He wanted more, wanted all of the beautiful man beneath his hands— wanted him forever.

He pulled his lips from Will's and smiled at the moan from the other man as he tried to chase his mouth. Grabbing the condom from the soap dish, he ripped it open with his teeth, pushing his hair back from his face and wiping the droplets of water from his eyes. Scott whined as he rolled the latex down his cock, the sound echoing off the tiled walls. The pre-come was leaking from him as if a faucet had been turned on, and he didn't think he'd be able to last if he didn't calm the fuck down.

"Scott, *please*. Do it."

Scott pressed a kiss between Will's shoulder blades and curled one hand around a lean hip, while the other pushed at Will's lower back, encouraging him to bend forward. Reaching down and lining the thick mushroom ridged head of his cock against Will's hole, Scott took a deep, steadying breath and eased past the rim. His eyes drifted shut at the sight of his length disappearing inside the quivering man before him. He couldn't watch their bodies becoming one; he would definitely lose it if he did.

In a way, keeping his eyes closed was almost worse than seeing the act itself, because every tiny sensation was heightened tenfold. Once the crown had slipped past the ring of muscle, it was as though he were falling as Will tightened around him and then pushed back, impaling himself on Scott's cock. The sound of Will's harsh breaths and pleas for more sent shivers vibrating up his spine, and his own cries fell from his lips. Wave after wave of pleasure washed over him and, when he was fully seated inside Will, surrounded by Will, engulfed by Will, he set up a slow rolling pace into dark, wet heat.

"Scott, *fuck!* Harder, baby. Give me more."

"Oh, God, Will," Scott groaned, the sound of his lover's voice, the desperation in his tone, filling him with a sense of power as he grabbed onto Will's hips and increased his pace. He knew by the high pitched mewling that came from the big man that he was hitting that sweet, sweet spot, and he angled his hips to try to hit it on every pass. "So tight," he gasped, hanging his head over Will's back and watching in stunned amazement as the sweat ran off him and onto Will's skin. "So fucking… hot… so fucking… beautiful."

"Love you inside… me. Don't stop… oh, fuck… don't stop."

"Gonna make you… come so hard, baby. So… good, love fucking… you." Scott knew his fingers would leave marks on Will's smooth skin when he had finished with him, but he didn't care. He wanted to mark him. Wanted everyone to know Will was his. "So close… oh, fuck… Will, say my name… wanna hear my name." He pounded relentlessly into Will, his balls pulling up tight as he held onto the last vestige of his control. "Gonna come, baby," he grunted, his body curling over Will's and reaching around him with one hand to join Will's fingers as they jerked his cock. "*Will!*" Scott cried out when the first pulses of Will's orgasm warmed his skin, the sensation sending him over the edge, his own orgasm slamming into Will as he thrust in uncoordinated release. As he filled the condom and spurted inside Will, the man beneath him cried out a single word on an almost feral growl.

"*Scott!*"

Scott laid his head between Will's shoulder blades and pressed open-mouthed kisses to the honey-toned flesh as he rode the waves of his release. "Jesus, fucking Christ," he rasped, his voice raw and cracked.

Easing himself upright, he gripped the end of the condom and slowly pulled out, stripping the sheath of latex off and tied it, quickly opening the shower door and tossing it into the trashcan by the sink. He squawked when Will's strong arms came around his waist and pulled him back under the spray of the shower. "Dude!" His tone was one of mock complaint, a complaint soon forgotten as Will kissed him softly. Noting the frown creasing Will's smooth brow as he pulled back, Scott reached up and tried to remove it with the sweep of his fingers. "What? Tell me," he said as he watched Will's cheeks flush.

"I don't know." Will shrugged and leaned down so that their foreheads were resting against each other. "I was just thinking. In the middle of the fucking nightmare that's this fucked up community—is it wrong to feel this fucking… I don't know."

"This fucking what?"

"*Good.*"

****

When Todd opened the door half an hour later, Will's heart tightened in his chest. The fear in Todd's deep blue eyes was palpable, only softening when he realized it was them. Will's gut clenched with anger at the bastard Todd had been terrified he would find on his doorstep.

"Hey guys, come on in," Todd smiled, standing back to allow them to step into the hall, closing the door behind them. "I've just put some coffee on. Would you like a cup? Or I've got some beer in the fridge?"

Scott followed Todd down the hall and Will brought up the rear, switching into cop mode, although still allowing his gaze to linger on the sway of Scott's hips. In the kitchen, Will sat down at the table beside

Scott and leaned back in his chair. He couldn't resist the smile that curved his lips when Scott moved close enough so that their shoulders brushed against each other. His gaze flew over to where Todd stood at the counter as a loud crash echoed around the kitchen. "Todd? Are you okay?"

Todd nodded, picking up the pieces of the cup he had dropped. "Fine, fine. I must have gotten up on the clumsy side of the bed today."

"I know how that is," Will replied, trying to keep his smile natural and his expression neutral. He could practically see Todd shaking from across the room. *Clumsy my ass! He's terrified!* Looking down at Scott's hand on his thigh, Will took a couple of steadying breaths, grateful for the pressure of his fingers reminding him why they were there.

"Where's Marcus?" Scott asked, taking the cup that Todd held out to him.

"He's gone out of town on business. There's a new band he's hoping to sign to the label. I've been listening to them actually, he left me their demo. They're really good."

"How long is he away for?" Will asked, lifting his cup and sipping at the hot coffee, feeling the warmth of it slide down his throat and expand in his chest. He didn't miss the flicker of fear in Todd's eyes at being alone.

"Only overnight," Todd answered, folding his legs underneath him on the chair and picking up his own cup.

"Does he go away often?" Scott asked.

Will sat back and casually draped his arm across the back of Scott's chair. He recognized the subtle change in Scott's tone, the softness being one he used when interviewing a confused victim. Knowing that Scott was beginning his attempt to get Todd to open of his own accord. If they tried to force any information from the man, all they would succeed in doing was scaring him even more than he already was. He sipped at his coffee as he watched Todd's shoulders relax a little, some of the tension leaving him.

"Too often," Todd said ruefully. "But it all adds up, and the more bands he signs, the more money that comes in, and the closer we are to our dream." His lips curved up in a wistful smile.

Will couldn't help smiling back at the expression on Todd's face. "Your dream?"

"Yeah," Todd leaned his elbows on the table. "It's kind of corny really. But I've always dreamed of living on a ranch somewhere. Nothing huge, you know, just a few horses, maybe some cattle, with nothing around for miles and miles, nothing but me and Marc."

"You really love him, don't you?"

The gaze Todd fixed on Will was unwavering as he said simply, "He's everything."

"It must have been nice to have Cory and Jon to keep you company while he was away," Will pressed. *Shit! He should have left this to Scott!* He wished he could bite his tongue off, furious with himself when Todd's gaze wavered and flitted between him and Scott nervously. "I mean, they must have been a great comfort to you. You must get lonely when Marcus is gone."

"What are you suggesting?" Todd's was affronted. "They were my *friends*, nothing else. They were willing to help me in ways you could never imagine..." He trailed off, and ducked his head.

"Todd, Will wasn't suggesting anything, dude. He just meant it was good that you had friends like them. Good friends, who were willing to do anything they could to help you." Scott's tone was placating.

"Oh, God." Todd's eyes widened in disbelief.

"Todd." Will reached out a hand across the table and glanced at Scott when Todd flinched at the movement, and looked around him as if he was expecting someone else to appear.

"You *know*. You *saw*." Todd got to his feet and spread his arms out to the side. "Did *He* send you? Is that what all the friendly concern is about? Did he tell you to come get a piece?" His breath caught in his throat. "Go on then. Get it over with. What do you want? One at a time? Both together? I'll do whatever you want just… just *please*… don't hurt me."

Will watched in stunned silence as Todd began to undress, shaking fingers struggling with the buttons on his shirt. Pushing his chair back, he rose to his feet slowly, his heart aching in his chest as all life left Todd's blue eyes at his approach. Reaching out he put his hands gently on Todd's shoulders and pulled him into his arms. The anger roiled in his gut, burning his throat when Todd stiffened against him, but didn't move away, as if he was resigned to more abuse. Will tightened his hold, keeping his voice low, but firm, as he held Todd to him. "Todd, it's okay. We're not here for that. We're here to help you, man. We want to make sure no one ever hurts you again." He gazed at Scott when his lover's arms came around both him and Todd.

"Todd… please, let us help you. Tell us who it is. Help us make it stop," Scott said softly, nothing but compassion in his tone. "Did he hurt Cory and Jon?"

Todd pushed them away at that and shook his head. "I can't. *Please*. Just leave. You can't help me. *No one* can. He'll…" The tears already coursed down his face. "Just go. Get out. *Please*."

Will watched, his own tears spilling from beneath his lashes as Todd turned and fled from the kitchen, his feet pounding on the stairs, followed by the slamming of a door. He was half way to the stairs when Scott grabbed his arm. "What?" He frowned at Scott.

"We can't leave him up there. We've got to get him out."

"We can't," Scott said, pulling on Will's arm and urging him toward the front door. "What are you going do? Blow our cover? Take him to the station? Put him in lock up? Baby, he's not going to tell us anything. Not right now. We've got to let him come to us."

"So what the hell are we supposed to do?" Will said, running a hand through his hair in frustration. "Scott... his face... he's so scared, we can't leave him." He sighed heavily as Scott pushed him over the threshold and closed the front door behind them.

"We have to. All we can do now is watch, and wait."

****

He watched Scott and Will walk back to their house, jealousy and fury building within him. What did Todd think he was doing? He knew he wasn't supposed to have other men in the house when he was alone. Did Todd think he wouldn't find out? That he wouldn't see what was going on under his very nose? Surely by now Todd knew that he saw everything. His lips curved into a predatory smile as he closed the door behind him, his fingers tightening around the nylon cord he had taken from the drawer earlier.

Todd felt the hairs on the back of his neck stand up when he heard the first footfalls on the stairs. *Oh, God. Please don't let it be Him. Please be Marc, please be Marc.* He swallowed down the wave of nausea that rose in his throat as the bedroom door opened slowly and He closed it behind him. When he looked into those icy blue eyes, the saliva dried in his mouth and terror flashed through him like quicksilver. He knew that look—he'd been bad—he was going to be punished.

"Did you think I wouldn't be watching, Todd?" The voice was smooth and soft, like a lover's touch. "Did you think I wouldn't see, wouldn't know?" With each word, He took a step closer. "Which one of them fucked you, my pretty little whore? Which one of them put his hands on you?" He tilted his head to the side and smiled, blue eyes darkening. "Or was it *both* of them? One in that beautiful ass and one between those gorgeous lips?"

"Baby, please... I didn't do anything... I *swear*. I didn't let them touch me... didn't tell them anything... *please*." Todd held out his hands, pleading with the man who was now so close that there was barely a breath between them. He cried out when harsh fingers tangled into his blond hair and yanked his head back painfully. Todd tried desperately to breathe around the hot, wet lips that were sealed over his, and the tongue thrusting into his mouth. Closing his eyes tightly, he waited for it to be over. Tried to respond as best he could, knowing it would be so *very* much worse if he didn't. Finally, his lips were released and he gulped in desperately needed oxygen.

"Maybe I should tell Marcus what you've been doing? What you've let *me* do to you. What you've *let* the other men I've brought here do to you, in *his* bed. Maybe I should tell him what a whore you are, right before I kill him. Wouldn't that be a wonderful memory to send him into the ever after with?"

"*No!*" The word screamed from Todd's lungs, and then he quickly hung his head in submission at the flare of anger in the other man's eyes. "Please... don't take him from me... I'll do anything. I'll be good." Swallowing against the bile that he could taste in the back of his throat, Todd lifted his hands and stroked them over the other man's ass, attempting to appease.

Blue eyes darkened further as they raked over Todd's lithe body. "Oh, I know you'll be good, baby. Now—take off your clothes."

****

"Something's not right," Scott said rubbing his eyes as Will came in with yet another cup of coffee. They'd been watching Todd's house all day and they'd seen no one go in and no one come out. To all intents and purposes, it looked like any other house in the cul-de-sac. Even the lights had been turned on in the living room and there was a muted glow from the master bedroom. But there was a niggling feeling in his gut that told Scott there was something wrong with the perfect picture. The fear in Todd's eyes was eating away at him as he sat in the darkness of the living room so he wouldn't be seen watching the house. He took the coffee from Will's outstretched hand and leaned into the other man's warmth when he sat down on the arm of his chair. "It's too quiet. I don't like it." He sighed heavily. "It feels like the calm before the storm, you know?"

"Scott?"

Scott gazed up at Will from over the rim of his coffee cup. He'd immediately picked up on the nervousness in Will's tone and knew something was going on in that head of his. "What are you over-thinking, Harrison?" He stroked Will's denim clad thigh with gentle fingers, and waited for the other man to speak.

"Are we... Is this... What..." Will blushed and took a deep breath. "What is this thing? You know, between us?"

"Fantastic, hot, best sex I've ever had. Do I need to go on?" Scott waggled his eyebrows teasingly at Will, and immediately wanted to kick himself when he saw hurt flash across those beautiful brown eyes. *You asshole, Turner!* "I'm sorry, Will. This is why I suck at relationships." he sighed. "I mean *really* suck. I've always been so afraid of anyone in the department finding out I'm gay, I've never even come close to a relationship. I guess they got tired of waiting for me to commit and left."

"They left because you're an asshole, you asshole," Will said sarcastically, downing another mouthful of his coffee.

"Well, yeah, that too." Scott nudged Will's arm with his shoulder and smiled softly at him, the smile widening when Will finally relented and met his gaze. He watched as Will put down the cup and swung onto his knees in front of him, positioning himself between his open thighs and caging Scott in.

"Thing is," Will began. "I like you. I mean, *really* like you and I want there to be an us when this is all over. I mean, I'm fully prepared to overlook the fact that there's barely enough room in the bed for both of us and your ego, and the fact that you snore like a freight train. Oh, and I'm even willing to ignore the unbelievably unhealthy fascination you have with *Days of Our Lives*, and assist you in the unmanly cuddling you like to do after sex. What do you think? Is it something that you might want to try?"

Scott's heart swelled in his chest at the uncertainty and hope in Will's eyes, making him look like a five-year-old who had just been told that Santa might not be real. If he was honest with himself—*Yes, Scott, by all means be honest*—he wanted to grab the beautiful man and kiss him senseless and tell him he wanted to be with him forever, but he couldn't. *You mean you won't. Not everyone out there is Paul Turner. When are you going to realize there are some things worth taking a chance for?* "Will—" His words were cut off by a knocking at the door. "Who the hell is that? It's ten thirty for Christ's sake."

****

Will sighed heavily and eased himself to his feet. "I can't wait to get out of here; these people have no understanding of personal bubbles." He glared down at Scott and bent to kiss him, swiping his tongue across Scott's full lower lip. "This conversation is not over, Turner," he warned, ignoring Scott's attempt to grab a hand to pull him back down and padding down the hall to the front door. His eyes widened in disbelieving horror at the man who almost fell over the threshold.

Blood dripped from the fat lip Todd was sporting, and his right eye was almost swollen shut. Nylon cords were tied around both his wrists and one arm was wrapped protectively around his midriff. Will could only stare as Todd moistened his bloody lips and croaked, "Help me," before collapsing into Will's arms.

"Scott!" Will shouted, lifting Todd into his arms, kicking the door shut, and heading to the stairs. "First aid kit!" His gaze locked with Scott's as the other man ran from the living room, quickly took stock of the situation, and sprinted down the hall to the kitchen.

"Hurts," Todd whimpered when Will laid him on the bed in the master bedroom.

Will could clearly see that Todd's stomach was distended and from the way he was breathing he was sure he had at least a cracked rib or two. "Todd," he said, smoothing back the sweat dampened hair from Todd's clammy forehead. "We need to get you to a hospital." He looked up as Scott ran into the room with the first aid kit in his hand and knelt down on the floor beside Todd's head.

"No… no hospital," Todd said, his voice almost unrecognizable around his swollen mouth. "Just… make it stop...Will...please."

"Will."

Will glanced at Scott and followed his horrified gaze. "Oh, Jesus," he breathed at the bright red stain seeping through the ass of Todd's jeans and onto the sheets beneath him. "Todd, you're bleeding, we need to call an ambulance."

"No!" The cry had Todd coughing harshly, spots of blood decorating his lips. "Marc. He'll know... he'll know what I am... what I let Him do. Please don't.... just want... to stop. Don't let Him... hurt me."

Will leaned down and pressed a kiss to Todd's forehead. "I won't, baby. It's okay. You're safe now."

X

"Scott," Will said urgently as he filled a bowl with warm water while Scott grabbed some towels. "He's bleeding. We need to get him to hospital."

"I know, I know." Scott nodded, his voice low. "Who the fuck is doing this? Why won't he give us the name?"

"I don't know," Will snapped, running a hand through his hair and picking up the bowl. "Let's get him cleaned up and into the car. I don't care what he says; we're going to the hospital."

The two men worked together to ease Todd out of his clothes and slipped a towel beneath him. Will used the scissors from the bathroom cabinet to cut the cords from Todd's wrists, while Scott cleaned the blood from the injured man's swollen face.

****

"Sorry, dude," Scott said softly, wincing right along with Todd when he cleaned around his lip. He tried to distract Todd while Will unwound the heavy cords and began to wipe a fresh towel across the welts on Todd's flesh. "We need to tell you something—about us." He saw the immediate fear in Todd's eyes and soothed him gently. "It's okay, I promise. Will and I are detectives with the White Plains PD. We were sent here undercover to try to find out what really happened to Cory and Jon."

"What?" Todd hissed, trying to sit up.

"Don't move, dude," Will said softly. "I'm pretty sure you've broken some ribs."

"Just… bruised," Todd said on a low chuckle that made him cough again. "Broken ones feel different."

Scott nodded reassuringly, gently feathering his fingers through Todd's hair while he spoke. "We need you to tell us everything, Todd. We want to put him away so that he can't hurt you, or anyone else, ever again." He smiled softly, as Will dropped the towel and took one of Todd's hands between both of his.

"Talk to us, Todd," Will murmured. "Help us stop him. Who's doing this?"

"You're here for Cory and Jon?" Todd whispered, tears slowly rolling down his face. "They loved each other so much. I don't know how He managed to convince everyone that Cory killed Jon; how anyone could believe that Cory would ever hurt Jon." He groaned loudly as he shifted on the bed. "But then He's good at convincing people, making them see what He wants them to."

"Todd," Scott said softly, rubbing a gentle hand up and down Todd's arm. "I'm going to need to see what he's done. I need to make sure you're okay." He squeezed Todd's arm at the man's quick nod and glanced up at Will, who immediately helped to maneuver Todd onto his side. Scott parted Todd's ass cheeks as gently as he could, not wanting to cause him any more discomfort. His gaze flew to Will's and he motioned toward the bathroom with his head, smiling encouragingly as Will stood and walked into the en suite. He didn't want Todd to see the un-tempered rage on Will's face at the sight of the abuse Todd had been subjected to.

"It's all right," Todd's voice was small and embarrassed as he explained. "He took me dry... it'll stop."

Todd had an obvious tear to his rectum and although the bleeding had slowed, the tissue was red, inflamed. Scott had to swallow down his own anger when he saw the semen mixed in with Todd's blood. He'd obviously not only been taken dry, but without protection. "Will," he called out in a conversational voice. "I need some sort of container." He pressed a gentle kiss to Todd's shoulder. "I'm going to take a sample for evidence. I'll try not to hurt you, is that okay?" Nodding, Todd buried his face into the pillow as Scott took the Q-Tips Will held out to him. As gently as he could, Scott collected a couple of samples of the semen and put the Q-Tips into the plastic bag Will had brought in from the bathroom.

When they had finally managed to get Todd comfortable, having cleaned his ass, padded his injuries with some gauze, then slid a clean pair of shorts and one of Scott's T-shirts on him, they sat on the bed and Todd began to talk.

****

"When we first moved in here, it seemed perfect. Marcus and I had been together for about a year, and I was just starting to make a name for myself, you know?" He couldn't bring himself to look at the two men listening to him. The compassion in their eyes was too much for him to handle. The last thing he was deserving of was compassion. He'd brought all this on himself, hadn't he? *He'd* said so.

"The whole gathering thing came about when He suggested it one night over dinner. At first we all thought He was kidding. But we were all a little toasted by then, and it sounded like a bit of harmless fun. It was never supposed to be anything heavy, and we'd always said we'd participate in the petting, but we never wanted it to go further. We had each other, we'd never had, or needed, anyone else in our relationship and we didn't want to start.

"The first gathering, He cornered me straight away, kissed me, and touched me. Damon had gone off with Marcus and so I just went with it. I mean, He's gorgeous, I was flattered and it was nice. Hell, I enjoyed it." He rubbed a hand through his hair, wincing as the action pulled on his bruised side. "But afterward,

He approached me in the kitchen, grabbed my arm, and told me how much He wanted to fuck me. Of course, I said no, that that was not what Marcus and I had agreed to. I didn't see the anger in him, beneath the surface. Didn't expect it from him, not *Him*, so why would I have been looking for it? He seemed okay, and everything was fine.

"Until the next gathering—Marcus was away. I didn't want to go, but the others said it would be fine and if I didn't feel comfortable, I could just watch. Hell, even Marc told me I should go and that if I wanted to kiss and touch, he was fine with that. We had already laid down the ground rules as to how we were going to play the whole situation and so he wasn't worried. He made it sound like it was stupid for me to sit at home alone when I could have a drink, hang out, and maybe even get off. That there was nothing to be afraid of..." His lips curved into a rueful, joyless smile. "Hindsight is a wonderful thing."

****

Will reached out with one hand and rested it on Todd's ankle, wanting to comfort and reassure him. With the other, he grasped Scott's hand and lifted it into his lap, keeping their fingers entwined. For a reason he couldn't begin to explain, even to himself, he felt the need to have Scott connected to him while they listened to Todd. Needed to know Scott was safe and right there beside him. Scott's fingers curled around his and when the other man's thumb began a gentle sweeping motion on the back of his hand, the tension seemed to flow out of him. "Then what happened?"

****

"I got drunk. I didn't mean to, but He kept giving me drinks and, thinking back on it, He probably wasn't giving me singles. Before I knew it, I was in David's arms, with Cal giving me a blow job. But He was watching me the whole time. Even when He was touching others, being touched by others, his eyes never left me and I suddenly felt afraid. I couldn't even explain why. His eyes, they bored into me like He wanted to eat me alive. I tried to leave... no one really cared, they were all too drunk or high and there were more than enough bodies around to replace me." His breath hitched in his throat.

"He stopped me in the hallway and pushed me up the stairs. I told him I had to go, that I didn't feel so good, but He just said that He'd make me feel better, and locked the bedroom door. He... He," Todd swallowed audibly. "He... hurt me. Tied me to the bed… forced me. He kept telling me how good I was, how much He knew I wanted it. That no one would believe I hadn't, that if I told Marcus He would just tell him I'd instigated it. That no one would believe a useless, white trash whore like me. I was just some sleazy musician they'd let in because Marcus was an up and comer. Eventually He untied me and I got home as fast as I could. I spent over an hour in the shower with the water so hot it turned my skin red—trying to scrub him off me."

"What happened then?"

Todd sighed. "Nothing, for a while. Every time He saw me, when no one else was looking, He would make gestures at me. Gestures that made his intentions clear. He'd stand as close to me as He could get away with, make any hug or kiss look like an affectation, He made sure no one would ever question the way He acted toward me. But I felt his eyes on me all the time, and the look in his eyes if Marcus touched me, or kissed me in his presence. It scared me. *Really* scared me. He knew I wouldn't tell Marcus. How could I?

"When I met Marcus I was a struggling musician, singing in a bar for drinks and tips. Meeting him was the best thing that ever happened to me in my pathetic little life and He knew that. Knew how much we loved each other and that we'd promised we would never fuck anyone else. He was right, I couldn't tell

Marc what had happened, what I'd *let* happen. I thought I could put it behind me. I would just make sure I was never alone with him again and everything would be okay. Then Marcus went away on business."

"Was there another gathering while he was away?" Scott asked.

"No." Todd shook his head. "All I remember is being asleep and waking up when I felt someone get into bed beside me. I remember vaguely thinking Marcus had come home early and I rolled over to cuddle up to him. I was only half awake, but I knew the moment I felt his lips on mine, that it wasn't Marc. I tried to fight him, I think I even got in a punch or two, but I saw it in his eyes—He liked it. The more I fought, the more excited He got—the more excited, the more violent.

"It became a kind of twisted routine after that. Every time Marcus was away, He would suddenly be in the house. I'd sit, shaking, for hours sometimes, just waiting. But He always came. He was careful not to make the bruises show, but I had to become quick at explaining any that Marc saw. Then He started to bring other men so that they could do things to me while He watched, while He took pictures."

****

Scott saw the guilt, the humiliation flood Todd's eyes, knowing he was thinking of the pictures that he and Will had seen. He let go of Will's hand and moved to sit beside the beaten man. He slid a comforting arm around Todd's shoulders and said softly, "Todd. Look at me, please." Lifting Todd's chin, he looked into his tear filled eyes and said firmly. "*None* of this is your fault. Do you understand me? *You* are the victim here. He raped you. He abused you. He took away your right to say no. He is to blame. Not you."

"You don't understand." Todd gasped in a breath as fresh tears began to fall. "It is my fault. If it wasn't for me, Cory and Jon would still be alive. If they hadn't tried to help me..." He trailed off and buried his swollen face into Scott's shirt.

"Todd," Scott soothed, stroking the back of Todd's neck gently. "What happened to Cory and Jon?"

Todd sniveled and wiped at his face. "He killed them. They were trying to get me away. They were trying to save me. And He killed them."

"Can you tell us what happened?" Scott continued to stroke Todd's neck and whispered words of comfort as Todd laid his head on Scott's shoulder. "Take your time."

"We went out for dinner, Cory, Jon, and I. Marcus was working late and the four of us had become close friends so we used to go out together a lot." He sighed, adjusting his position slightly on Scott's shoulder, but not moving away. "I went into the bathroom to take a leak and didn't hear Cory come in behind me. He saw the bruising on my back when I was at the urinal. I didn't realize my shirt had rucked up and he could see the marks that He'd left a few days before. They were particularly nasty and still really painful— I'd been pissing blood for days. I had a hard job explaining those to Marcus. Said I'd taken a spill off my bike in the park and landed on some rocks. Unfortunately, that one didn't quite wash with Cory." He chuckled half-heartedly. "He was such a big mother hen. He packed us into the car and we drove around while I talked and talked and talked. Everything came out. I *couldn't* let them think it was Marcus. I had to tell them the truth. Once I started talking, I couldn't stop. That's when they started planning on how to get me out."

"Is that when they bought the bus tickets to Phoenix?" Will questioned.

"Jon said they'd be harder to trace. *He'd* always said if I tried to get away, He knew people. He would find me, and He would make Marcus take my place. I couldn't let that happen." He wiped at his face again. "Cory said that until things were sorted, when Marcus was away, I would stay with them. For the first time since it started, I felt safe, really safe. It was also the last. That was the night they died.

"I woke up in their guestroom and He was standing over me. I cried out but He punched me in the gut and dragged me into Cory and Jon's room. I don't know how, but He knew we were planning *something*. He must have been watching us those last few days, we were never apart. There was arguing and Cory tried to hit him. Told him they knew what He'd been doing and they were going to call the police. He flipped out. I'd never seen him that enraged. He totally lost it. I didn't even see the gun. Honest I didn't. If I'd known He would go that far, I'd never have gotten them involved. You have to believe me."

"We do," Will urged. "We do believe you, Todd. Just like Scott said, none of this is your fault. The blame lies on his shoulders, not yours."

"He killed Jon first and then when Cory was leaning over him screaming, He shot him too. I think I screamed, I'm not sure. I must have, because He hit me and knocked me out. When I came to, I was on the floor in their bedroom and the first thing I saw was Jon." He closed his eyes. "Half his head was just... gone. I'll never forget it. Cory was lying across him, He had a hole in his temple and the gun was in his hand.

"He said that's what happened when I tried to get away. I got people killed. He said if I tried it again, Marcus would be next. Said that I *belonged* to him, and that He would tell me when He'd finished with me. I had no choice. I couldn't let him hurt anyone else. I couldn't let him hurt Marc.

"He was excited by what He had done and He made me... made me..." He hung his head. "Right there on the floor, with Cory and Jon lying dead in front of me. Told me I enjoyed it because I came." He began to sob. "I *came* while my friends' blood was on my hands. I'm so *sorry...* so, *so*, sorry."

"You listen to me," Will said, gripping Todd's ankle in his anger. "Anything he did to you, any reaction he got from you, he would have got from anyone, from me, from Scott, hell even from Marcus. Your body had a physical reaction to this bastard. Not your heart. It was not you. None of this was you. You didn't deserve any of it. Do you hear me? Do you *hear* me?"

"And tonight?" Scott prompted as Todd nodded.

"He arrived about fifteen minutes after you left. After He was finished, I waited for a while before I came over here, to make sure He wasn't coming back. I didn't know where else to go."

"This was the right place, Todd. He's not going to hurt you again," Scott whispered into Todd's hair. "I promise you. You're safe now."

"If *only* that were true."

Three pairs of eyes flew to the bedroom doorway. Scott tightened his arm around Todd as the man's eyes filled rapidly with tears and he glanced over at Will, the disbelief clear in his lover's gaze. Then Scott's gaze came back to the owner of the voice and his stomach bottomed out as he registered the gun.

XI

"*Jay?*" Scott gazed in disbelief at the man lounging comfortably in the bedroom doorway. "*You?*" He couldn't believe it. Couldn't even begin to process what he was seeing. He was totally stunned. He would have never in a million years thought Jay would have been capable of the atrocities he'd visited upon Todd.

"Funny," Jay said, running a hand through his blue-black hair. "That's exactly what Cory and Jon said." He gave a mock shudder. "I just got a major deja vu. I *know* it's always the quiet ones you have to watch out for." His lips curved, but the smile didn't reach the cold, blue steel of his eyes. "Todd, *baby*," he said softly, clicking his tongue against his teeth and tutting. "You really should learn to stay like a good dog. I'll have to think up something nice and painful for you later."

****

Will could tell from a mere glance at Scott that he was weighing their options, and knew that Scott would see the same in his. *Fuck! Think, Harrison, think.* His gun was in the drawer of the nightstand and he knew Scott's was under the mattress. There was no way that he would reach his gun before Jay got off a shot. So he did what Will *'Do you ever shut the fuck up?'* Harrison did best. He began to speak. "Why, Jay?" His tone was low and unthreatening as he turned so that he was facing Jay. "What about Erik?"

Jay's eyes narrowed and he pointed the gun at Will. "You leave Erik out of this. He has nothing to do with this."

"Why? Doesn't he know what a sadistic bastard you are?"

Jay was across the room in three large steps and punched Will across the cheekbone with a clenched fist, sending Will backwards onto the mattress. "I would never hurt Erik... *never*..." He glared down at Will sprawled on the bed. "Well... apart from that one time. But I couldn't control myself. I let it get out of hand. Still, every cloud has a silver lining... it led us here."

Will's eyes widened in stunned comprehension. *It was him? But he loves him. I've seen it in his eyes.* "It was you? *You* attacked Erik and put him in the hospital?"

"It wasn't in the parking lot. That's just what I told the police and Erik. It was in our bedroom and, like I said, things got out of hand. The crack he took to his head means that he doesn't remember that night. Neither do I, if I'm honest. I just remember being inside him and then everything whited out. When I came out of it, he was covered in blood and barely breathing. I couldn't take the chance that I would lose control again, so I had to get my," he paused as if searching for the right word, "*other* pleasures elsewhere after that. Of course, I had to pay for it, but believe me, they earned their fee." His gaze rested on Todd where he was pressed up against Scott.

"Then came *Todd*, with those doe-eyes and that trusting nature. Not to mention that beautiful ass and, *God,* how I wanted it. I would have just fucked him a few times and that would have been it—but he said no. Can you *believe* it? He refused me, teased me with those long lashes and the sway of those hips. What can I say, I don't handle rejection well, makes me a little cranky. I wanted to taste him on my tongue. Feel him struggle beneath me. Hear him moan, longed to see him *bleed.*" His lips curved in a cruel smile. "My own little personal whore for free and, just like the whore he is, he takes it all and more... don't you, baby?"

****

Scott kept one arm around Todd while the other reached out and gripped Will's shoulder, noting the swelling on his face, the skin already purple. He was trying to keep a clear head, but the sight of Jay's mark on Will had him on the verge of doing something reckless. He breathed deeply and glared at Jay. He wanted nothing more than to wipe that smirk off the man's face, and possibly shoot him while he tried to escape. A million thoughts skittered across his brain, but one kept flashing at him in its own bright neon sign. *What about Stamford?* Pulling Todd even closer, he raised an eyebrow at Jay. "I take my hat off to you, Jay. You fooled everybody. I mean, I thought you had a meeting in Stamford. I'm guessing everyone else thinks the same?"

Jay shook his head, his tone sarcastic. "If anyone thought about it hard enough, they'd notice that my business trips always seem to coincide with Marcus's. I don't like to be restricted by any schedule other than my own." His gaze raked over Todd. "I like to take my time, don't I, baby? Todd likes it too; of course he'd never admit it. Did he tell you how hard he came just inches from Jon and Cory's dead bodies? How he moaned and shook when I pounded into him? He's quite the *willing* victim." He grinned lasciviously. "He likes you, Scott, I can tell. He likes tall, dark, and fucking beautiful. Would you like to try him? I don't mind. I like to watch. Or..." His gaze shifted to Will. "We could trade..."

"Fuck you," Scott ground out, moving his body as if to form a barrier between Todd, Will, and Jay. The way the bastard talked about Todd as if he were a used car that he should take for a test drive sickened Scott and he hissed through gritted teeth. "You'd have to kill me before I'd let you touch either of them."

"Oh, don't worry, I'm going to kill you— eventually."

"There's something else that's bothering me," Scott said, increasing his grip on Will to keep him from doing anything drastic.

"What?" Jay said scathingly. "More than the gun and the fact that I'm gonna put a hole in your head?"

Ignoring Jay's attempt to goad him into action, Scott continued. "How do you get in? I know you're the architect, but even you couldn't have had the foresight for anything intricate."

Jay's laugh was a harsh and cruel sound in the room. "What, Scott? You think I built a series of tunnels in the walls? Little trapdoors everywhere? Nothing so high tech I'm afraid." He reached into his pocket and pulled out a key ring with a bunch of keys on it. "I have keys to the front and back doors of every house in Laurel Heights. I kiss Erik goodbye and then I drive to the woods at the back of the houses and drop in, unseen, to spend a little quality time with my whore." He smiled at Todd and his tongue snaked out to lick his lips. "So simple, it's genius. And you know what I love most? I love the wait. Knowing that he's all alone, just anticipating when I'll come to him, wondering what delights I have planned for him, knowing how he moans when I tie those cords nice and *tight*. How those acres of soft white skin feel beneath my fingers. You just can't buy that kind of perfection."

The strong scent of urine filled the room and, glancing down at the man he still held in his arms, Scott saw the darkening stain on the boxers Todd wore. His gut roiled. The desire to hurt Jay so strong that, for a split second, he almost forgot he was a cop. It was only the physical shaking of Todd's entire body that kept him in place. He tightened his hold on Todd and noted the way Jay's eyes narrowed when he looked at the arm around Todd's slender shoulders.

****

"So what are you going to do?" Will said quietly, watching Jay's every movement. "You going to convince everyone that Scott and I argued and killed each other? Just like Cory and Jon? Isn't that a little dicey, using the same excuse twice?"

"Depends on how you would like to be remembered. Could be a crime of passion. Or a sex game gone wrong," Jay replied, waving the gun in a circle expressively. "I could even tell them how I heard Todd screaming and came to the rescue, because I have keys, you see, being the landlord so to speak... so luckily I could let myself in. And there he was, tied to the bed, being raped and beaten by the two of you. *You* took him dry with that huge cock of yours, Will. How could you? You quite literally ripped the poor boy a new one. Then one of you came at me with a gun and I had to act, I mean, Todd's my close friend, I couldn't stand by and let him be abused so badly." He suddenly emitted a fake sob. "It was so awful, Officer, seeing him trussed up like that, I just had to do *something*. There was a struggle for the gun and it went off— twice." He smiled, his blue eyes gleaming in the light from the bedside lamps. "I'm sure Todd would corroborate my story and be very, *very* grateful."

"Jay," Todd whimpered. "I'm *sorry*. Let them go and I'll do anything you want. They won't tell anyone. Please, baby—" His words stopped at the lift of Jay's hand.

"I didn't tell you to speak, bitch," Jay said dismissively. "Okay—let's get this show on the road. Will, take off your clothes. We need to make the scene look authentic. Don't worry, if it makes you feel better, I'll let you fuck Scott one last time—as long as I can take pictures." His lips curved into a lascivious sneer.

"No," Will snapped, determined brown glaring into cold blue, uncaring of the gun pointed at him. He gasped as Jay smiled and pulled back the hammer until it clicked home, the sound loud in the spacious room. Will's stomach tightened when Jay pointed... at Scott. *Fucking bastard! I'm gonna kill him. Slowly.*

"Will. Take. Off. Your. Clothes."

"You really don't want do this, Jay," Will said, dropping his tone and keeping it conversational, as if he was imparting a guilty secret.

"Oh, don't I?" Jay sneered.

Will shook his head slowly. "See, killing me and Scott is only gonna open a whole can of extra whup up on your ass. The cops won't accept your elaborate little story, and you won't be able to sweep this one under the carpet with talk of scorned lovers or kinky sex games. You wanna know why?"

"Enlighten me," Jay drawled, not lowering his aim.

"The White Plains Police Department doesn't like cop killers." He could see that Jay was thrown by his statement, that it was obviously the last thing the other man had expected him to say. Blue eyes widened as his words sank in and Jay realized what Will was saying.

"No," Jay shook his head in denial. "You're lying. You're not cops."

"Are you willing to take that chance?" Will said, menace in every word. "We were sent here to find out what happened to Cory Philips and Jon Webber. See, not *everyone* in your little community fell for your story, Jay. There are some who knew Cory would never hurt Jon and," he paused, leaning slightly in the hope that he could get nearer to the nightstand, and his gun, "it would seem they were right." Will saw fear in Jay's eyes for the first time since he'd walked into the room. Not much, but enough. He had no idea how this information was going to make the man react. If there was one thing worse than a crazy, sadistic bastard, it was a *cornered,* crazy, sadistic bastard. The stakes had suddenly been raised.

There was, however, only one clear thought in Will's mind, wiping out all others. *Scott.* He'd die before he let Jay touch him. He suddenly knew what

Todd meant. When the threat of danger to the one you loved more than anything was so strong, you'd do anything, submit to anything, whatever it took, to ensure their safety. If it was the last thing he did on this earth, he would make sure Scott was unharmed. He'd rip Jay's throat out with his bare hands and spit in his face with his last breath, if it meant keeping Scott safe.

"But, we could *help* you, Jay," Will said coaxingly, deciding to try a different tack, seeing if he could throw Jay completely off balance. "We can get you the help you need, dude. We can talk to the judge, get you a lighter sentence in a minimum security facility. It'll just be like an extended vacation." He shuffled forward on the bed, his hands raised, palms up in a placating gesture. "All you have to do is give me the gun, Jay. We'll take care of the rest."

"No," Jay kept the gun trained on Scott. "I'll just have to change my plans a little. I'll just have to take Todd with me. Kill you and then take Todd somewhere no one will ever find us. Where no one will hear him scream. Do you like that idea, baby? You and me, all alone, miles from anywhere. I know I do. *God,* the sounds you'd make..."

"What about Erik?" Scott hissed. "He loves you and I know you love him. I've seen it."

Jay's eyes glittered as he nodded his head. "I *do* love him. Have *always* loved him. But Todd fulfills a need in me that no other man can, not even Erik. No one else gives me the total release, body and soul that I feel when my whore is sobbing around me. Erik would never understand. Just like you don't. I need Todd, he makes me whole." He smiled ruefully. "I'm sorry."

Then he pulled the trigger.

The shot sounded like thunder in the quiet of the room and Will cried out at the whoosh of air that escaped Scott's lips when the force of the bullet entering his body threw him against the headboard.

Everything seemed to slow.

Will's eyes locked with Scott's as the other man pitched forward onto the bed, blood blossoming in a dark red stain on his shirt. "Scott!" He wasn't sure if he'd actually said his name or just thought it. Then pure instinct took over.

Will flung himself from the bed without a second thought and lunged at Jay. His hands grabbed for the gun and he tried to wrestle it from Jay's grasp. He managed to get a kick to the other man's shin, loosening Jay's hold on the grip, but not loose enough. The gun turned and a second shot split the air.

Will grunted as the bullet entered the meaty flesh of his thigh and his leg went out from under him. The pain was white hot and momentarily clouded his vision, but he didn't let go of the gun. Tightening his grip, he pulled Jay down to the floor with him. Jay tumbled to his side and Will forced his hands over his head, holding the gun away from their bodies.

"Will! Move!"

Scott's voice was harsh and cracked, but the sweetest sound he had ever heard. Will pushed hard at Jay's shoulders and rolled away, just as the third gunshot rang out. He heard Jay's gasp of stunned pain as he and the gun fell from his hand. Ignoring the fire in his thigh, he rolled back and grabbed the gun, training it on Jay. "Party's over, Randall."

Will panted harshly as he pulled himself across the carpet toward the bed and gazed up at Scott, kneeling on the bed, his gun still clasped in the hand that was pressed to his side. Blood seeped through his fingers from his wound, and beads of sweat had broken out on his face, but Will didn't think he had ever seen a more beautiful sight in his life. "Are you okay?" he gasped, pressing his own hand on the bullet hole in his thigh.

****

Nodding, Scott eased himself down to the floor next to Will, biting his lip to stop himself from crying out. "I think I'm holding something on the outside that really should be on the inside, but aside from that, I'm fine. What about you?" His breath fell from his lips in gasps, unable to draw in enough air. The pain in his side was indescribable and he felt woozy and lightheaded, but that didn't matter. Only Will mattered. He looked down at Will's leg and hissed in concern at the amount of blood pumping from the wound. "Will, I think he nicked an artery, put more pressure on, you're losing too much blood. Todd?" He gazed over at Jay who was moaning on the floor, his hand clutched to the wound in his shoulder. *Nothing less than you deserve you fucking bastard!* "Todd? Are you okay?" He'd shoved Todd down onto the bed when he'd reached for his gun, hissing in his ear to stay down.

"I'm okay," Todd's voice was small and terrified, but it was there.

Scott leaned his head back against the foot of the bed as they heard feet pounding up the stairs and Brent skidded to a halt in the doorway. "Yay," he mumbled weakly, "the calvary."

"What the fuck is going on in here?" Brent shouted, gazing in stunned amazement around the room.

Scott gave a pathetic half-chuckle, knowing they must look like a Greek tragedy. Three of them with gunshots, Todd lying beaten on the bed, and blood everywhere. Behind Brent crowded David, Cal, Damon, and Erik.

"Jay?" Erik choked in disbelief and ran across the room, dropping to his knees beside his lover.

"Cal," Will rasped. "Call nine-one-one and White Plains PD, ask for Detectives Cassidy and Bates, then hold a gun on Jay. Damon, take care of Todd. It's okay, we're cops," he nodded at Brent. He turned his head and smiled at Scott beside him. "I'm going to pass out now. Is that okay?"

"Jeez, a thigh shot and you need to pass out. You're such a lightweight, Harrison," Scott replied, pressing a kiss to Will's temple as the big man's eyes closed and he slumped against his shoulder. "But I love you," he whispered, closing his own eyes and leaning his head on Will's as he slipped into semi-consciousness. Everything was a blur after that as Scott drifted in and out.

Brent, Mr Sleaze himself, turned out to be quite the white knight. He ripped a towel in half and tied it around Will's upper thigh, literally ripping the towel rail from the wall to wind in the knot to form a tourniquet on Will's leg, to try to stem the still steadily flowing blood. He eased Scott down on his back and Cal and he packed towels beneath the gaping hole in his side and then pressed more towels on his stomach.

David had pulled Jay up and sat him in the easy chair in the corner of the room and stood watching his every move.

Damon and Cal sat either side of Todd, holding him while he sobbed quietly; the relief that it was finally over being too much. A heartbroken and devastated Erik, after listening to what Todd had to say, could do nothing but murmur, "I'm sorry, so sorry," over and over again, staring at Jay as if he had never seen him before. Jay stared into space, not making eye contact with anyone in the room.

Scott groaned loudly in relief at the sound of sirens and the screech of tires outside, heralding the arrival of the professional calvary. He heard Grace before he saw her as his name was called over and over on her way up the stairs. *Jesus, she makes a lot of noise for someone so small!* "Keep it… down," he mumbled as her face swam before him. "Trying… to sleep."

****

"Not yet, you don't, asswipe," Grace said, quickly summing up the situation and switching to full on cop mode. "The ambulance is on its way," she said softly, kneeling beside him and removing the now sopping blood red towel from his side, so that she could evaluate the damage. *Fuck!* Her heart leapt into her throat at the vicious wound the bullet had torn into Scott's flesh. *That's bad, that's really bad! Shut up, Cassidy, focus!* "It's not too bad," she said confidently, proud of the way her voice only wobbled slightly as the lie fell from her lips. "Hold on, babe. They're coming." She glanced over at Julie as Scott passed out again. "How's Will?"

Julie swallowed hard, her face impassive, but her eyes terrified. "He won't wake up. He's lost a lot of blood and his pulse is really thready. Where the fuck is that ambulance!"

"Are they okay?" Todd croaked from the bed. "Are they okay!"

Grace stood and walked around the bed to clasp Todd's outstretched hand. "Todd? I'm Grace, Scott's partner. How are you doing?"

"Forget me. I've had much worse than this. Are *they* okay?" Todd's voice cracked on a sob. "They saved me. Please let them be okay."

"They're both hurt quite badly, I won't lie to you," Grace said in her no-nonsense manner. "Will's lost a lot of blood and Scott's—" She paused, not trusting herself to continue.

"The ambulance is here," Cal interrupted from where he was stood at the window.

****

It was in fact two ambulances. The paramedics carried in stretchers and dealt with each man in turn. Scott whimpered when they removed the bloody towels and packed his side with gauze before lifting him onto a stretcher. He slapped weakly at the hands pushing an oxygen mask over his face. "Will? Where's Will," he croaked. "I want to see, Will." Not wanting to give in to the darkness again, he tried to push himself up on the stretcher, fighting against the hands pushing him back down. "Get off me," he growled. Didn't they know he needed to stay where Will was? Needed to see he was okay? Didn't care what happened to him as long as Will was okay? "Grace!" His voice sounded canned to him from behind the oxygen mask a paramedic was holding onto him, forcing him to breathe in the pure air.

"I'm here, Scott," Grace said softly, taking his hand while they strapped him to the stretcher.

"Need to… see Will. Is… he okay?"

"They're strapping his leg now. Everything's gonna be okay. You're going to be fine, Scott." She gripped his fingers tightly and smiled down at him.

"Crap… liar, Cassidy," he rasped, his eyes closing. He knew how bad his wound was. He wasn't stupid. That's why he needed to see Will, needed to hold him, tell him. Who was he kidding? He could still feel the blood oozing from his side, the wetness of it against his skin. He may not survive to tell Will anything. "Tell him," he gripped Grace's fingers weakly. "You tell him... I *love* him. Tell him… I'm… sorry."

"Fuck you, Turner," Grace ground out through clenched teeth. "Tell him yourself. Come on!" She yelled at the paramedics. "What's the hold up?"

One of the paramedics working on Will suddenly shouted, "He's not breathing!"

"I gotta get him to the ER, ma'am." The man holding onto Scott's stretcher, grabbed Grace's upper arm and leaned in to stress the urgency of the situation. "The bullet went straight through one of his kidneys and out the other side. The more time we waste, the less chance he has."

"Take him, take him," Grace said, squeezing Scott's fingers one more time.

"No… not yet… Will!" Scott's voice was barely a whisper. "Will—"

The noise of the monitor's continuous monotone followed him into the dark as blackness surrounded him and held onto him tight.

XII

Todd's eyes opened slowly. He could feel the coolness of the crisp sheets beneath him. Wincing at the throbbing ache in his backside, he tried to shift his position. He'd had to have surgery to repair the damage Jay had caused. He had a catalog of contusions and heavily bruised ribs, along with a fractured cheekbone which may need plastic surgery later down the line. *As if he needed additional reminders of his degradation. Every second of it was already imprinted on his brain. Would he ever be free?*

They had been able to perform the surgery under an epidural and after much shouting, screaming, and general menace on Brent's part, Damon had been allowed to gown up and sit with Todd while they did the repair. Unfortunately, the epidural was now wearing off and the throbbing ache in his ass was worsening. As he moved, a soft moan fell from his lips.

"Do you need some pain relief?"

Todd turned his head to see a sleepy looking Marcus sitting in a chair by the bed. Shame washed over him. Marcus *knew*. Todd closed his eyes immediately and turned away, unable to face the recrimination in Marcus's gaze.

"Don't you do that," Marcus said, his voice unwavering. "Don't you turn away from me. Not *ever*. Look at me, baby, *please*."

Opening his uninjured eye, Todd looked into deepest blue and saw only love. "I'm sorry," he bit his lower lip, the tears falling unheeded down his cheeks. "I'm *so* sorry."

"You have nothing to be sorry for. It's okay, I'm here now. Everything's going to be okay." He pressed their lips gently together, his own tears mingling with Todd's. "Why didn't you tell me?"

"He said... he said he'd deny it. That no one would believe me over him. He said… he said he'd tell you… hurt you. I didn't want you to stop loving me. *Please* don't stop loving me," Todd rasped, his voice thick with tears. *Please don't hate me.*

"Nothing could ever change the way I feel about you, don't you know that? *Nothing.*"

Todd sobbed in the haven of Marcus's arms. Sobbed out all the hurt and the pain, knowing that it was over and he was finally safe.

****

"Why?"

Jay's gut clenched at the sound of that voice. He couldn't look at him. Knew the pain and hurt he would see in those blue eyes. Turning his head toward the window and away from the man standing in the doorway, he let his eyes drift shut. The doctor told him that they'd removed the bullet from his shoulder and that there was no major damage. He would be sore for quite a while, but he would heal. Then the doctor had left the room while Detectives Cassidy and Bates read him his rights and slipped a set of handcuffs around his wrist and the side bar of the bed.

"Wasn't I enough? I *loved* you." Erik's breath hitched in his throat, his voice thick with unshed tears. "How could you hurt Todd and what you did to Cory and Jon—" he bit back a sob. "Say something, you bastard!"

"Is Todd okay?" Jay heard the pain in the harsh sobs Erik could no longer hold back, but he couldn't deal with his pain. He needed answers and no one was giving them to him. The heavy door slammed as Erik left the room and Jay finally opened his eyes and stared up at the ceiling. Was Todd in the next room? Down the hall? He needed to know. His anger began to boil in his gut. What was the bitch telling people? Was he spinning some ridiculously pathetic story about how Jay had hurt him? Was he fooling them into thinking that he wasn't responsible for everything? He'd better be keeping his mouth shut, or he'd pay... God how he would make him pay.

****

"Hey, handsome."

Grace's voice seemed to come from far away and Scott frowned, trying to latch onto the sound above the annoying beep filling his head. She said his name again and he felt as though he should at least make an effort to respond. Forcing his eyes open, he blinked owlishly above the clear mask strapped to his face. Grace's face swam above him and he turned his head slowly and squinted until she came into focus. Her fingers felt cool on his forehead and his tongue snaked out to moisten his lips.

"Is this... heaven?" He rasped, wincing at the dryness of his mouth.

"Would I be here if it was?" Grace teased, her smile soft as she gazed down at him. "You're okay," she said, taking his hand in hers, stroking his skin softly.

"What?" Scott tried to convey the question he was asking with his eyes, hoping she would understand him, as he didn't have the energy to do anything more right now.

"The bullet went through your left kidney, and they had to remove it," she said softly. "You had a lot of bleeding and it was touch and go there for a while, but they managed to get it under control. You're gonna be okay, you lucky son of a bitch."

"Not… me," he huffed, lifting the hand without the clip on it that read his oxygen levels, wondering briefly why his arm weighed a hundred pounds all of a sudden, and pulled the mask off his nose and mouth, so it was hanging on his chin. "Will?" His throat felt raw, as if he'd been gargling broken glass and his voice didn't sound as though it belonged to him. "Where's… Will? I heard… he wasn't breathing."

"That's 'cause you were boring the shit out of me," a voice to his left said. A deep, croaky drawl. "Passing out was the only way I could get you to shut up."

Scott tried to sit up and he groaned as Will pushed the wheelchair he was sitting in, closer to the bed and put a steadying hand on his shoulder.

"Don't you dare, sexy. If you're gonna bust your stitches, it's gonna be during hot butt sex, not because you're being your usual meat-headed, asshole self."

Scott grabbed the hand that Will held out to him through the side bars of the hospital bed. *He's alive. Fucking asshole. I'm going to kick the shit out of him!* "Hot butt sex? You wish," he rasped. "Lukewarm butt sex maybe." He pinched Will's arm hard, causing the other man to give a squawk of pain. "*Son of a bitch!* Scared the fucking shit out of me. I thought you were dead you big freak. What did you stop breathing for? You only got shot in the thigh!" When he'd heard that monotone as he'd passed out for the final time, he had silently asked God to take him, too. He didn't want to live in a world that didn't have Will Harrison in it.

Will huffed indignantly beside him. "Fuck you, Turner. I was pumping out blood faster than they could get it in. Artery was like a geyser, you should have seen it. Trust you to turn this into a "my gunshot's bigger than your gunshot" pissing contest."

"At least I didn't flat line on your ass and I was holding my guts in my hand!" Scott croaked back. "I've half a mind to make sure you never get *any* kind of butt sex again." The way his eyes were roaming over Will's face as if to memorize every curve, every line, softened his threat.

"Can we keep the talk of butt sex to a minimum, please," Julie said, walking into the room with a coffee for Grace and one for herself. "Hot or any other kind."

"You're just jealous 'cause you wanna tap my ass too," Will shot back, his fingers tightening on Scott's, his gaze never leaving Scott's face.

"I'd rather floss with Grace's twat hair," Julie deadpanned, sipping at her coffee. Scott raised an eyebrow and glared at her meaningfully, grinning when she stood up. "Gracie, why don't we go tell the nurse he's awake?" she said, nodding her head toward the door.

"Subtle, Bates," Scott said hoarsely.

"It's my middle name," she grinned, closing the door behind them.

Scott couldn't take his eyes off Will. His bandaged leg was supported on pull out slats and there was a bag of blood attached to the IV in his arm, hanging on a stand fixed to the back of the chair. Noting the pallor of his skin and the dark circles beneath those soulful brown eyes, Scott frowned. "Shouldn't you be in bed somewhere, geyser boy?"

"You trying to get rid of me? After all the fuss I caused getting in here?" Will grinned. At Scott's raised eyebrow he explained. "I may have made one of the doctors cry when they said I couldn't come in here and wait for you to wake up." He shrugged. "It's not my fault he's a wimp, and the gun wasn't loaded. Hence the paraphernalia strapped to the chair. My leg hurts like a son of a bitch, I'm woozy, and my butt's gone to sleep, but you're not getting rid of me. I've been waiting three hours for those beautiful eyes to open, Turner."

"Don't ever do that again."

"What? Threaten the hospital staff, or wait for those beautiful eyes?" Will said softly, reaching up to brush Scott's hair from his forehead.

"I thought you were dead." Scott pulled on Will's wrist and dragged his hand down to his lips, pressing them to the palm, kissing the soft flesh. A smile curved Will's lips and he bit Will's thumb gently in retaliation. "Freak."

"Asshole," Will responded, smiling wider and wider. "You were *worried* about me."

"No, I wasn't."

"Yes, you were, don't deny it. I heard you, you know."

"Heard what?" Scott frowned, shifting in the bed and grimacing at the flash of pain in his back and side. The painkillers were obviously beginning to wear off and his whole left side was beginning to beat out a steady throb in time with the beat of his heart.

"I heard you tell me that you love me."

Scott felt his cheeks fill with warmth. *Shit! He was supposed to be unconscious!* "I was delirious," he huffed. "And I thought you were going to die. Hell, I thought *I* was going to die. It was just a heat of the moment thing… like saying it during sex."

"Uh-huh, no way, I heard you say it. It's out there, you can't take it back." Will grinned, lowering the side of Scott's bed and repositioning himself. "Luckily, I know what a commitment-phobe you are."

"Oh, God, you're not going to go all Oprah on me, are you?"

"Maybe. You *lurve* me," Will drew the word out in a singsong voice.

Scott closed his eyes at the teasing grin on Will's face. "Great," he mumbled. "We have a moment when we're both close to death and you mock me. Nice, real classy, Harrison."

"Would it help if I said it back? Oh, wait a minute."

Rolling his eyes at the mock horror on Will's face he then shook his head, his expression rueful. "I'm going to regret this—what?"

"With your declaration of undying love and the bedside vigil and everything," Will deadpanned. "We're heading dangerously close to relationship country. You think you can handle that, Detective?"

"Meh," Scott replied, closing his eyes at the feel of Will's lips teasing the inside of his wrist. "If you wanna give it a try, I guess that'd be okay. But I can't guarantee I'll be any good at it. You know, what with me being such an asshole."

"Will you hold my hand in public?" Will asked, flicking his tongue against the inside of Scott's elbow.

"If it's dark," Scott replied, tired of waiting and lifting his head to urge Will on. He needed his lips on him now. Needed to know that he was really there, that he wasn't just delirious, that Will was really alive.

"What about making out on the desk?" Will was less than a breath away.

"If it's after hours and we're the only ones there... *Will*." His name was a whimper. Scott wanted him to bridge that breath and stop torturing him.

"Sex in the bathroom at work?" Will grinned.

"Definitely," Scott grinned back, lifting his hand and pulling Will's head down, sealing their lips together in a soft, gentle, tender kiss. When their lips parted, Scott brushed waves of honey-blond hair from Will's face and pressed their foreheads together. "I love you."

"I know, you already told me." Will's smile was soft and gentle and he didn't tease for long. "I love you, too."

****

THREE MONTHS LATER

Will yawned widely and tipped his head back beneath the spray of warm water from the shower head. He was tired, the kind of tired that made your bones ache. Reaching up for the soap, he washed himself, taking care around the scar where the bullet had entered his flesh. Not that he hadn't recovered well, he had, but he'd been on his feet for more than a large portion of the day, and it was throbbing ominously. He groaned quietly and rinsed himself clean, turning off the shower when he was satisfied all the soap suds had washed down the drain.

Stepping out of the shower, he grabbed a towel off the rack and briskly dried himself before wrapping the towel around his waist and then taking another to rub over his hair. He dropped both of the towels into the laundry hamper, and opened the medicine cabinet, taking out a bottle of Tylenol. Popping the cap, he shook two into his hand and tossed them into his mouth, running some water into his cupped hand and then slurping the pills down. He grimaced at the taste left behind on his tongue and grabbed his toothbrush, squeezing toothpaste on the bristles and brushing his teeth. He paid particular attention to his tongue, trying to scrub away the acrid chalkiness. Rinsing his mouth, he washed out the glass and snapped off the light before he opened the bathroom door.

Will padded barefoot down the hall and into the bedroom. His tiredness seemed to drain away as he took in the sight before him. Scott's profile was illuminated in the muted glow of the bedside lamp, and a book lay open on his stomach. He smiled, this was the third time this week he'd fallen asleep reading while he waited for Will to come home. Crossing the room, he gently maneuvered the book from beneath Scott's fingers, popped the bookmark inside to save his place, and then put the book on the nightstand beside Scott's cell.

He stretched his arms over his head, biting his lip as his vertebrae realigned and his muscles complained at the harsh treatment they were receiving. With some of the tension eased, he slid as quietly as he could between the sheets, not wanting to disturb the sleeping man beside him. He rolled over onto his side so that he was facing Scott and slipped one arm beneath his pillow, rubbing his cheek against the soft cotton of the pillow case, another yawn opening his mouth wide.

Will gazed adoringly at Scott, following each line and curve of his face in the glow of the lamp. In repose, the other man looked like a teenager, his skin tanned and smooth, full lips parted slightly and long dark lashes fluttering like butterfly wings against his cheeks. *Jesus, Harrison. He's right; you have got to stop reading Sue Brown!* He knew he was acting like some love sick moron, but he couldn't help it. He just thanked God every day that Scott was alive.

Closing his eyes, he let the memory of Scott's hospital stay wash over him. It had been the third day after the shooting. They'd been sharing Scott's room as Will had insisted on being moved so he could be with him. One minute they had been bickering over the remote for the TV and the next Scott's temperature had suddenly spiked and he'd had a seizure. Will had watched the infection rage through Scott for almost a week. They kept pumping antibiotics into him and for a few hours he would be lucid and then his temperature would go haywire and they'd be back to square one. At one point, they'd even mumbled that Will should prepare himself for the worst, and say his goodbyes. He'd very politely replied, "Fuck *that*!" and told an unconscious Scott in no uncertain terms that if he thought he was going to wimp out now, he had another think coming. It must have worked, because nine hours later, his temperature dropped and stayed that way. But Will didn't breathe a sigh of relief until Scott's navy eyes opened later that day.

Recovery had been arduous after that, and it was three weeks before they finally let Scott out of the hospital, although they wouldn't let him even consider returning to work for another nine weeks. Will smiled fondly. Yesterday had been Scott's first day back on the job and Will had watched him like a hawk. The doctor had said that he was only allowed to do light duties for the first few weeks, because he would tire easily, so Will had made sure he followed the doctor's orders to the letter. Much to Scott's annoyance. In fact, Will bit back a chuckle, by ten-thirty, Scott had dragged him to the bathroom and told him that if he didn't leave him the fuck alone, he was going to drown him in the toilet. Will had backed off, after Scott had agreed to leave the office by five every night until he was stronger.

"Stop staring."

Scott's deep voice was thick with sleep, and Will moved closer, draping his arm over Scott's slender waist. "I thought you were asleep," he murmured, pressing his lips to the other man's temple.

"I was," Scott complained, "but this creepy-assed freak keeps staring at me."

Will chuckled as Scott rolled away from him and then shuffled backwards until they were comfortably spooning. "It's your own fault for being so Goddamn hot. Did you eat? Are you hungry—?"

"Will?"

"Yeah?"

"Stop talking."

"Okay."

****

Scott stepped out of the shower and wrapped a towel around his lean hips. Wiping the condensation from the mirror, he studied his reflection objectively. He'd lost a little weight over the last three months, but he was gaining it back now, so his face wasn't as haggard as before. The infection he had developed in the hospital had knocked him for a loop and he'd had to spend an extra three weeks stuck in that bed after Will had been released, not that he remembered much.

His fingers brushed softly against the scar on his left side. The doctors had assured him that he was in great physical shape and living with one kidney was something he could adjust to with some relatively simple measures. He had to increase his fluid intake and drink at least two to three liters of water a day, change his dietary habits, and maintain a healthy lifestyle. This, combined with regular six month check-ups to ensure his remaining kidney was not under any undue stress, meant that there was no reason why he shouldn't live a long and healthy life.

Yesterday had been his first day back at work. He sighed as he squeezed toothpaste out onto his toothbrush and began to clean his teeth. As expected, the good-natured ribbing had started almost as soon as he'd walked through the door. The rubber ring on his chair, because they figured it must be hard to sit down, what with Will being such a big boy. The condoms and lube in his desk drawer and the GQ magazines stuffed into files. Scott had tried to take it all in good fun, the way it was meant, but he had found his gut tightening with every crack. This had been one of the reasons why he had kept his sexuality to himself. He'd rolled his eyes and thrown the magazines in the trash and then settled down to work, glancing over at Will briefly and wondering just how nasty the ribbing might turn if they knew what had really gone on between them in Laurel Heights, or that they were now practically living together in Scott's modest home.

Turning on the faucet, he cleaned his toothbrush under the flow of water before rinsing his mouth. When he was finished, he wandered back into the bedroom and smiled slowly at the vision waiting for him. The early morning sun sent shafts of light through the chink in the curtain, and fell on the miles of honey-toned skin currently sleeping soundly in his bed. Scratch that, *their* bed. The sheet had inched its way down Will's back, barely skimming the glorious curve of his firm ass, baring a large amount of cheek to Scott's gaze. His cock thickened and filled, tenting the towel knotted around him, and his lips curved into a wicked smile as he crossed the room.

Crawling up the bed, he straddled Will's thighs, keeping his stance wide and being careful not to lower his weight down onto the sleeping man. Scott slowly peeled back the sheet, raising high onto his hands and knees. Bending his head and parting his lips, he ran the tip of his tongue down Will's lower back and over the curve of his ass. Will's skin twitched beneath his tongue and he tried not to chuckle when the other man grunted loudly into the pillow at the first flick of Scott's tongue against his rim.

"Ugnh," Will breathed, fingers clawing at the sheets beneath him.

Scott felt the groan Will emitted against his lips as it vibrated through the other man's body, the groan turning into a high pitched keening as he pointed his tongue and breached the ring of muscle, pushing inside.

"*Scott*!"

"Yes, baby?" Scott said, pulling back to scrape his teeth across the soft flesh of Will's ass cheek. Reveling in the sound of the whine at the removal of his tongue. He placed a hand on Will's ass, as the other man pushed backward, seeking his touch. "So impatient," he crooned, nipping at the globes of flesh and suckling on smooth skin.

"Don't stop," Will begged. "I love the way you rim me… oh, God, *Scott*."

Scott tapped Will's ass lightly and worked his tongue inside of the quivering man again. Moving his hand down, he alternated between rolling Will's balls in his palm and stroking the length of his hard shaft, smoothing his thumb over the already leaking head. When he slid a finger alongside his tongue, pushing hard, Will cried out harshly from deep within his chest. Scott smiled against Will's hole and licked at the rim in short, stabs, loving the sounds that came from his lover, loving that he was responsible for them.

"Scott, fuck me, baby, *please*."

Scott stabbed at the ring of muscle with his pointed tongue one more time, before scrambling up the bed to grab a condom and the lube from the nightstand drawer. Quickly slicking up his fingers, he rolled Will over onto his back and slid a pillow beneath lean hips, before sliding back into the writhing mess that used to be Will *'I'm a big tough cop'* Harrison.

"I'm right here, beautiful," Scott crooned, sliding in a second, then a third finger, pumping them in and out, stretching the muscle while ripping the condom open with his teeth. "You like that?" He gasped at the animalistic cries falling from Will's lips when his fingers slid over that sweet bundle of nerves inside dark, wet heat. "Fuck, Will. The way you sound... just the sound of you makes me wanna come." Scott pulled his fingers free slowly, quickly rolling the condom down his painfully hard shaft and lifting Will's legs onto his shoulders. Leaning down, he kissed Will deep and dirty as he pushed into him.

Scott couldn't stop the whimper that mingled with Will's when the head of his cock slid past the ring of muscle and into the dark heat beyond. When he was all the way in, he panted desperately into Will's neck, licking at the sheen of sweat in the hollow of his throat. Will's muscles clenched around him and he took that as his cue. Locking with brown eyes that had darkened to burnt chocolate, Scott began to thrust in earnest.

The room filled with the sounds of their harsh breaths and ragged moans as Scott moved within Will, *his* Will. He was still constantly amazed at how perfectly they fit together. Two halves of one whole, moving in sync with one another, so close they could read each other's movements before they were even made. He'd never loved anyone as deeply as he loved Will—hadn't thought he knew how to love, not like this. He angled his hips and Will cried out again and again, meeting him thrust for thrust as he hit that spot deep inside.

"I love you," he groaned closing his fingers around Will's leaking cock, stroking him in time with the rolling thrusts of his hips. He was unable to drag his eyes from Will's when the other man reached up and cupped his face in shaking hands as he came, pulsing over Scott's fingers. He breathed harshly, watching the pleasure blow Will's pupils almost completely, thrusting deep inside and holding himself there as his own cock twitched in his orgasm and spilled hot and heavy into Will's ass.

"*Will,*" Scott breathed, collapsing against Will's chest as long legs fell from his shoulders and wrapped themselves around his waist. "Jesus, fuck," he said eloquently, sliding his lips across Will's and kissing him slowly, pouring his heart into the kiss. A kiss filled with every corny romantic line he could never come up with to express how much he loved this man. He wished he could find the right words to explain to Will how, just when he thought it was impossible, he fell in love with him just that little bit more. That every damn day his heart felt that little bit fuller, whether it just be a look, or a word, or the sound of Will's laughter—but every day he found himself falling deeper.

Withdrawing slowly, Scott kissed soft lips in apology for the hiss of complaint Will made, and quickly stripped himself of the condom and tied it off, tossing it into the trashcan by the bed. He grabbed the towel he had been wearing when he came out of the shower and wiped off Will's belly before curling around his warm, sweat slick skin. Resting his head on the other man's muscled chest, he sighed contentedly, completely boneless in his satiation. "You're thinking," he drawled, circling Will's nipple with a gentle finger. "I can hear you."

****

Will pressed a kiss to Scott's hair. Every muscle in his body pulsed with tiny sparks in the afterglow of his orgasm and he lifted a hand to feather his fingers through the soft, dark strands that lay against Scott's forehead. "I was just thinking about yesterday, you know, your first day back. It wasn't too bad, was it?"

"Once they'd got all the butt-fucking jokes out of the way," Scott said derisively.

"It's just harmless banter, babe, you know that," Will reassured, continuing to stroke his fingers through Scott's bangs. "They're all glad to see you back. I got the same treatment my first day, except they'd replaced my desk chair with a wheelchair covered in pretty pink bows and blown up condoms." He smiled when Scott snorted inelegantly at the picture he was creating. "They'll get bored with the whole, Will and Scott's fabulous undercover adventure soon enough." Scott mumbled into Will's neck and he pulled him closer.

He understood how Scott felt about the ribbing, knew the reasons. But he'd tried to impress upon him that their colleagues were just making a big joke about the situation, not about their sexuality. No one knew the truth. Will sighed heavily and rubbed his cheek against Scott's hair, inhaling the scent of the shampoo he had used earlier. As much as he may want them to.

The moment the doctor had told him that Scott was going to be all right, he'd known being together behind closed doors was not something he wanted for forever. He'd been so happy and so relieved that he hadn't lost the giant asshole, he'd wanted to run screaming through the streets of New York shouting his love for the other man to the sky. But he hadn't. Instead, he'd found himself in a quiet stairwell as he'd slid down the wall, ignoring the pain in his thigh as he sobbed like a baby.

He loved the man beside him, without condition. Loved everything about him, including his insecurity and foolish fears about letting the outside world know who he really was—who *they* really were. Scott had his reasons, he understood that. Had spent long nights talking until the small hours about Paul Turner and his utter decimation of his son's confidence; the fear the man had planted in Scott's head that everyone would treat him the same way his father had, once they discovered the real him. He just had to cling on to the hope that one day, Scott might love him enough to get past that and be able to embrace their relationship in the light, instead of wanting it kept in the dark. Because he knew one thing for certain, Scott was it for him, now and forever—for better or worse.

"I love you," Scott murmured, stroking his fingers up and down Will's side.

"I love you," Will replied, capturing Scott's lips in his and kissing him deeply. "And as much as I'd love to spend the rest of the day in bed showing you just how much, if we don't move it, we're going to be late."

He ignored Scott's grumble and slapped his firm, round ass before he clambered off the bed. "Come on, asshole. We've got to be there in an hour."

Today was Jay's sentencing hearing.

****

"Scott?"

Turning at the sound of the voice, Scott grinned widely at Todd, pulling the other man into his arms for a warm hug. "Hey, Todd, how are you?" Scott said softly, looking into deep blue eyes.

Todd shrugged. "I'm doing better. How about you? They finally let you go back to work I see."

"Yeah, I think I was driving Will crazy. He's been back for a month now and every time he got home I grilled him for hours. I'm glad to be doing something again. Although the doc's put me on desk duty for a while, at least I'm out of the house." Glancing over Todd's head, Scott smiled at Marcus who was chatting animatedly to Will. "How's Marcus?"

"He's great, *really* great. We've been going to counseling together and it's helping. He thinks it's his fault. That he should have known. Shouldn't have left me alone, shouldn't have just accepted the excuses I came up with." Todd gazed at the big man with an adoring smile on his face. "Of course, it's not his fault, and I think he's finally beginning to accept that. There's still a long road ahead, but we're getting there. And we're moving at last. We've bought a little place near Fort Worth; it's not huge, but just what we've always wanted. It's a brand new start, for both of us, and Erik's gonna come out and stay with us for a while. What about you and Will? Still in the closet?"

Scott chuckled at Todd's good-natured tease. "We're good. Really good. Let's just say both our closets are now in the same house."

"But the doors are still firmly closed?"

"For now," Scott conceded, squeezing Todd's shoulder. He didn't miss the look of regret in Todd's eyes at his confession, but today wasn't about him and Will. Today was about justice for Todd. He smiled at Marcus and accepted his hug as the big man and Will came to join them. "Marcus, good to see you, man. Todd was telling me about the ranch. Sounds like everything's going well." He glanced up at the clock on the wall above them. "Are the others coming?"

"They're planning to, well, everyone except Erik. He's having a real hard time." Marcus sighed heavily and slipped his hand into Todd's. "He blames himself. Thinks he should have known. I know how he feels. We did debate keeping Brent away, but he's promised us he won't be leaping across any tables to kill Jay with his bare hands." Blue eyes hardened. "Not that I would be rushing to stop him if he did."

David and Brent walked through door, followed by Damon and Cal, taking the time to greet Scott and Will before huddling around Todd and Marcus, pack-like in their stance. Their support for their friend palpable.

"So," Brent said, his hand firm on Todd's shoulder. "What do you think the judge will do? Can Jay appeal against the judge's decision? We don't want Todd to have to go through another trial."

Will shook his head reassuringly. "I don't think there's any danger of that, Brent. Jay can appeal all he likes, but any appeal could take years. When it comes down to it, he committed a capital crime. He killed two people in cold blood, not to mention what he put Todd through, and the whole attempted murder of two police officers. It was obvious that the defense was going to try to come up with an insanity plea, but the psychiatrists already debunked that. Jay's a sadistic sociopath; he knew exactly what he was doing." He ran a hand through his hair. "The sentence itself will be decided by the same jury who sat at the trial. The judge then has the option to modify the sentence within the confines of the law. The prosecution and defense will offer the jury facts from the trial, but I know there are no witnesses scheduled, so it will just be a summation. Then the jury will retire and when they've reached a decision we'll be called back in to hear the suggested sentence."

"He deserves the death sentence." The voice behind them was quiet but firm, and they all turned to face Erik. "I want him to pay for what he's done." He leaned into the comforting arm that Cal put around his shoulder and grasped the hand that Todd reached out to him as he was pulled into their communal embrace.

"Gentlemen," the attorney for the prosecution said gently, putting his hand on Will's arm. "It's time. The judge is ready."

The men filed into the courtroom and sat down on the side of the prosecution. Will reached across Scott and squeezed Todd's fingers when the side door opened and two guards brought Jay into the room, and his gaze followed the man as he walked to the table where his lawyer waited for him.

Jay wore an expensive navy suit, a pale blue dress shirt and a navy tie, his loafers polished to a high shine. Will thought he looked like he was heading to a meeting, not to hear the decision on where and how he should spend the rest of his life. As Jay sat down in the chair his lawyer held out for him, Will tensed as the man turned, focused cold blue eyes on Todd's face— and smiled.

"All rise. This court is now in session. Honorable Judge Slade presiding."

Once the judge was seated, he banged his gavel and the bailiff called, "Be seated." Putting his glasses on, he looked down at the brief in front of him and leaned back in his chair. "Would the defendant please rise," he said firmly, waiting until Jay was on his feet. "Jared Randall, you are here today for sentencing. You were found guilty by a jury of your peers for the murder in the first degree of Cory Philips and Jon Webber, for the vicious, continual assault and rape of Todd Campbell, and for the attempted murder of Detectives Scott Turner and Will Harrison of the White Plains PD." He paused, pouring himself some water into the glass beside him and taking a sip. "You may sit. Okay, the court notes that counsel for the defendant is Maurice Wheeler and the counsel for the city of New York is Andrew Bennett. Mr Wheeler, you may address the jury."

Will glanced at Scott and his lips lifted in a brief smile as his partner closed the infinitesimal gap between them on the bench and he felt the heat of Scott's thigh warming his. Jay's lawyer began his summation and Will settled back in his seat. Sentencing could sometimes be harder than the original hearing itself, with both sets of lawyers going over every little piece of evidence, re-hashing everything and then trying to convince the jury that the defendant deserved either the most lenient, or most aggressive sentence within the constraints of the law. And all the while the victim had to sit back and listen to every last detail of the crime being picked over like vultures tearing the last vestiges of meat from a rotting carcass.

He found himself wanting to wipe the smirk from Jay's face as his lawyer droned on about his difficult childhood, his inability to rationalize his feelings for Todd, and even asked them to remember that although Mr Campbell was undoubtedly a victim of abuse, who was to say that *every* incident was non-consensual? Will's mouth dropped open on its hinge at that last statement. How on earth did the man have the nerve to say that? Will couldn't believe what he was hearing. His glance flitted to the jury and he was glad to see that some of the jurors obviously felt the same. A young woman was glaring at the lawyer, her cold stare almost demanding that he take it back, and a couple of men were shaking their heads in stunned amazement. But he knew they were not here to try Jay. He had already been convicted, today was merely to see how long he would have to pay for his crime. Of course, if it were up to Will, Jay Randall would sit in a cell on death row until they shot him full of that special little cocktail and sent him to the big psycho ward in the sky.

Will felt a surge of pride at the impassive mask Todd wore. Both he and Scott had warned him that the defense would try every trick in the book to get Jay a more lenient sentence, including tearing Todd's character to shreds. That Todd should hang on to that fact during the summations and remember that Jay was guilty, no matter what trash his lawyers dragged out. That Jay would be looking for the slightest reaction from him, however small. He glanced at Todd now and saw the only reaction was the whitening of his knuckles where his hand was clasped in Marcus's.

Then it was the turn of Andrew Bennett, from the District Attorney's office, who reminded the jury of the psychiatric reports by both the defense's and prosecution's expert witnesses. That Jay's own expert agreed he is a sociopath. Will gazed at Jay's profile as the lawyer continued. He could tell by the tightening of his jaw and the tendons in stark relief against his skin that Jay was holding onto his control by the skin of his teeth.

Will turned his attention back to the jury and studied their faces as Bennett spoke, realizing that Jay could see the same revulsion on their faces that he could. His gut warmed with satisfaction as he realized Jay knew there was a real possibility he would get the death penalty for what he'd done. That he couldn't charm his way out of this one. That twelve women and men, strong and true, held his life in their hands.

When Bennett had finished his closing statement, the Judge turned to the jury and bestowed upon them a beatific smile. "Ladies and gentlemen of the jury, you have listened to the arguments of both the defense and the prosecution. If you would kindly retire to deliberate, and return to this court when you have reached your decision on the sentencing of Mr Randall. Court adjourned." He banged his gavel and stood, followed by the loud instruction of the bailiff for everyone to rise as the Judge left the courtroom.

They were back inside the air conditioned courtroom before they'd even had the chance to finish the awful coffee from the vending machine one floor down. Will glanced at Scott and raised his eyebrows in surprise, acknowledging the shake of Scott's head. A quick decision by the jury was not always a good thing. After they had all taken their seats and the jury had filed in, Jay was brought in from a side room and followed the guards to his counsel's table. Will reached across David beside him and put a steadying hand on Marcus's knee as Jay's lips lifted in a cruel sardonic smile as he took his seat. "Don't give him what he wants," Will said softly, giving Marcus's knee a reassuring squeeze, smiling at the way Todd's hand slipped into his lover's to ground him once more. He felt the warmth of Scott's thigh beside him and a sharp wave of longing washed through him, wishing he could as casually touch his own lover the way Todd touched Marcus.

"All rise," the bailiff called out in a loud booming voice as the door to the judge's chambers opened. "This court is now in session. Honorable Judge Slade presiding. Be seated."

Judge Walker turned to the jury and pushed his glasses further onto his nose. "Mrs Foreman, members of the jury, have you reached a decision?"

Will watched as a business woman in the front row got to her feet, "Yes, Your Honor."

"And you reached this decision unanimously?"

"We did, Your Honor." The woman handed a piece of paper to the bailiff who passed it to the Judge, who read the same and then nodded to the jury.

"Thank you, ladies and gentlemen of the jury, you are now dismissed."

Will's stomach churned as the Judge took his time in reviewing the paper in his hand and after what seemed like an hour, but was in reality a minute, if that, he looked over his glasses at Jay and said, "Will the defendant please rise. Mr Randall, do you have anything to say before the sentence is entered into the record?"

"Yes, Your honor," Jay said quietly, his voice shaking on the words. Will's gaze narrowed, wondering what the man was going to say. "I'm sorry, so sorry for the decisions I made. For the hurt I caused, to those I loved and who loved me. I know there is nothing I could do to make right what I've done. I took the lives of two of my friends, ruined the life of another and broke the heart of the man who stood beside me. For that I am truly sorry."

"Thank you, Mr Randall, please remain standing," Judge Walker said, leaning back in his chair and keeping his gaze trained on Jay. "Before I read the sentence, which I wholeheartedly agree with, I have a few things I want to say myself. I too have read both of the extensive psychiatric reports by Dr Logan and Dr Brown and, as far as your plea of diminished responsibility due to temporary insanity is concerned, I have come to the conclusion that, Mr Randall, if there is anyone more in charge of their faculties than you, I have yet to meet him. You knew *exactly* what you were doing every step of the way, and have shown no remorse for your actions at any point. Your little speech was nothing but the grandstanding of a master manipulator. You used Mr Campbell for your own amusement and gratification and, when Mr Philips and Mr Webber tried to remove him from the situation, you killed them in cold blood, without hesitation, taking the lives of two young men who had everything to live for, and you almost took Mr Campbell's spirit in the process."

The judge's gaze shifted from Jay to the men surrounding Todd on all sides and smiled encouragingly. "I am glad to say, you appear to have been unsuccessful in that endeavor and, surrounded by the love and support of the community you so viciously betrayed, I think he's going to be just fine.

"The shootings of Detectives Turner and Harrison were, in my opinion, Mr Randall, the stupidest move you could have made. This Court doesn't take kindly to the attempted murder of our city's officers." He looked down at the piece of paper in his hand and began to read. "Jared Andrew Randall, you will serve two life sentences for the murders of Cory Philips and Jon Webber. You will serve no less than 25 years for the rape and torture of Todd Campbell. And you will serve a further 25 years for the attempted murders of Detectives Will Harrison and Scott Turner, all of which are to run consecutively. You will now be taken from here to Rikers Island, where you will be held without the possibility of parole." He closed the papers in front of him and banged his gavel. "Bailiffs remove the prisoner."

Will could tell by the set of Jay's shoulders and the way his fists clenched at his sides that he was not going quietly. He nudged Scott with his shoulder and hissed, "Something's going down." Grateful when Scott stood up with him. He was right.

As the Bailiffs tried to lead Jay from the room, the man wrenched free of their grasp and launched himself toward Todd. Will threw himself in front of

Todd and out of the corner of his eye he saw Scott grab Marcus's arms and hold him fast. "You bitch! You think you're free of me? You'll *never* be free of me!" Jay struggled as the guards grabbed his shoulders, pulling him from the room as he strained to get to Todd. "You're *mine*! I'll make you scream you whore, do you hear me? I'll make you *bleed*. It'll never be over! Never!"

"You bastard!" Marcus yelled, held back by Scott and Cal as they dragged Jay through the door to the side rooms and it slammed behind them. "You'll never touch him again! I'll kill you first! I'll kill you first!"

The gavel banged again, sharp repetitive raps, until the furor in the court had subsided. "Mr Campbell," the Judge said compassionately, his kind gaze level and unwavering on Todd. "I am sorry you were subjected to that, but I can assure you, here and now; you will never see that man again. I wish you all the best, young man. Court dismissed."

Outside the courtroom they huddled together, each man comforting the other. Erik standing tall and strong with his arms around Todd, the other men's arms around the two of them. Scott and Will stood to the side and watched the circle, gentle smiles on their faces, their shoulders pressed together. When Damon and Cal held out their arms, they stepped inside the circle and they all stood quietly together in their relief.

****

After about ten minutes, Will smiled ruefully and indicated that they had to get back to the station. With more hugs and promises they would stay in touch and, if any of the guys ever needed *anything*, they knew where to find them; they ignored Brent's mumblings about unpaid parking fines, and took the elevator down to the parking lot beneath the courthouse.

As Will unlocked the SUV, he gasped at Scott's searching hands on his waist, turning him and pressing his back to the side of the car. "What—?" His startled eyes fluttered shut as Scott's lips sealed themselves over his, hungry, desperate almost, his tongue delving deep as he stole his breath. When Scott finally drew back, Will panted harshly, his chest heaving. "Wow, what was that for?"

"Just felt like it," Scott replied, straightening his tie and walking around to the passenger side.

Will climbed behind the wheel and gazed over at Scott, completely stunned. He wasn't used to public displays of affection outside of Laurel Heights, and it had thrown him. Licking his lips, he inserted the key in the ignition and started the car. *It must have been the emotion of the sentencing. Yeah, that's what it was.* Putting the car into drive, he maneuvered out of the space and drove toward the exit, turning left and heading back to the station.

The ride was silent—too silent. Will kept glancing over at Scott, noting the set of his jaw and the obvious tension in his shoulders. He had his thinking face on, which wasn't always good, and Will couldn't help but wonder what had caused the frown creasing his lover's brow. "We couldn't have asked for a better result. I knew Walker wouldn't be fooled by the temporary insanity crap."

"Yeah."

"Are you okay?" Will asked, pulling into his parking space at the station and setting the handbrake. He turned off the engine and put his hand on Scott's thigh. "What's wrong?"

"Nothing, I'm fine," Scott replied, unbuckling his belt and clambering out.

Will watched in amazement as Scott slammed the door and didn't even wait for him to get out before he headed for the elevator and stairwell. "Scott!" Will cursed under his breath and grabbed the files off the backseat before climbing out and locking the car behind him. "Fuck it," he hissed when he skidded to a halt at the elevators. Scott was nowhere to be seen. He couldn't have been waiting long enough for an elevator to arrive, so Will surmised he'd taken the stairs. But why? Something was going on in that illogical head of his, and Will needed to find out before whatever was bothering him festered and got blown completely out of proportion. Stepping into the elevator, he leaned back against the faux granite wall and rode up to the fourth floor, his foot tapping in agitation.

When the doors opened, Will was greeted by balloons, and colleagues dressed in party hats, blowing whistles. Julie and Grace smiled widely and clapped as he walked out of the elevator, catching Scott out of the corner of his eye walking toward them down the corridor from the stairwell. He turned and waited for the other man to join him. He knew his gaze clearly said *"What the fuck?"* but Scott only glanced at him briefly and then turned his attention to their captain.

Captain Hall poured some orange juice into two glasses and handed them to the two men. "Congratulations on a job well done, boys. You caught the bad guy and saved the day. I think there may be some commendations coming your way. You guys make quite a team."

"Thanks, Cap," Scott smiled, lifting his glass of orange to his lips, and downing it in one. "Right, back to work," he said briskly and batted a balloon out of his way to sit down at his desk.

Will caught the look that Grace threw him, but all he could do was shrug as he sat down at his own desk, leaning down to switch the computer on and then picking through the pile of files in front of him. He couldn't give her any insight into Scott's mood, because he had no idea what had caused it. Was he annoyed that he'd given in to the urge to kiss Will in the parking lot?

Was he now worrying that someone had seen them? Running his hands through his hair, he tried to concentrate on his paperwork.

An hour later, the balloons had been popped, the streamers and glasses cleared, and the phones were ringing off the hook as usual. And Scott had still not looked at Will. Not once. In sixty whole minutes not one glance—not even an accidental meeting of a passing gaze. Nothing. Zilch. Nada. Will didn't know how much more of the silent treatment he could take. Stupid Scott *'You have to guess what's wrong with me'* Turner. Picking up his cell phone, Will ran off a text, not even raising his head when he heard Scott's cell beep across the way.

Are you going to tell me what's wrong?

His cell vibrated in his hand moments later.

Nothing's wrong.

Liar.

I just need to figure some stuff out for myself.

What stuff?

Can we talk about this later?

No—what stuff?

Later.

You're freaking me out.

I know. I'm sorry.

Will bit his lip hard enough to draw blood. His stomach was tied in knots and he was, as he'd just said, freaking out. What the hell was going on? They were fine a few hours ago and now all of a sudden Scott had to 'figure stuff out', what the fuck was that? He was just about to rattle off another reply when Hall came slamming out of his office.

"Harrison! Turner!" he yelled across the room. "There's someone here from the local press. Wants to take a picture of our two top detectives now that they're both back at work. Chief's orders, so come on." He clapped his hands together and nodded to the photographer next to him. "How do you want them?"

The small, dark haired woman smiled appreciatively at both Will and Scott. "Over by the door would be good, then I can get the department logo in the background." She ushered a very quiet Scott and a mildly pissed off Will to where she needed them, and then smiled encouragingly. "Could you turn to each other and shake hands or something? You know, smile, and look like you're happy to be back."

Will turned to Scott and held out his right hand, forcing a smile to his lips. He waited while Scott stared down at his hand, then continued to stare, and then stared a little bit more. "Scott?" Will hissed through his teeth, noting how everyone around them had stopped working to witness the little scene playing out in front of them. "What's wrong with you?" His stomached tightened as a thought suddenly occurred to him. "Are you sick?"

****

Scott's gaze traveled from Will's hand to those deep brown eyes he loved so much. Eyes that told him he was loved in return with merely a glance. Eyes that were now looking at him with confusion and fear, but he was the one who had been afraid—not anymore. Not with Will beside him.

"Yeah," he replied, his voice scratchy and raw as he stared at Will. "I *am* sick. Sick of lying, sick of being afraid, sick of pretending the person I love most in the world isn't standing right in front of me." He slipped his fingers into Will's and before the other man could register what was happening, Scott pulled him up hard against his body and kissed him, deep and tender.

When he pulled back, he stared into Will's astonished eyes.

"I know I've been freaking you out, and I'm sorry," he said softly. "But when I saw Marcus, Todd, and the others at court, the way they held each other without even thinking about it, without looking over their shoulder to make sure no one was watching. I wanted that, too—so badly I could taste it. I wanted to hold you in my arms and let the world know that you're mine. But I was still too afraid of what everyone else would think, and then it suddenly occurred to me. I'm a good cop. A *damn* good cop, and so are *you*. We've both worked hard to get to where we are and we've earned it, and the respect of the team.

"If that changes because we're together, then I'm not sure I'd want to be a cop anymore. Because, you know what?" He smiled softly at the bewildered shake of Will's head. "I can do without the force, but I can't do without you." Lifting his hand, he smoothed Will's hair back from his forehead. "I love you, Will Harrison, and I don't give a shit who knows it." He turned to the watching room. "Did you hear that? I am in fucking *love* with Will Harrison!" Scott gasped as Will pulled him into his arms and kissed him soundly. He wrapped his arms tightly around Will's neck and kissed him back with everything he had, as the catcalls and whistles from their colleagues started. Grace and Julie being louder than everyone else, of course.

"Did you get your picture?" Hall rasped at the photographer. At her amazed nod, he turned to the two men and said, "Can I see you two in my office, please?"

Scott tightened his fingers on Will's, his stomach churning but his gaze unwavering, as they walked across the department to Hall's office. The captain's face had been expressionless, but his gray eyes had glinted hard cold steel as he glared at them. "It'll be okay," Scott hissed at Will, who looked decidedly pale beneath his tan. "I can apply for a transfer, just let me do the talking."

"No," Will replied, his fingers tightening on Scott's. "If anyone is applying for a transfer it's me. You've been here for five years, you shouldn't have to leave. I'll go."

"Today, assholes!"

Scott swallowed hard and gave one last squeeze to Will's hand before they stepped into the captain's office and closed the door behind them. "Cap—"

"Sit!" Hall barked without looking up from the file on his desk.

Scott opened his mouth to respond but Will pulled him down onto the chair beside his and threw him a glare that had his lips snapping shut. His stomach was in knots. Not that he was about to take back a single word he'd said, but he knew the man sitting behind the desk had the power to make or break both their careers. After what felt like an hour of silence, he couldn't take it anymore and cleared his throat to speak.

"I'm the one doing the talking here," Hall said, closing the file and leaning back in his chair, his gaze cool and assessing. "I'm guessing you're both thinking which one applies for the transfer, right?"

"Well—" Scott's mouth snapped shut when Hall held up a single finger.

"Do I look like I'm finished?" Folding his hands across his stomach, Hall's gaze flitted from one to the other. "This is how it's gonna go down. No longing looks across the room at each other. Any domestic shit will be left at the door. While you are in my department, your hands will remain visible at all times. And if, for one minute, your relationship affects the way you do your jobs I'll kick you *both* out on your little pansy asses. Understood?"

"We can stay?" Scott stammered incredulously. "Both of us?"

"Just don't give me cause to change my mind."

"And it doesn't bother you?" Will said, his voice holding a note of disbelief. "The gay thing?"

Hall huffed out a laugh, "Have you met Damon? Listen guys, I don't care who you fuck as long as it doesn't interfere with the job. Like Scott said out there, you've earned the respect of your colleagues time and time again but, if anyone gives you any grief beyond blown up condoms, I wanna know about it. I won't have that kind of shit in my house." A smile briefly lit up the older man's features, "Now fuck off, you've got work to do."

"Thanks, Cap," Will said, standing up and shaking Hall's hand. "We won't let you down."

"So, as long as we don't bring anything into the department, we're cool?" Scott queried, nodding at Hall's affirmation. "As Will said, Cap. Thank you. You won't be sorry." Scott followed Will out of the captain's office and shut the door behind them. Quickly making sure they were out of earshot of their colleagues, he pulled on Will's sleeve and hissed, "Follow me." Ignoring the question in Will's gaze, he strolled across the department and out of the door, heading down the corridor.

"Where are we going?" Will hissed.

"Didn't you say something about sex in the bathroom?" Scott smiled wickedly at him as he pushed open the door to the men's bathroom.

Will pushed him into one of the stalls, the grin on his face widening. "But what about what Hall just said?"

Reaching around Will and jamming the lock home, Scott chuckled, his fingers fumbling with the belt on Will's pants. "He said we weren't allowed to do anything in the department, we're not in the department."

"I can't believe you did that. I'm so proud of you," Will murmured, groaning when Scott's fingers found their mark.

"Will?" Scott murmured, licking at the sensitive skin behind Will's ear.

"Yeah?" Will gasped.

"Stop talking."

"Okay."

EPILOGUE

The clanging of a stick against the bars heralded the arrival of the guard. "Randall," Guard Thompson's voice was gruff. "Back against the wall. Your lawyer's here." The short stocky man waited until Jay got to his feet and moved to the bars of his cell, sliding his hands through the slot in the door. Guard Thompson unlocked the cell and stared Jay down while he cuffed his wrists, daring him to make any sudden moves. Once the cuffs were secure, he indicated that Jay should move back and then unlocked the door, before pulling him forward and pushing Jay along in front of him.

Inside the meeting room where the inmates met with their lawyers, he pushed Jay into one of the chairs at the table, undid one of the bracelets then attached it to the arm of the chair. Taking another set of cuffs from his belt, he slipped one half of the cool metal around Jay's ankle and then the other to the chair leg and snapped it shut. Once he was satisfied that Jay was secure, he got to his feet and went to open the adjoining door. "You can come in now, Mr Kent."

"Thank you, Roy. You can leave us alone," the well-dressed lawyer said briskly. "I have confidential matters to discuss with my client about his case." He smiled up at the guard confidently, charm oozing from every pore. Once the guard had left to stand outside the door within shouting distance, the man sat down at the table opposite Jay.

"Mr Kent?" Jay drawled, shaking his head slowly. "So you're my new lawyer, huh?"

"I thought I looked every inch the part," the man replied, straightening his tie and smiling confidently. "We don't have long." He dropped his voice an octave and Jay gasped as the other man's socked foot slid up the leg of his orange jumpsuit, caressing the skin of his ankle. "I miss you," the man's voice was soft and low.

"What do you miss?" Jay hissed, biting at his lower lip, his gaze falling to the man's mouth.

"You hands, your tongue," the man whispered, his voice raw and his eyes darkening. "I miss you inside me, making me scream." He hissed when his foot reached the crotch of Jay's pants and he rubbed his sole against the hard shaft tenting the material. "I miss the way you tie me down and punish me when I'm bad, the way you punish me more when I'm good, and I've been *real* good, baby." He whimpered low in his throat. "I need it, Jay, all the marks are gone, and I need you so bad."

"Stop." Jay groaned, his cock rock hard in his pants at the images the man's words invoked. "Have you gone to him yet? Did you find the keys?"

"Exactly where you said they'd be. I had a little scout around last night and I took these for you." He picked up the briefcase on the floor and snapped it open, handing two photographs to Jay.

Jay's lips parted on a gasp and he reached out to stroke Todd's sleeping face with his fingertips. "When is *he* going away?"

"Thursday. He's away for three days, tying up loose ends before they move to the new place. Todd's been nervous, but I told him he was perfectly safe, I'd take good care of him while Marcus is away. In fact, I may have offered to stay overnight so he's not alone."

"Good," Jay said softly. "Take *real* good care of him, Mr Kent. Make him scream—I want him to scream."

"He'll scream. You taught me well. I'll be back next week," the man snapped the briefcase shut and smiled as he slipped his shoe back on. Standing, he looked toward the door and quickly moved around the table to slant his lips over Jay's, tongues colliding, delving deep. "With lots of photographs. Goodbye, Mr Randall."

Jay licked the man's taste from his lips slowly and smiled as the other man knocked on the door to alert the guard they were finished.

"Make sure you tell Todd I said hello."

THE END

ABOUT THE AUTHOR

I live in a small seaside town just outside London, on the South East coast, that boasts the longest pier in the world; where I am ordered around by two precocious children and a dog who thinks she's the boss of me.

I've been writing seriously for three years now and loves giving voice to the characters warring to be heard in my head, and am currently petitioning for more hours in the day, because I never seem to have enough of them.

Website:
http://lisaworrall.com

Facebook:
Lisa Worrall Author

Twitter:
Lisa_Worrall

Blog:
http://lworrall.blogspot.com/

Email:
lisaworrall69@gmail.com

Google+:
Lisa Worrall

Fanclub:
http://myawesomefans.com/index.php/groups/viewgroup/10 lisa ε lovelies

ALSO BY LISA WORRALL

Available from **Dreamspinner Press**:

Bank Job

"U.S. Male" in *Uniform Appeal*

No Strings Attached

Unshakeable Faith

Running from the Past

I Can See for Miles

Thirst (Coming Soon)

Available from **White Stiletto Press:**

Always Hope

Is Love Still Enough?

Summer Heat

Not Just for Christmas

'Tis the Season

Too Much Christmas Spirit

Westford Hall

In the Heat of the Night

Halloween Duo: Dreaming of You /

Halfway House

New York Cowboy

Laurel Heights

Laurel Heights 2 (Coming Soon)

Marshall's Park, The Complete Series:

Monty Gets Arrested

Monty's First Date

Monty Meets the Ex

Meeting Monty's Parents

Monty Loses His Head

Moving Monty In

Monty Meets the Parents

Monty's Trick or Treat

Monty Punches Pocahontas

Monty Gets Married... Doesn't He?

Left at the Crossroads Series
by Lisa Worrall & Sue Brown:
Book 1 - Un-Expected by Lisa Worrall

Available from **JMS Books LLC**:
"Frozen Angel" in *Tea and Crumpet*

Available from **UK Mat Publishing**:
"Reunion" in British Flash

Awards:
Unshakeable Faith
Rainbow Awards 2012
Honourable Mention
and One Perfect Score

Printed in Great Britain
by Amazon